I0656756

Richard Strange

The life of St. Thomas of Hereford

Richard Strange

The life of St. Thomas of Hereford

ISBN/EAN: 9783741189579

Manufactured in Europe, USA, Canada, Australia, Japa

Cover: Foto ©Andreas Hilbeck / pixelio.de

Manufactured and distributed by brebook publishing software
(www.brebook.com)

Richard Strange

The life of St. Thomas of Hereford

NOTICE.

THE author of the *Life and Gests of St. Thomas of Hereford*,—which is here reprinted without any alteration, except what is involved in the adoption of the modern orthography of English words—was Father Richard Strange, S.J., a Northumbrian, born in 1611. He entered the Society in 1631, taught at the Jesuit College at St. Omer, served on the English Mission, was Rector of a house at Ghent, and in 1674 was made Provincial. His name is very prominent in Dr. Oates' 'true and exact narrative.' After some marvellous escapes from pursuivants related in Father Hamerton's personal narrative, he died at the age of seventy-one at St. Omer.[1] This is a reprint of his book, which is extremely scarce, and yet the only English Life of St. Thomas Cantilupe. Some few verbal changes have been made to make the meaning clearer. As the Life is full of unction but somewhat meagre in fact, a supplement has been added with additional particulars. These are drawn from various sources, but

[1] *Records of the English Province S.J.* vol. iv. p. 623.

mainly from the Bollandist Life and Mr. Webb's
Notes to the Swinfield Roll.

It may be of interest to append a few characteristic
anecdotes of the Saint, drawn from the evidence of
witnesses who knew him well. As to his outward
appearance, Brother Robert, the sacristan at St.
Bartholomew's, London, describes him as 'having
an angelic face, a complexion white and ruddy, a
good beard and a long nose, with flaxen hair.' Hugh
the Barber tells the Papal Commissaries, not without
a certain pride, that his master 'was no hypocrite or
humbug (*papelardus*), trying to make himself out
better than other people; that in dress and other
things he was not different from his equals; that
when at the Universities he wore indoors a mantle
and a cassock (*garnochiam*) like what Prelates wear
(for he was Archdeacon of Stafford). Out of doors
he had furred garments and a furred coverlet to his
bed.' After the Saint's death, William Gandro, his
body-servant, and the heir to his wardrobe, says that
so anxious were the Saint's relatives to get keepsakes
of him, that he had to tear to pieces both cassock and
tunic, but the mantle and hood he kept for himself,
though a Welsh rector offered twenty pounds for it.

A story is told of the Saint's hair-shirt, which he
inherited from his uncle, the Bishop of Worcester.
The Saint did not find it hard enough or knotty

enough for him, so he sent it to Oxford to have it roughened and hardened. This he wore to the day of his death, and Robert of Gloucester, the witness, says it was the hardest that could be found. The same witness says that once he ventured to expostulate with the Saint on his excessive abstinence, saying, 'You eat and drink too little, my lord; you wont be able to last out. Getting no answer he repeated the remark, when the Bishop said, 'Eat and drink what you like, and hold your tongue and leave me in peace.' Robert rejoined, 'My lord, I will not do so, because I don't want you to die, for I should lose the promotion I am hoping for from you.' St. Thomas answered, 'You want to flatter me.' But it would seem that he did get his promotion, for he became the Bishop's official, and was in some sense the occasion of his master's death and his own excommunication.

A story of much the same sort is told of William de Montfort, the Dean of St. Paul's. Noticing the Saint's extreme abstinence, he told him that he could not make out how it was that he, who eat and drank so little, and thus weakened his health, could venture upon such arduous enterprize as his suits with the Earl of Gloucester and Archbishop Peccham. 'Cousin,' said St. Thomas, 'you mustn't watch what I eat and drink, but you, being a great dignitary, eat and drink what you like. But as you are a priest like me, I will tell you a thing you must not reveal in my lifetime—after my death you may if you like. For the last two-and-thirty years I have never risen from table without feeling as hungry as when I sat down, yet I am strong enough to venture on a battle with you.'

This Dean Montfort was one of the Saint's executors, but he did not long survive the Saint, and is said to have died of fright at having to make a speech before the King. Soon after the Council of Reading, Robert of Gloucester was grumbling about the number of Papal Provisions and the sort of men who were put into benefices, saying that these Prelates acted so presumptuously that people would not obey them, and would care no more for the Roman Church than for the Sultan. Then St. Thomas, moved with indignation, rebuked him, and told him never to say such things again, saying 'that the Primacy of the Roman Church would last for ever.' The following anecdote is told of the Saint's last illness. His chaplains, seeing that he could not recover, said to him, 'My lord, would you not like to go to confession?' And he looked at them and said, 'Foolish men.' After a little pause they said to him again, 'Do you not know that your time is drawing near? The leech says you cannot live much longer. Would you not like to see the confessor?' He said, 'Foolish men.' A third time they said the same thing: 'The time must be near; would you not desire to make your peace with God.' And a third time he made the same answer, and so he died. 'Afterwards it was found that he went to confession every day. He had no need of their counsel; but he had no will to reveal what had been the habit of his life.'[2]

Feast of the Nativity of our Blessed Lady,
1879.

[1] *Glories of the Sacred Heart*, p. 237.

CONTENTS.

xiv   *Contents.*

Contents.

CHAPTER I.

The time and circumstances of the Birth of St. Thomas.

THE Church of God, since the primitive times of Christianity, scarce ever flourished under a happier constellation of saints than in the thirteenth age, when conversation with Heaven was not confined to caves and deserts, but found admittance both in cities and courts; when Christian humility sat as well upon the thrones of kings as in cells of hermits; and true poverty of spirit knew how to vest itself, as in sackcloth, so in purple. This was the age—a golden one in this respect—when virginity was preserved and flourished not only in the sanctuaries and inclosed gardens of religious cloisters, but, like a lily among thorns, in the very midst of worldly delights and greatness, even in the state of wedlock and highest fortune. Then it was when princes had no other interest of state but the glory of God, nor any other ambition but to dilate His Kingdom, which they endeavoured at the expenses of their crowns and lives, and were more employed in fortifying their

B 30

country with religious convents than forts and citadels,
when they held it a greater strength and honour to
their royal families to espouse their daughters to
Christ crucified, in the greatest rigour of penance
and poverty, than to see them seated on the highest
thrones of monarchs; when, in fine, those two great
patriarchs, St. Dominic and St. Francis, peopled the
world with so many choirs of angels, brought Evan-
gelical perfection out of unknown retirements and
solitudes to the common habitation of men.

Our country of England, though separated by
nature from the rest of the world, was not excluded
from that universal influence of Divine grace wherewith it pleased God to bless those times.   The blood
of the glorious martyr St. Thomas of Canterbury, as
the true seed of the Catholic Church, was not spilt
in vain; and being in this age yet fresh and warm,
brought forth special fruit both in laity and clergy.
But in all none more eminent than another St.
Thomas, another Chancellor of England, another
prelate, another champion of ecclesiastical liberties,
and though not slain by the sword, yet lost his life
in the cause.   Thus the mercy of God poured down
sweet showers of Divine blessings upon that kingdom
by the merits of this holy martyr: yet His justice
laid not down the sword of due revenge for that
bloody sacrilege, nor was it yet satisfied with the

personal disasters of that unfortunate King, Henry II. who found as many Absaloms as he had sons, ready to tear the crown from his grey hairs, and to bury him alive who had given them life; and after he had seen two of them lead him the way to his grave, he followed not long after, and left the other two his curse for inheritance, of which they had each one their share by succession.

The former of whom was Richard I., third son of the aforesaid King, who though otherwise a valiant and great prince, and therefore surnamed Cœur de Lion, yet for that curse entailed upon him by his father (and much more if there were true cause of deserving it), had his crown torn from his head by a violent and untimely death. And that it might not fall to a more innocent hand, left no child, but a brother far worse than himself, who, that his royal purple might be of a more lasting tincture, gave it the second dye with the blood of his nephew Arthur, next heir by birth to the crown of England, as son of Geoffrey, Earl or Duke of little Brittany in France, which Geoffrey was fourth son of Henry II., King of England. And though it is not certain that Arthur was murdered by his uncle's own hands, as the French do tell us, yet all agree that Arthur was put in prison at Rouen by his uncle, King John, and never appeared after: the manner of his death

is best known to God alone, before Whose invisible
eyes all things lie visible. However, King John,
fifth son of Henry II., and surnamed Lackland,
makes the land his own; and on this wrong builds
all his right, which he ever managed with an equal
tenor, as weakly as he did wickedly; till at last,
called to an account by a stranger for oppressing
his country, left the world like an outlaw, and a
poor child to pay his forfeit. This child, Henry III.,
though otherwise most innocent, could not altogether
plead not guilty, seeing that he claimed all his right
from so great injustice.

In the midst of this dismal and dark cloud our
morning star first appeared. In the height of this
horrid storm, which threatened no less than a total
destruction of the nation, it pleased God to give a
pledge of atonement between Heaven and earth, to
bless the world with our glorious St. Thomas Cantilupe
as a rainbow after a deluge of blood and misery,
whose birth did not, like another Benjamin, purchase
his own life with his mother's death, but finding his
country in agony, restored life. Neither was he only
a common benefit and happy presage to the public,
but a special blessing and reward for his father's
loyalty. For when the greatest part and power of
the kingdom, either out of personal offence and
hatred of the deceased King, would yet pursue him

in his image, or led by interest, the common idol of the world, thought fit to combine with the stronger party, and rather adore the prevalent might and fortune of an invading foreigner than to support the weakness both in years and forces of their native Prince. William Lord Cantilupe, father of our glorious Saint, looked upon the present state of things with another eye, and was resolved to lay down his life and fortune at the feet of justice, leaving the event to the Divine balance, whether he stood or fell being secure of victory, which ever crowns them who sacrifice themselves to truth and loyalty. Wherefore, as a person of eminent ability and honour, he gives strength to the better but lesser party; and as he ever maintained his faith inviolable to the father, though a Prince of most odious and lawless government, he could never forget the respect of sovereignty, so he continued the same unto the son, with all the disadvantage of human interest.

The barons, with their French protector, were not only masters of the field, both in strength and number, but also many months possessed of the head city of the kingdom, a thing ever held of highest consequence, as being the ordinary residence and Court of kings, and whosoever wins it seems to wear the crown. The little King at nine years of age, being solemnly crowned at Gloucester, was in a

manner confined to that city and two others—Bristol
and Worcester, though some other particular places
and castles in several parts of the kingdom stood
firmly to him. And chiefly Lincoln, which was our
Orleans, where a lady,[1] not inferior to the French
shepherdess in courage, as she was far above her in
birth and quality, defended the castle of Lincoln the
space of a whole year against Gilbert de Gand, a
prime commander of the French forces, though he
had possessed himself of the town, and pressed the
castle with a vigorous siege. The King's honour,
besides his interest, was conceived to be not a little
concerned in the relief of so much fidelity, especially
of so rare and unusual example in the weaker sex.
The Lord Cantilupe, therefore, with other nobles of
the royal party, accompanied likewise by the Legate
of the See Apostolic, with what power they could
make, marched forth upon this design. Being arrived
within eight miles of Lincoln, they all confessed and
received the Holy Eucharist, with a plenary indul-
gence which the Legate granted them, and solemnly
declared the adverse faction separated from the
communion of the Holy Catholic Church. Thus
armed and encouraged from Heaven, they fell on
with such irresistible violence that, though the
defendants exceeded the assailants far in number,

[1] Nichola de Camville.

besides the advantage of their walls and trenches,
the town was soon gained, with a total defeat of the
enemy, Thomas Earl of Perche, a person of highest
nobility and command in the Barons' army, allied
both to the crowns of England and France, being
with many others slain upon the place, besides
fourteen earls and barons and four hundred knights,
with their servants, horse and foot, taken prisoners.
This victory cut the sinews of the Barons' confede-
racy, and blew off all foreign storms from our English
coast, the French Prince thinking fit at last to look
back upon a safe retreat, and to quit another's right
not to lose his own. In fine, our young King was
so settled hereby in his throne, that from this day
no rebellion durst presume upon the minority of
his years, nor attempt his fortune. And for the
space of thirty-four years, as long as William Lord
Cantlupe, the father of St. Thomas, lived, no man
had the power or courage to make head against
him.

These happy tidings welcomed St. Thomas into the
world, or rather he brought them with him; these
laurels of victory crowned the cradle of our holy
infant, or rather he was given from Heaven as a
crown of his father's loyalty, and as a pledge of the
Divine protection over the little King, who, though
a child, was better read than most men in that maxim

of wisdom,[2] that crowns and kingdoms are disposed
and swayed by the hand of God; and therefore,
seeing himself, at the first step into his throne, so
strongly opposed or rather thrust out by the violence
of a foreign adversary and faction of his native
people, could think of no other refuge but God.
And as an author[3] of credit writing of those times
recounts, he betook himself to little Jesus in his
Virgin Mother's lap, and with as innocent, as sweet
a confidence, presents his petition in these words:
' I beseech Thee, who art a King and Child, govern
and defend me henceforth who am a King and child.'
That this petition was not in vain, is sufficiently
manifest by the event and strange overthrow of such
powerful designs, which could only be controlled by
the hand of God. Neither did the Divine mercy
make a stop here, but gave a further assurance of His
holy protection by the happy birth of St. Thomas
Cantilupe, who was not only a presage of better
times, but in a particular manner designed for a
main support and strength both to King and kingdom in the highest seat of government, and to be a
mirror of justice in the tribunals both of Church and
State. [1.][4]

[2] Prov. viii. 15.

[3] Henry Knighton, *De Eventibus.* ' Rogo te puerum Regem ut
me regem puerum de cætero regas et defendas.'

[4] The references in brackets all through this volume are to the
numbered paragraphs of the supplementary Chapter (ch. xxvi.).

CHAPTER II.

Of the parents and descent of St. Thomas.

NOBILITY, though in the most civilized nations it hath ever had a special prerogative in the general conceit of men, yet with this abatement and restriction, that the wiser sort never looked upon it otherwise than an extrinsical and borrowed light, shining more by the reflection of other's deserts than any worth in itself. Which well interprets that ancient custom of the Roman nobility, who wore the figure of a moon upon their shoe as a distinctive mark of their rank and quality. Neither had that golden grasshopper, which the gentlemen of Athens wore upon their garments as a badge of honour, any other meaning but to admonish them that nobility, though it seemed a specious and glittering thing, yet was but a mere airy and idle fancy if, like the silly grasshopper, they contented themselves to sing and chant their ancestors' renown and greatness, and would not take the pains to lay up store, and make themselves a stock of true worth and honour by their own industrious and noble actions. Virtue, like the sun, shines with its own light, and needs no supply from any other; it lives not with the breath of other's fame, nor rakes up honour out of dead men's ashes.

It may seem, therefore, a very unnecessary, if not preposterous diligence, to be inquisitive of the pedigrees of saints, whose purity and holiness of life hath raised them above all the height of flesh and blood, and, by a strange adoption, made them brothers and sisters and mothers of God Himself.[4] Nevertheless, if the wisdom of God allows of a mutual reference and communication between the parent and the child, so as the shame and honour of the one reflects upon the other; if the eternal Providence hath a special and mysterious design, even in that lineal succession of nature, as it appears by the style of Holy Scripture, and remarkably in the genealogy of the Word Incarnate, where the finger of God points out all particulars with such exactness, name by name, both good and bad; in fine, if the excellency of virtue doth not seldom more appear by a parallel of former times, either in similitude and imitation of worthy actions or a generous renouncing and detestation of the contrary, it cannot but conduce to the better knowledge and esteem of saints to be informed of what

[4] St. Matt. xii. 50.

stock and condition they are. If noble and of high
extraction, like a diamond bred in a mine of gold,
worthy to be observed, that by their own virtue they
surpass the glory of their birth and ancestors, and not
by idolizing and adorning, but treading upon worldly
greatness, they make it an ascent to raise themselves
from earth to Heaven. If of a mean and low degree,
like an Oriental pearl in a coarse and rugged shell,
the workmanship of Divine grace is the more to be
admired that can raise children of Abraham from
stones, and frame such precious rarities out of gross
materials; as the happiness and glory of the saints
themselves is likewise more remarkable, seeing they
owe nothing of their greatness to earth, but receive
all from Heaven. In a word, it cannot be denied
but that nobility and renown of ancestors (as an
impartial witness[5] well expressed it), is a visible light
which makes the actions of posterity more conspicuous, be they good or bad.

Having upon this occasion digressed thus far, give
me leave to add one word more, and let our nobility
know that this business of descent, be it never so
noble, is a mere airy thing unless it be supported and
illustrated with virtue and piety. When it is thus

---

[5] Sallust. 'Majorum gloria posteris quasi lumen est, neque
bona eorum neque mala in occulto patitur' (Speech of Marius).—
Bel. Jug. c. lxxxviii.

mated it both gives and receives great advantages, and the one sets off the other extremely. True it is that everywhere, even alone, it ought to have its due respect, and none that I know denies it besides the Quakers, but when any brag of it they boast of what's not their own, and show thereby rather their own emptiness than its worth, and themselves to have more of the man than Christian. For Christian nobility derives not its pedigree from flesh and blood, but grace and sanctity, according to the saying of St. Ambrose, the "lineage of a just man is virtue and perfection, for by it souls are ennobled and dignified," as families are by antiquity of blood, not only ennobled but deified to a participation of the Divine nature. This is true nobility indeed, and worth standing on, and adds great lustre to the other, as the mixture of a nobler metal doth to another of an inferior alloy, yet still we must so commend the one as to leave the other in its due reverence and esteem.

To come now to our blessed St. Thomas. His father was William, Lord Cantilupe, a person for his worth and greatness often mentioned in the English history and records of heralds. The father of this lord was also another William, who jointly with his son stood ever firm in the Barons' Wars to both the Kings, whose favour in employments of highest trust and honour they well deserved. Though, as a known historian[6] of those times affirms, their family received not so just a measure as their merit required. Yet the father of our Saint bore no less a charge in Court than that of Great Master or Lord Steward of the King's house. Which, as in other kingdoms, so in this of England, was ever esteemed of chief favour and dignity, being the eye and hand of the King, not only at a distance and in absence, but commanding all in his very presence, and in a manner seated upon the same throne. Neither was this honour or whatsoever also they received from their Sovereign above the rank of their birth and quality.

The Cantilupes, or Cantelowes (vulgarly so called from the original Champ de Loup, or Campus Lupi), were a noble family of special note and eminency among those brave adventurers who followed the Norman Conqueror in his enterprize of our English monarchy, and purchased him that crown with the hazard of their lives and fortunes. And as they brought with them a fair inheritance of estate and honour, so they still continued their course with successive increase, as great rivers the further they go the more they dilate themselves with the reception of other streams. The heirs-general of the Strongbows and Marshalls, Earls of Pembroke, of the

[6] Matthew Paris.

Fitz-Walters Earls of Hereford, of the Breoses, or Breuses, Lords of Abergavenny, left their estates and greatness by right of marriage unto the Cantilupes. Such was the paternal line of St. Thomas, and his father, a person of so high command and credit, the King, upon an exigence being to make a voyage into France, could not think of a more powerful and faithful hand, beyond all exception and envy, to intrust with his crown and kingdom than William Cantilupe.

It was an equal match between this lord and the Lady Millicent, Countess of Evreux and Gloucester, mother of our Saint. She was daughter of Hugh, Lord Gournay, and the Lady Juliana, sister to Reginald, Earl of Dammartin and Boulogne. The Gournays were of the prime nobility of Normandy, nearly allied to the sovereign Dukes of that country, and as near to our glorious and blessed King Edward the Confessor. The Counts of Dammartin were of an illustrious family in France, matched with the greatest princes of Europe. And this Reginald, uncle to the Lady Millicent in right of his wife Ida, grandchild to Stephen, King of England, became Earl of Boulogne, which title he transferred again with his daughter Matilde, married unto Philip, Earl of Clermont, only brother to Louis, the eighth King of France, and uncle to St. Louis. This then was

the alliance and descent of that noble lady : she
was first married to Almeric Montfort, Earl of
Evreux, in Normandy, as also of Gloucester, in
right of his mother Mabel, eldest daughter and heir
to William, Earl of Gloucester, grandchild to Henry,
the first King of England. This Almeric, being head
of that illustrious family of the Montforts descended
from Robert, surnamed the Pious, King of France,
and dying without issue, was the last of that race
in Normandy, leaving his noble and virtuous consort
the Lady Millicent to be blessed with a happier and
more fruitful marriage, especially in this her son,
who alone illustrated that renowned family with
more honour than all the greatness and titles of
their famous ancestors. [2.]

CHAPTER III.

Childhood and domestic education of St. Thomas.

To look into the infancy or childhood of saints may seem as little pertinent to their merit, as to the glory of God : that part of the life of man being commonly held for a mere prologue or dumb show before a tragedy of miseries ; a dream or slumber before the soul awakes to the light of reason ; a state of neutrality betwixt man and beast, as incapable of praise as blame, and only happy in this, that it is insensible to all un-happiness. Yet experience and reason teach us that this twilight of life is not so dark, but that we may read sundry characters, though written in a small letter by the hand of God : this mute part of the age of man is not so speechless but that it foretells us much of what will follow. In fine, even childhood itself hath not so little of the man, but that it is capable of deep impressions both of grace and reason : as the lovely and sweet variety of colours in many flowers receive their first tincture in the very root ; and the value of pearls depends much upon the first drop of dew which falls into the shells when they are newly engendered. That the Divine Providence hath a special eye upon the infancy of man is an undeniable truth both in human and Divine history: neither doth this only consist in certain prodigies and demonstrations of a power above the reach of nature, but also, and that most usually, in a particular favour and protection of the Divine hand by connatural means of education and other circumstances, to withdraw from evil and lead to virtue.

The whole sequel of our St. Thomas's life clearly shows how highly he was privileged with both these blessings from Heaven. A nature he had, elevated above the common strain, a mind full of generous heat and vigour, ever tending to a higher sphere, like a fire without smoke or mixture of proper elements, which met with so noble a temperature of body, that though of a prosperous and lively habitude, he never knew in his whole life what anything meant which was not agreeable with the purity of angels. He, the first fruit of that happy marriage, was born at a manor of his father's in Lincolnshire, Hameldon[1] by name, where he also received the

---

[1] Hambleden in Buckinghamshire, about four miles from Great Marlow, but in the diocese of Lincoln about the year 1218 (*Acta Sanct.* vol. xlix. p. 494).

Sacrament of Baptism, regenerated thereby to the
precious adoption of the children of God. In
memory whereof Edmund, Earl of Cornwall, son
to Richard, once King of the Romans, and a great
admirer of our Saint's perfections, built there an
oratory to the honour of God and this Saint, in the
which oratory our Lord is said to have wrought
frequent miracles by the intercession of the same
Saint. Besides him, his parents were blessed with
a numerous offspring of three sons and ʼthree
daughters, which like so many young olives environed their table to their great joy ; and the latter
were all bestowed in an honourable wedlock.

To cultivate duly these hopeful endowments both
of nature and grace by a good education was the
care and endeavour of his pious parents; who, as
in his infancy they had provided him of a virtuous
nurse (the process of his canonization calls her
devout, noble, and holy, insomuch that even together
with his milk he sucked in sanctity), so in his childhood they were no less wanting to furnish him with
fit masters for his instruction in these first rudiments ;
and this was to be done under their own eyes, that
they might be witnesses of all. They knew right
well how important the first impressions are in
children, and consequently how choice they ought
to be, since that tincture is retained a long time,

and gives ordinarily a relish to their proceedings.
His parents were so chary in this point, and
solicitous to have the blessing of Heaven second
their industry, that we may say they imitated daily
the ancient Illyrians, who, when they gathered their
sweet Fleur-de-lis, lifted them up as an offering
to Heaven, from whence they had received them :
so these noble personages, looking upon their first
fruit as a gift of God, and acknowledging it to be
more His than theirs, endeavoured with all gratitude
to make him a fit present for the Divine hand, and
to raise him from earth to Heaven by careful and
virtuous breeding.

Their usual habitation was at Court, by reason
of the charge which the father of our Saint bore,
and the obligation he had of personal attendance
for the daily service of the King. The reputation
of Courts hath ever been as of a place where virtue
is laughed out of countenance and denied admittance,
as too coarsely clad for such fine company. Infamy
is nowhere more in credit, nor vice so canonized : it
is a school of Egyptian hieroglyphics, where beasts
and monsters are supposed to signify heroic virtues.
What care, therefore, and vigilance were these pious
and noble parents to use in preserving this sweet
flower from blasting under so malignant a climate !
What caution and prevention to banish all folly

and vanity from the sight of those innocent eyes, to stop his ears from the least whisper of charming pleasures! What a perpetual watch and ward, not to let a word fall, not the least action or gesture appear before this little one which might have any noxious impression in his tender soul! Though to say the truth and to give those happy times their due (which is also to be observed as a special providence of God towards the advancement of our Saint in all perfection), the style of that Court was far different from the usual course of others, and might well be termed a sanctuary of piety and school of virtue.

Such an influence hath the example of princes over the hearts of men, drawing them whither they list with a kind of magnetic force either to good or evil. We had then a King who thought it no under-valuing of majesty to visit hospitals and alms-houses, to serve and feed the poor with his own hands, to embrace and kiss lepers. Instead of revels and masques, his chief pleasure was in his chapel, where he heard every day three Masses with solemn music, and never omitted to be present at the rest, as long as there was a priest at the altar; where he ever used this ceremony in honour to the King of Heaven —to support the priest's arm whilst he elevated the Sacred Host, then with reverence to kiss his hand.

Insomuch as his near kinsman and brother-in-law, St. Louis, then King of France, observing that out of his devotion to the Holy Sacrifice of Mass, he left no considerable time for sermons, advised him to allow some part of his pious exercises to the Word of God ; to which he answered, that for his part he had rather see his friend than hear him spoken of. Our Queen, as long as this King, her husband, lived, agreed with him as well in piety as in conjugal love, and as soon as his death left her free to her liberty, she retired to a cloister of consecrated virgins, where the world might see her heart had ever been.[2] The Consort of our Prince, son of Henry III., now King, and after successor by the name of Edward I., was a daughter of Spain, who was so little read in the Platonic of our days, that she knew not how to love anything but Christ and her husband, whom she followed through all hazards and terrors to the Holy Land, where the Prince, being treacherously stabbed by a Saracen with a poisoned knife, when no skill of surgery could prevail, the invincible love of this lady undertook the cure, and gave her the courage to suck out the poison and putrefaction of the wound with her own mouth, to make it good that love is

[2] Queen Eleanor of Provence took the veil in the Benedictine Convent of Amesbury, in Wiltshire, in 1287, where she died in 1292—permission being given for her to retain her dower.

as strong as death.[3] The piety of the whole Court
was answerable to their Sovereign's example, which
appears evidently in that so many of the prime
nobility devoted their lives and fortunes to the service of the Holy Land, and the greatest ladies ended
their days in holy monasteries.

Nevertheless, though that Court then was such a
Paradise, the pious and prudent parents of our Saint
knew well that serpents might lurk even there.
Vipers creep into gardens of balsam, poisons and
antidotes often grow in the same bed. They were
not strangers to the infirmity of human nature, especially in youth, which, like a distempered stomach,
longs for that which is most hurtful, and in such
variety of objects, as at a full table, seldom or never
feeds without a surfeit. They resolved therefore to
place this precious treasure which God had given
them in a safe retreat, as nature, or rather the Author
of nature, teaches the little pearls, when they are
soft and tender in the shell, to retire under shady
and hollow rocks, being otherwise not only exposed
to violence of waves and weather, but also subject

[3] Hemingford's account, quoted by Mrs. Strickland, makes
Eleanor of Castile's conduct the reverse of heroic. It is consoling
to learn that 'he (Edward I.) always attributed his recovery to
the tender care and attention of Eleanora ; but if there had been
any truth in the story of her sucking the poison, the narrative
of the scene which has entered into its details so minutely, would
not have forgotten this circumstance.'

to change colour and be truly sunburnt if they float in the open sea. They followed, therefore, the advice of the Holy Ghost given to all parents, if they love the safety of their children, to put them under the shade and protection of wisdom: 'He shall set his children under her shelter,' with a promise not only of security, but also of glory: 'Under her covering he shall be protected from the heat,' and in her glory shall he rest.'[4] This holy and prudent resolution of theirs was, it seems, much furthered by a near kinsman and friend, Walter Cantilupe, Bishop of Worcester, a person of mind and courage equal to his birth, and of such zeal that to advance the heroical design of Christian princes in the Holy Land, he went himself thither, accompanied with one of the greatest men of that age for piety and valour, William Longuespée, Earl of Salisbury, whose happy death in that quarrel was solemnised with a triumph in Heaven, as it was revealed at that very instant to his mother in England, who then led a religious life in a monastery of her own founding.

The said noble Prelate, Walter Cantilupe, being in familiar conversation with William, Lord Cantilupe, father of St. Thomas, and the child being present, the Bishop asked him what course of life

[4] Ecclus. xiv. 26, 27.

he would choose, what pleased him best? The
child freely answered him that he would be a
soldier. 'Well said, sweet heart,' quoth the Bishop,
'thou shalt be a soldier to serve the highest of Kings,
and fight under the colours of His glorious martyr,
St. Thomas.' These words proved not only pro-
phetical by the event, but also had such efficacy,
that the parents, as in obedience to a Divine decree,
directed the whole education of the child to piety
and learning. And the child himself, as if he had
learnt a new lesson from Heaven, thought no more
of those glorious fancies to which his own generous
nature carried him, and the examples of his illustrious progenitors incited him, but with the same
courage betook himself wholly to his book, and with
the little Solomon preferred it before thrones and
kingdoms. This resolution was truly to be admired
in the child, and no less in his parents, considering
not only the vehement inclination of men to live
after death in their image by posterity, but much
more the height of their fortune, with so rich a stock
of antiquity and honour, preserved and amplified for
so many descents; whereas if he took a course of
retirement from a worldly life and not compatible
with succession, as his education seemed to dispose
him, all must die with him and lie buried in the
same grave.

None of these respects could ever persuade the parents of our Saint to let him run the common race of the world in liberty, in plenty, in wantonness, in excess of vanity and pleasure, without restraint of anything that flatters the sensual appetite, foments self-love, and rejects all command of reason. These generally being esteemed in the depraved judgment of men as proper attributes of greatness, and, on the contrary, discipline, learning, and piety laughed at as a debasement of noble spirits and mere precisianism.. But these pious and prudent parents weighed things in another balance; they were fully satisfied of this truth, that nothing suits better with honour than virtue, and that nobility cannot live in a more immortal monument upon earth than in the shrine of sanctity. They knew that the nobler the mind, the more need of cultivating, otherwise, like a rich soil, more subject to grow wild and degenerate. They were not so solicitous to propagate as to illustrate their family, the happiness whereof they placed not in long continuance, but a good conclusion. And since families are mortal, and have their term of life as well as each particular man, they cannot come to a better end than to die in the bed of honour with integrity of fame and virtue.

CHAPTER IV.

St. Thomas goes to Oxford.

OUR little St. Thomas having now received the first
tincture and elements of learning at home, both the
authority of his parents and his own propension led
him to a place of higher improvement, the University of Oxford, which was at that time in the primitive
vigour, and esteemed by all as great a school of
virtue as of learning, and therefore the common
nursery of our chief nobility of England : a thing
continued even to our days, though with different
success, as but too true experience teaches us.   It
was hard to say whether Oxford in that age (though
it ever bore the pre-eminence of antiquity) or Paris
had the greater repute and fame of learning.   Yet
this noble strife bred nothing of that malignity to
which the emulous nature of man is but too prone—
yea, rather maintained a friendly commerce, and, as
it were, free trade between these two great marts of
wisdom and sanctity.   And as those times were
fertile of great persons in all perfections, neither of

these two renowned academies did engross any advantage to themselves, nor envy the other's benefit, but mutually imparted to each other what was rare and eminent.

The two glorious lights of the Catholic Church, the Orders of St. Dominic and St. Francis, illustrated the world at that time with their primitive splendour, and revived Christianity with new vigour of learning and piety. St. Thomas of Aquin, St. Bonaventure, and that Doctor of Doctors, Alexander of Hales, born in Gloucestershire, master of both these Saints, with many others of the foresaid holy Institutes, were the oracles of that age, and particularly enriched and cultivated the French and English Universities with their admirable doctrine. Among the rest that famous and learned Prelate, Robert Kilwarby, was highly eminent, who, bred and born in England, was one of the first of that nation who consecrated himself to God in the holy habit of St. Dominic.

But his great abilities and learning gave him not leave to enjoy the sweet retirement of a religious life. He was first called by the See Apostolic to the Primacy of England, in which charge he gave such testimonies of his incomparable worth, that Nicholas III., who then sat in St. Peter's Chair, a great admirer of learning and virtue (which alone he regarded

in all preferments), to have his nearer assistance in
the general government of the whole Church, thought
fit to create him Cardinal and Bishop of Porto, near
Rome, which is the second dignity among those
princes of the Church.   The holy Prelate having
received this new addition of honour, was so far
from that common disease and dropsy of souls, who
the more they have of greatness, the more they thirst,
that the first thing he did was to disburthen himself
of his Metropolitan charge of Canterbury, not without resentment and repugnance of the King and all
the nobility of England, who extremely affected and
reverenced him for his great learning and holiness
of life.   He left behind him a perpetual monument
of his piety and love to his Order, which is yet
extant, though applied to a different use, commonly
known by the name of Blackfriars in London.   This
place, when he was Archbishop of Canterbury, he
purchased, and built both church and convent for
his religious, whom he transferred thither from a less
convenient residence in the suburbs.   The modesty
and humble carriage of this great Prelate was no
less admired in the Court of Rome than his eminent
parts and excelling knowledge.   He would not
change his poor religious habit for the purple of
princes, and was the first Cardinal that retained his
habit in that dignity, as ever since his example was

followed by those who were promoted to that degree of honour from religious orders of monastic discipline. He never appeared in public but on foot, and never had other train but two of his own religious to accompany him, and two other attendants in the nature of servants. In fine, though he was admired and honoured as the oracle of those times, and mouth of the See Apostolic, as appeared in that famous treaty and letters written by him in the Pope's name to the King of Tartary, about the conversion of that nation to the Christian faith, yet nothing could ever lift him the least thought above himself out of the profound humility and poverty of a religious man.

It was a special providence of God that this great person was chosen to be the spiritual guide and governor of our holy Saint from his tender years, which we may esteem a mutual happiness and honour to them both, seeing that the wise child is the father's joy, as the father's worth is the children's glory. The learned and wise Prelate seeing how pure and generous a soul he had to manage, omitted no care and industry to set him forward to the highest perfection. Wherein finding his angelical pupil so ready and pliable, and even to outrun his wishes, he conceived such unspeakable joy and comfort, that all the days of his life he could never name him without exces-

sive admiration and praise. He never met with
stone or bramble in that soul to choke or hinder
the full fruit of the heavenly seed; he never found
weed in that bed of lilies; he never saw spot in that
virgin stole which he had received in baptism; no
flashes of levity, frowardness, or unconstant giddiness
so incident to that age. All his soul, in fine, like
that crystal sea of the Apocalypse, without wave or
wind, not disturbed with the least blast of disordered
passions, yet still in motion, abhorring nothing more
than that canker and bane of virtue, sloth and idleness.

He never omitted to be daily present at the Holy
Sacrifice of the Mass with all reverence and attention,
which he took for a common duty of all pious
Christians: and therefore would oblige himself to
a greater task, reciting daily, young as he was, the
Canonical Hours or Priest's Office, which in him was
a remarkable act of piety, and not only a presage of
his future intentions, but also a token not improbable,
that even then as much as lay in him, he devoted
himself to a clergy life: having otherwise no tie at
all, either of benefice or Orders; his years being
incapable of the one, and the discipline of those
better times not allowing ecclesiastical fruits and titles
to any other but such as for ability and age could
worthily perform the functions. In this manner did

our Saint pass his first course of literature, with such success and profit in the Latin tongue, that it gave him new appetite and courage to apply himself to the higher sciences.   As they who discover the first veins of a rich mine work on with more alacrity to attain the main treasure.   Wherefore, though at that time Oxford flourished with all advantage of learning, both for knowledge and discipline, and could furnish other nations with choice masters in all sciences, yet considerable motives drew St. Thomas out of his native country into France, and induced him to choose Paris for his school of philosophy.   [3. 4.]

CHAPTER V.

St. Thomas's Study of Philosophy.

THE fact that antiquity placed the temples of their goddess of learning and wisdom in forts and castles, seated upon a higher ground, and at a competent distance from the common habitation of their towns and cities, did not only signify that wisdom and knowledge is the chief protection and safeguard of men, and a thing highly elevate above the vulgar reach, but also that the proper seat of learned exercises is to be at a convenient distance from the throng and tumult of the world : this being no less an enemy to speculative and studious minds than smoke and dust to the eye, and a confused and jarring noise to a delicate and harmonious ear. This considered, the most populous city of Europe, and the greatest Court, might seem very improper for the improvement of St. Thomas in his studies : especially for him in particular, having more occasion of distraction than any other, by reason of his near relation and alliance with the greatest princes of that

Court, namely, Reginald, Count of Dammartin and Boulogne, great uncle to our Saint, and Matilde, Countess of Clermont, daughter of the foresaid Reginald, married to Philip, only brother to Louis the Eighth, and uncle to St. Louis, who reigned at that present time. These circumstances might well have put a youthful spirit upon other thoughts than serious and painful studies, and forced him even against his will to spend the greatest part of his time in receiving and paying courtly visits. But the generous resolution of the Saint, and the great light which he received from Heaven to make a true estimate of things, gave him strength and vigour to prosecute his course without diversion.

And such were those happy times, that he found rather help than prejudice in Court, where the King, a Saint, taught the world this truth, that the disorder of courts is not the fault of the place but the men, and that virtue is ever at hand where it finds admittance. Neither did the Court and army, the two proper spheres of this great prince and soldier of Christ, alone partake of his holy influences; he was as great a patron of learning as arms; and as piety and discipline is the chief support and advancement of both, his powerful example and industry, and the concourse of so many great persons renowned for learning and sanctity, invited thither by the fame of that happy reign, gave such life and vigour to the University of Paris, that it never flourished more than in those holy times. The famous College of Sorbonne, so esteemed even till this day, that it is a special mark of honour to be a member thereof, was then first founded, and owes the glory of so prosperous a continuance to that happy beginning, which made them heirs not only of the name and patrimony, but also of the eminent learning of their worthy founder, Robert de Sorbona. The persons also who then either taught or studied in that University are a sufficient testimony of the flourishing state of these times which bred them, whom the schools ever since have reverenced and admired as chief masters and mirrors of human and Divine sciences, and observe continually their method and form of teaching, as the ready and only way to attain solid and perfect knowledge.

That St. Thomas made the best use of these advantages appears evidently by the effect, and that public testimony of his singular ability and learning, when having finished that course of studies he proceeded Master of Arts, which honour in those impartial times was not to be bought with favour, nor upon any other account than desert. Neither did he satisfy himself with that specious ornament of his youth, as commonly persons of his rank and quality are wont to do, and then apply the rest of their life to the designments of ambition and pleasure. As after his return into England he changed not his mind with the place, but still continued, like a faithful lover, his constant affection to wisdom, whose amiable beauty had so possessed his heart, that it wiped away all other impressions. And that he might enjoy his happiness without disturbance, he retired from Court and the restless noise of the world to his known repose and first nursery of his youth, the University of Oxford.

But before he leave Paris, and we conclude this chapter, it will not be impertinent to our purpose to show what a lily he was at that time amidst those thorns of philosophy, able enough to choke all spirit and sentiments of piety and devotion, if great care be not taken; that is, how pure and nice a conscience he kept, how sensible of the least blemish of imperfection; and this will appear by an example which stands on record, and happened in this interim. While he studied his philosophy at Paris, the window of his closet was a little at fault, and to set it right without trouble or the help of a workman, he served himself of a stick or prop of a vine out of the next vineyard. The matter, God wot, so very inconsiderable, to an ordinary conscience would not have created any scruple at all; yet he, though otherwise not scrupulous, in his tenderness, apprehended the transgression so deeply, that even then for its expiation he enjoined himself a seven years' penance, and each year with great remorse confessed the same. From whence we may gather how angelically pure that blessed soul was which checked so resentively at so minute a thing, and how far it was from harbouring any great offence which deemed the least heinous. A tender conscience is like a tender eye, which the least mote disturbs and annoys, making it water to wash off the stain, and express regret that ever it came there. [5.]

CHAPTER VI.

Study of the Canon Law at Oxford.

THE resolution which St. Thomas took after he had ended his philosophy with such success and applause, sufficiently declares that his intention was not to make use of those studies merely as an additional ornament of his other eminent parts and quality, that as his birth and fortune raised him above the vulgar sort, so he might also excel them in perfection of mind and knowledge. Which could not but be esteemed a motive worthy of a generous spirit, in setting so true a value upon the better part of man, and not suffering the flower and vigour of his age to vanish and wither away without fruit. In prosecution of such happy beginnings, to carry all on before him, and perfect himself in each kind and for all callings, he resolved for his next task to apply himself to the civil law; which, though a hard and knotty knowledge, yet he hoped to draw some honey out of these flints for his improvement. He took it as the Israelites did the spoils of the Egyptians, to apply it to the service of

the true God, and hearing that there was a famous
professor at Orleans who read that lecture with much
applause, he betook himself thither, and frequented
his school with such esteem of progress, that he far
outstripped his fellow-students, being judged not only
fit, but fittest, to supply the chair in his master's
absence. This knowledge enabled him much as to
the management of secular business, which, though it
were not the thing he aimed at, yet did good service
thereby, and especially in the discharge of his double
Chancellorship.

Having possessed himself of this study he undertook another of some affinity with the former, but
more sacred, and that was the canon law. This
suited more with his inclination and intentions,
besides the special providence of God, which led this
Saint by the hand from his first infancy, and guided
him step by step to that height of greatness to which
He had designed him both in spiritual and temporal
government, for it seems evident that our Saint had
even then devoted himself entirely to the service of
the Church and a clergy life, otherwise what preten-
sion could a person of his condition have to apply
himself to that sad and laborious study of canon law,
as void of pleasure as profit, or any other ambitious
interest, for him in particular, seeing that nature and
fortune had raised him to such a pitch that he had

little need of skill and industry to advance him
further. The motive then of lodging his thoughts
upon this serious and learned study was to enable
himself for that holy function to which God had
called him from his very childhood. He knew that a
clergy life ought to be a shining light, not only in
itself, but to illustrate others as well by doctrine as
example. He was assured that ignorance in such a
state was blindness in the eye, deafness in the ear, a
palsy in the limbs, and a whole privation of life and
vigour through all the body. That it was to play the
pilot without chart or compass ; to command in war
without practice of arms or discipline ; to undertake
the cure of others without knowledge either of the
evils or remedies. Neither was the circumstance of
time unreasonable to undertake that study in the
prime and vigour of his years, when he had improved
himself in the perfect knowledge of philosophy, which
quickens the mind with a new life, teaches men to
speak and call things by their true names, gives them
eyes to see what is invisible, and makes the senses
own, what they never knew, upon the word of reason.

Much about the time while he was deliberating to
leave Paris, a General Council indicted at Lyons in
the same kingdom by Innocent IV., was to take its
beginning on the ensuing feast of St. John Baptist, it
being summoned not only upon the score of the Holy

Land, but also for redress of other ecclesiastical
abuses. The emulous spirit of our Saint, desirous to
benefit himself in each degree, repaired thither
together with his younger brother Hugh; knowing
well that such assemblies summon, as to a general
muster what is valiant, so to this what is wise, learned,
and in virtue eminent. He knew that a General
Council is like a constellation where many propitious
lights combine in one to the illuminating of the
Christian world, as the great interpreter of God's will;
as an oracle giving to know undoubtedly what we are
to believe and do, in the great practices of Christianity, and whither can one recur with more advantage and satisfaction than hither in doubts of this
nature? These two lesser lights even then darted
forth such conspicuous beams, that notice being taken
of them, they were both made chaplains of the said
Pope; and the rather for that, besides their own
merits, the presence of their father, sent thither by
the King of England, contributed not a little to their
dignity. The Council ended, our Saint returned full
fraught with what he had heard and seen, and taking
Paris in his way, hastened over to his Mother University of Oxford, towards the accomplishment of the
forementioned task of canon law; designing when he
had mastered it to proceed forthwith to his divinity
But we may say that in this he reckoned without his

host, and while we propose, God disposes much other-wise; for about fourteen years intervened ere he could begin the latter, and in the interim he was to undergo a double Chancellorship, both of University and realm; of both these we shall treat in the ensuing chapters.

Coming to this famous University he met, to his great comfort, and as great benefit of spirit, with his former ghostly father, Dr. Robert Kilwarby; who, as he had before not only known him from his child-hood, but also laid in him the first foundations of a spiritual life, so now he resumed again the same charge, and he willingly lent his best endeavour to a further advance. The spiritual advices of this good man were to our Saint as so many oracles, and as such he received them, animated thereby to a serious progress in both his undertakings of learning and virtue. For we are to advert that it was his settled maxim to make these two always individual com-panions, keeping them in an equal balance, so that learning should adorn piety and piety learning, each giving the other mutual assistance; insomuch that no application to studies could divert his mind, or lessen his fervour to devotion and virtue. He knew what the Apostle[1] said to be most true, that knowledge is a swelling vapour, and puffs up to danger of bursting if

[1] 1 Cor. viii. 1.

it be not kept down by the weight of piety, and
bounded with a profound humility.   Want of this
wholesome caveat makes many great wits miscarry,
while they will be more witty than wise, and learned
than virtuous.

As for the effect and success of these his present
studies, by consent of all, both friends and foes, that
is, enemies of God and themselves (for on the Saint's
part he never had any, nor opposition at all, but in
the behalf of God and His right, which he was
obliged to maintain), by common consent, I say, he
proceeded Doctor of common law; and so became
incorporated into that noble and ancient University as
a principal and conspicuous member with a mutual
honour to them both : from whom he was not to
part till by a special providence of God, not only with
common consent, but universal joy both of King and
University he was made their head.   [6.]

CHAPTER VII.

St. Thomas is made Chancellor of Oxford.

SOME space of time elapsed here in preparing for
this graduation; some also affirm that he presided
for some time in that study (canon law); however,
that intervening space gave the learned academy a
sufficient knowledge of his singular worth and
abilities, letting them know what a treasure they had
got among them. In the meantime the University
was deprived of its head, or Chancellor, and was to
to be furnished anew. Nothing seemed wanting in
our Saint towards a most satisfactory discharge
thereof, either as to moral parts of learning, prudence,
or what is also requisite for the support and coun-
tenancing of the same authority, splendour of birth
and great alliance. Having thus cast their eye upon
him, by the joint vote and concurrence of that
illustrious body, the King was petitioned for his consent, and all parties concerned most readily yielded
to the choice besides himself, who never was ambitious of any preferment.

What a Chancellor of an University is can hardly
be defined, seeing that his power and office wholly
depends upon the national customs and proper insti-
tution of the founders.   But this is generally received
by all, that the Chancellor is truly head of the
University, not only in points of doctrine, but also
in moral discipline and comportment both of masters
and students.   In England, as this office was ever
of high esteem and honour, so even in these later
times it is for the most part borne by persons great
either by birth and dignity, or of eminent power and
favour in Court.   This being held necessary to support and protect that learned and united body from
all disturbance and disquiet, which that valiant and
great Prince, King Edward III., took so to heart,
that though he seemed wholly employed in arms
and warfare, yet upon an abuse and affront offered
by the city to the students of that University, he
divested the Mayor and magistrates of their power
they had before, and gave the Chancellor of Oxford
the only view of the excise of bread, ale, and wine,
and other victuals, excluding the Mayor utterly from
that office.[1]   This King, though he was deeply
engaged in wars abroad with such victorious success
and conquests, as none before or after him perhaps
had the like, yet was so present in the government

[1] Stowe, *Anno Regis* 29, 1355.

of his kingdom at home (especially what concerned the nobler and most important part of the commonwealth), that is, the education of youth, both clergy and laity, in learning and virtue, that it might seem the final mark he aimed at, and for all his successful prowess abroad, that he took it for the greatest honour to be a feudatory to the supreme dominion of wisdom, and in real effect did profess that infallible and everlasting truth: 'By Me kings reign and princes rule.'[2]

In this chair of, authority was St. Thomas set, and it was his singular integrity and upright demeanour which purchased him this great and general esteem. The truth is, there is no such purchaser of true worth and ascent to honour as virtue, and this is confessed both by friend and foe—even the latter deems it praiseworthy, though he cannot imitate it, but beholds it, as the owl doth the light, with disdain. Of his demeanour in this office, the record testifies thus: 'In which office of Chancellor, as also in every other which he bore, he demeaned himself with such uprightness and integrity, that he never swerved from the path of truth which he once trod, but went on always advancing from good to better.'[3] This advance was made by exalting

---

[2] Proverbs viii. 15, 16.
[3] Compend. Vitæ, *Acta Sanct.* vol. xlix. p. 541.

virtue and learning and depressing vice, and idleness
its nurse, by an impartial administration of justice
to all, giving every one their due, by maintaining
discipline in its vigour, without slackening the reins
to a noxious liberty. And as his authority extended
both to masters and scholars, and even to the citizens
themselves, so far as to impede any abuse towards
the former, so he carried an equal hand over all, and
failed not thereby to please all. How resolute and
active he was in this his proceeding is witnessed
by a scuffle or riot, which happened at that time,
betwixt the southern and northern scholars upon some
quarrel of emulation, in which the disorder grew so
high, that to part them he was fain to hazard his
own person, and to throw himself into the middle of
the throng, out of which he came though with a
whole skin, yet not with a whole coat, his gown
being torn and he beaten ; yet he mastered the multitude, reduced them to order, and made them do
penance for their insolency.

This of Chancellor was the first public office which
St. Thomas bore; this was that candlestick of gold
which first showed that burning and shining light to
the world ; this was that hill, where that well-built
city by the hand of God Himself first appeared, and
where there never was heard any other note but of
joy and comfort. And happy would that University

have deemed itself if it might still have been ex-
hilarated with these sweet notes, enlightened with
his knowledge, and refreshed with the streams of his
wisdom, of which they drank with much gust, and he
no churl in communicating them. But they, like the
fountain of Paradise, were not to be confined to so
narrow a current, fit to water the surface of the whole
kingdom, to which they were both sufficient, and
the King, at the loud report, which sounded even to
Court, designed them. He thought that famous
University too little a sphere for so great abilities,
and that it was an injury to the the whole realm to
confine such a person to any particular place though
never so honourable, and therefore resolved to make
the whole partake of this universal benefit. [7.]

CHAPTER VIII.

St. Thomas is made Lord High Chancellor of England.

KING HENRY III., a pious and gracious Prince, loved to employ and prefer the virtuous to great offices, as knowing that weighty affairs were never better managed, and consequently thrive better, than in the hands of such. For, besides the peculiar blessing and light which they receive from Almighty God, virtue gives them both industry and application, and removes many impediments which lie in others' way towards a due discharge of their trusts. And therefore, since our holy Saint carried in the opinion of all such a commendatory of sanctity of life and integrity of conversation, and withal his natural abilities corresponded to his supernatural, completing him in both, I wonder not at all that the good King cast his eyes upon him, and intrusted him with the great office of Lord Chancellor. As to the Saint himself, as he never sought the employment—nay, resisted what he could—so he came with a disinterested heart, disburthened of all respects but what he owed to God and his King, but seeing himself in the eyes of the Court and kingdom, he thought it needful to be more circumspect in his actions and behaviour, and therefore the author of his life says, 'Raised to that dignity, he endeavoured to square his actions and proceedings according to a straighter line of perfection.' He had learned to be so far master of himself, that no exaltation could raise him above himself, so that his heart and eyes were the same, nor did he now walk *in mirabilibus super se,*[1] in the clouds of wonders above himself. He knew he was made the vicegerent of Divine wisdom as to this pittance of trust, and therefore he said as it taught him, 'Arrogancy and pride, and wicked ways, and a double-tongued mouth I do detest :'[2] and I wish all that bear the place would say the same, and especially the last, of a double tongue, fit only for a double heart, destroying all sincerity and plain dealing. He owned and practised that which follows, 'Mine is counsel and equity, prudence is mine, strength is mine,'[3] and how he behaved himself in these particulars shall be shown in the end of the narrative.

To give now a small hint at the nature of this office, it may be observed that the word Cancellarius

[1] Psalm cxxx. 1.
[2] Proverbs viii. 13.   [3] Proverbs viii. 14.

or Chancellor signifies, not only now, but many ages
ago, an employment or trust of highest concern and
honour, next the King himself, most eminent for
power and authority, and till Sir Thomas More's
time, when worse changes and innovations followed,
the dignity of Chancellor was conferred upon single
or not married persons, though laymen, as not to be
incapable of ecclesiastical prelacy, either Archbishops
or Bishops, as the ordinary style of England was.   As
to the etymology of this word, Cassiodorus, that
learned and grave person, derives it from Cancelli,
that is, the grated inclosure wherein the Chancellor
separated from the common throng, not to be disturbed in his office, accessible only to men's eyes,
and therefore the same author calls these bars or
cancells lightsome doors, open cloisters, gates with
windows.   This was a friendly admonition or caveat
given by Cassiodorus to a Chancellor newly exalted
to that eminent office, to put him in mind that
though he was raised, and separated from the
common rank of men, yet he was exposed to the
common view of all, and therefore must proceed
accordingly—not please himself as if he were to
dance in a net, but to assure himself that he was
like to have as many censures and sharp judgments
on him as men had eyes.   Others say he is so called
because the Chancellor is, as it were, the mouth, the

eye, and ear of the Prince or Sovereign, and hath the receiving of all memorials or petitions presented to the Prince, and even decrees of the Prince himself; what he finds not convenient to law, or prejudicial to the Prince's or public good, it is his office to cancel or cross out as void and not to sign it. From this cancelling or crossing out with such uncontrolled authority, they will have the name of Cancellarius or Chancellor derived.

As for the Chancellor of England's office, it is a dignity that makes him esteemed in the kingdom above all, and next to the King himself. Insomuch that on the other part of the King's seal (whereof the custody belongs to the Chancellor) he signs his own orders, that the King's chapel be in his disposal and care, that the vacant archbishoprics, bishoprics, abbeys, and baronies falling into the King's hands, be received and kept by him that is the Chancellor, who likewise is to be present whensoever the King sits in council, even when he is not called, that all things of the clerk or clergyman who carries the King's seal be signed by the Chancellor's hand, that all things be disposed of by the advice and counsel of the Chancellor—in fine, that by the grace of God, his desert and merit concurring, he never ends his days but in the see of an archbishop or bishop, if he will accept of it. And for this reason

the office of Chancellor is never to be bought, as
having so much connection and relation to a clergy
state, for danger of incurring simony.   The manner
or ceremony of creating Chancellors in the reign of
Henry III., who installed St. Thomas in that dignity,
was to hang the great seal about the chosen Chancellor's neck.   But afterwards both the ceremonies
of instalment and his Court of Chancery were aug-
mented, and he had three seals, one of gold, two
of silver, a great one and a lesser; and for the lawyers'
abuses, and quirks in the common law the Chancellor's Court or Chancery was erected to moderate
all as umpire, merely out of equity and justice, inde-
pendent of sophistical tricks and verbal cavils.   This
was the office of the Lord Chancellor of England
since the Norman Conquest for the most part, with
some ceremonial changes, rather accidental than in
substance, as the kings who reigned thought fit.

In the administration of this office, as our Saint
showed great wisdom, so did he also great integrity,
and these two completed his justice, so that the
former secured him against mistakes and ignorance,
the latter against bribes and extortions, neither of
which either was or ever could be justly laid to his
charge—nay, he was so scrupulously nice in the
latter, that he would not have so much as the
shadow of it to approach him.   It is recorded par-

ticularly that certain religious men who had a suit depending at law applied themselves to him for his favour and furtherance in the despatch of the same, and thereto presented him with a jewel of value, which he rejected not without indignation, asking them whether they thought him to be won with gifts. Nor was his courage inferior either to his wisdom or integrity, upon which account, when reason and equity dictated that such a thing was to be done, he was undaunted as to the execution, even though the King himself stood in the way, yet none more observant of his Majesty than he. This may be confirmed by what happened at the council-table, and was driven on by many great ones who persuaded the King to confer an office upon a new converted Jew, whereby he was empowered over the lives and persons of such subjects as were found to be coiners of false money. He opposed it with much earnestness, saying it was too unlimited a power over Christians to be committed to a new converted Jew, who might easily be tempted according to his former ill habits to abuse it, and therefore besought his Majesty with tears either to revoke it or give him leave to absent himself, for he could not approve it. The King, moved with his tears and candour, as well as the force of his reasons, bidding him sit still, changed thereupon his determination. I shall say more relating to this in the last chapter. Now, how satisfactory his management of affairs in this ticklish charge was both to Prince and people, is evidenced by this, that the King ⁻upon urgent occasions, being called into France, left to him, during his absence, the trust and charge of the whole kingdom. [8.]

CHAPTER IX.

King Henry dies, his son succeeds. St. Thomas, with licence, gives up his Seal and retires.

IN this equal track of justice, declining neither to the right hand nor the left, did our Saint walk all the respite of King Henry's life. Full often during this space of time did he sigh after his former retirement, and ceased not upon fit occasions to importune the same ; but the good King, who had found his assistance and dexterity so serviceable in the despatch of affairs, would by no means hearken to that request, giving him leave to groan under his burthen, and he, in compliance with his will, submitted to it, making the best of the worst, and a virtue of necessity. At last, having finished the course of nature, as well as of a virtuous life, he paid the common tribute of mortality to death, and Edward, his eldest

son, called the First of that name, immediately succeeded in the throne, of whom it will not be amiss
to give some short account, as also how things went
in the course of affairs.

This Edward was not only a warlike but a wise
Prince, and as he had received both crown and life
from his father, so he restored both again, by cutting
off with his own hand the last and most · dangerous rebellion of all. This was raised by Simon
Montfort, a great soldier and of·high spirit, otherwise a pious and gracious person to most men, by
reason of his forward zeal to engage in what he
conceived did concern the common good, which
cost him first expulsion out of France, and after his
being received in England, and made Earl of Leicester,
no less than his life. This great warrior, observing
the march and approach of Prince Edward to give
him battle, turned to his commanders, and thus
advised them : ' Let us commend our souls to God,
for our bodies are theirs,' as it fell out, and he
died with the rest. The same great Prince Edward I.
after he had brought the kingdom of Scotland to
the utmost extremity, but prevented by death, could
not complete the conquest, charged his son
Edward II., or of Caernarvon (called so from his
birth in that castle) not to inter his body till he
finished the work begun by him, of which little

remained to be achieved. But those Court parasites, the young King's favourites, hating as death the life of a soldier, drew him off from that noble design to Court again, to the shame and infamy of the English nation and wretched end of that unfortunate Prince. A sad example of disobedience to the last words of a dying father, and such a father as England had scare his like for valour, conduct, and wisdom.

In the very beginning of King Edward's reign, and first step into the throne, St. Thomas, as his place and office required, brought him the great seal of England, with most humble acknowledgment of his obligation to his Majesty's father for honouring him above all desert with that eminent charge, which he now resigned into his Majesty's hands with this humble petition, that with his Majesty's approbation and leave, he may retire to that known mother of learning and wisdom, Oxford, where he may more enable himself for the service of God and of his Majesty and the assistance of his country. To which the King answered, first with thanks, as the manner is, for the great service done to the King and king- dom, and for his petition he assented to it, and for the present gave him full liberty to dispose of him- self as he thought fitting. This was what our Saint, much more addicted to the schools than to the Court, so earnestly breathed after, and as cheerfully

hastened to them as a stone to its centre or fire
to its element : *Trahit sua quemque voluptas.*

And here I cannot but pause awhile upon this
noble and heroical act of St. Thomas, which if we
measure by a human ell and man's natural inclination
to greatness, was perchance one of the noblest of his
life. For where in the world shall one find even
virtuous and holy men who make not preferments
a part of their aim and reward of their studies, much
less who will divest themselves willingly of it, especially the highest, when they have it in possession.
Honour is called the Nurse of Arts, and suits much
with the propension of man, who naturally loves
precedency and pre-eminency, as the milk he sucked
from his mother Eve, and few part with it but against
their wills. It is more than probable for divers
reasons that St. Thomas might have continued his
office had he not solicited a release from the same,
and such a solicitation upon the prudential motives of
a virtuous humility argues a profound sanctity and
contempt both of himself and worldly things. Had
he continued in his charge, the ordinary course of
such proceeding would have installed him in the
see of some great prelacy, of which, if he had been
more ambitious than of a private retirement, he
would have made it his business as he did this.
But saints see with other eyes than those of nature ;

they are guided by better lights, which partake more
of truth and less of vanity; they see honour to be
nothing else but a bubble and a burthen, and on
both scores worthy of despisement, since the former
is as empty as the latter troublesome, to say no
worse. To discover the emptiness of honour is a
point of wisdom, to contemn that which all dote
on, a point of sanctity; true wisdom makes them
know it is but a shadow, and that they ought not
to content themselves with shadows but solid sub-
stances, nor play the dog in the fable, who while
he more greedily than prudently snatched at the
shadow lost the bone. True sanctity tells them that
the truest honour is to contemn all honour besides
the honour of God, which, while they labour to
advance, they honour both Him and themselves, not
with an empty airy honour, but permanent and
eternal, whose shadow the other is.

Such good solid principles made our Saint do
what he did, that is, play the saint, that is, despise
and trample upon that idol of the world for the love
of Heaven and a virtuous life. But though the
King licensed him at his request from the Chancellorship, yet he still retained him during life, of
his Privy Council, as I find upon record in the
process of canonization, where his advice proved
many times advantageous above others, as I shall

hereafter have occasion to relate, and things were so ordered at present that no let or stop was put to the actual design of prosecuting his studies. [9.]

CHAPTER X.

St. Thomas returns to Oxford. Proceeds Doctor of Divinity. The testimony given of him.

OUR Saint, as we have said, being with licence and approbation of the King free from Court and the Chancellor's office, so much admired and wished for by the rest of the world, sung with the royal Prophet, 'The snare is broken, and we set at liberty;'[1] and like a dove or pigeon with eyes sealed to the lower world, soars upwards as far as his wings can bear him, to enjoy God and what leads nearest to Him, that is, true knowledge of Him, which, from the things it treats of, is properly and commonly called Divinity. In which study, having exercised himself with his wonted application, free from all other distraction and adhesion to terrene things, he made such progress, that by the votes of all, in due time he proceeded Doctor of that highest of sciences, which, as the angelical St. Thomas explicates it out of the Proverbs,[2] sits like a Queen

---

[1] Psalm cxxiii. 7.   [2] Chap. ix. 3.

in Court, and all other intellectual arts serve her as handmaids. And what wonder if his flight were so soaring, since he had the wings of a dove—I may say of an angel or bird of Paradise, by reason of his purest soul, cleanest heart, and angelical conversation; and as the clean of heart see God best, and He so attractively amiable, why should they not make great advance towards Him? As wisdom doth not enter a malevolous soul, nor dwell in a body subject to sin,[3] so when it finds one symbolizing with its humour in point of sanctity, and capacitated thereto, it communicates light as plentifully as the sun his beams to the crystal.

How joyfully he was received in that University, and what welcomes he had from all the degrees of the same, as a thing of course is needless here to be expressed. He coming now in the quality, not of a public person, but private student, to gain more time and sit closer to his task, waived what he could all such diversions—his entertainment was among his books, and his content in his devotions, and there he never found himself less alone than when most. He knew what a precious treasure time is, and esteeming it as such, was loth to lose the least parcel thereof. This he did both for his own benefit and the example to others, to make

[3] Wisdom i. 4.

them less wasteful of what the most part are lavish. To this good management of time and his other devotions he joined works of mercy, and especially relief to poor scholars, to many whereof he gave a daily maintenance, enabling them thereby to go through with their studies; and to this kind of charity he was much addicted, as we shall further show in the thirteenth chapter.

His thoughts, thus divided betwixt his studies and devotions, gave him the fruits of the former's industry, and the blessing of the latter's light. Amidst these he prepared himself for his great acts or commencement, at which his ancient friend and master in spirit, who had taught him many a good lesson in that kind, would be present—I mean Robert Kilwarby, who though at the time of his presentment he were Doctor of the Chair, yet before the time he was to stand in the act, his great knowledge and eminent virtue had received a condign reward of both from the hands of Pope and Prince, the see of Canterbury. This made the new Prelate not stand upon his points, but as the truly humble, the more they are exalted the humbler they are, so this preferment rather furthered than retarded him in the respect and honour he intended his friend. Friendship is never better grounded or supported than with piety, none knowing the

laws of the one better than the other, or keeping
them more inviolably as least swayed by interest.
Though the merits of our Saint were such that
they needed no commendatories, yet to observe
form and the usual custom, after his examen he is
bid to withdraw. That done, the Archbishop, who
came down purposely to perform the ceremonies of
his creation, gave an ample testimony of him, and
that upon oath to the present auditory, at what
time the Saint was no less than fifty-four years of
age. He commended him first from the four cardinal
virtues, and his eminent perfection in each, next
from his singular purity of body and mind, as pure as
to both as he was the first day he came into the
world. 'And if,' said he, 'you demand of me how I
come to have such a confident assurance thereof, I
answer, in the presence of God that I have read
it all along as clearly in his life and conscience,
by hearing his confessions even from his youth,
as any of you in a book legibly writ can read
characters laid open to your eyes; nor do I fear
but God, a lover of purity, Who has thus long preserved him without spot, will keep him spotless even
till death.'

This was a rare eulogium of the virgin integrity
of our Saint well worth our admiration and veneration, I may also add imitation, it falling especially

from the mouth of one who might be accounted an oracle as to truth, and as free from flattery as interest by it. Why then should any one suspect such a disinterested testimony of a sacred personage far above censure, and not rather censure those that censure him ? Everything is as it is taken. I read this eulogium of a venerable prelate, and I think I do prudently in framing thereupon a most high conceit of the Saint's purity—why should I not, he being one of unquestionable credit ? Another comes, and he censures all, both primate and Saint, both the testimony of this and the integrity of the other. I hold this discourse because Dr. Godwin once pretended Bishop of Hereford and Recorder of all the English bishops' lives, upon the rehearsal of this very passage, makes this reflection by way of a prudential note : *Omnis homo*, saith he, *mendax*—' Either confessor or confessed or the reporter lied, I doubt not.' Whence may be seen what gloss this historian puts upon so grave an asseveration, and how easily he waives any authority besides his own. What means the man by, *Omnis homo mendax*? Doth he aim at the Saint or the primate, or at himself? For if all be liars, by consequence he too ; and how nonsensically is this thrust in ! What need he doubt but such a point of perfection may be asserted, and neither confessor nor confessed nor reporter a liar ?

By what divinity doth Dr. Godwin conclude this ?
It may be a wonder beyond belief in the Protestant
Church that any one keep his baptismal purity in
an integrity of body and mind, but in the Catholic
it is not at all ; and I doubt as little of this as he
of the other.   How should we know the gests of
saints, since we have them not by revelation, but by
the relation of creditable men ?   No more certainly
is required here than suffices to ground a prudent
belief.   If every grave historian pretend to this, even
Dr. Godwin himself, how much more a prelate and
primate ?   But enough of such stuff ; he would only
have showed a piece of his divinity, and confirmed
it with an ' I doubt not,' and it suffices to have taken
notice of its strength.   I doubt not for all his doubt
but the primate's testimony will stand good, since so
many great virtues give force and warrant to his
veracity, and upon the same, that our Saint, as he
deserves, will be thought to have preserved his
unblemished integrity in the candour of its first
innocency.

About this time it was, while St. Thomas was
attending his studies, that Gregory X. gave a beginning to the Second Council of Lyons, and that
an interruption to him from the said studies.   The
improvement which he found by the former would
not let him slip the opportunity of redoubling the

same by the latter. A General Council is the school
of the age in which it is held, the great mart of
knowledge where one may buy wisdom at an easy
rate, and become acquainted with all the worthies
of all nations. An observant bee, he comes hither
as into a garden of choicest flowers, where it may
pick and choose the honey of all good improvement at pleasure, whether it be in point of virtue,
or whether it be in point of science, here he may
find patterns of the former, and no 'less of the
latter; here he may hear the orator perorate, the
philosopher discourse, the divine dispute, the interpreter expound, the antiquary impart his hiddenest
treasures of rites, customs, traditions, and the like.
For in the year 1274, upon the summons of the
Chief Pastor of God's Church, Gregory X., there
met seven hundred prelates in the city of Lyons,
Latin and Greek, gathered together from all the
parts of the Christian world to consider upon the
state of the Church; not only to seek a second
time relief for the Holy Land and its oppressions
by infidels, hut also to cement up the breaches of
the same Church, caused by that unfortunate schism
of the Greeks about the procession of the Holy
Ghost. Thirteen times had that perfidious nation
sworn and subscribed in full Council to an open
revokement and disclaim of that schism, and as often

had it relapsed to vomit; nor did it now any whit less as to both, submission and revolt.

Further account of this our Saint's journey than merely his going I find none; he went, I suppose, in the quality of a private person, because the record which mentions it specifies no more; and going as such (saints do not use to carry any great noise or clatter along with them) he returned when he thought good as silently as he went. And this must probably have happened after the time of his studies and graduation, because that passed and he commenced. I find he was immediately called to a chair in the same University, where having read and presided sixteen months, the fame of the indicted Council called him away, not by any other summons than those of his own improvement. For pretensions of advancement were as far from his thoughts as they were from his desires or heart; yet honours are like shadows following those that fly from them, and so they did him. For shortly after his return from the Council he was chosen to shine in the ecclesiastical magistracy, as he had before in the schools and secular tribunals; and how this came to pass must be the subject of the next chapter.

CHAPTER XI.

St. Thomas is made Bishop of Hereford.

WE have hitherto accompanied our Saint through the private passages of his life, and beheld him for the most part immured, as it were, within the walls of the school, attending chiefly to the perfecting himself, not others. Not but that he hath appeared, and very illustrious too, in the eyes of the world and glories of the Court, when made Lord Chancellor of England, he divided justice with such equal and satisfactory balance to the whole kingdom, that none besides himself was glad at the resignment. This was but a forced lending himself to what he could not withstand; or a voluntary admittance of what was put upon him, whether he would or no: otherwise, if it had been as much according to his gust as that of the rest of the world, he would neither have so earnestly sought his own release, nor joyed so much in obtaining it as he did.

Those great talents and abilities which rendered him so recommendable to secular did the same to

ecclesiastical promotions.   It is a prerogative which
God hath annexed to virtue, that it meets, though
not always, with many even temporal rewards when
it looks the least after them ; and indeed who deserves
them better, or when they have them can use them
with more integrity?   His nobility also and great
alliance gave no' small furtherance, whence it was
that he enjoyed at the same time by dispensation
many and fat benefices, all which, according to the
Collator's intention, he turned not so much to his
own interest as to the maintaining and recovering
of their rights, upholding privileges, conserving build-
ings, and relieving the poor of the respective neighbourhood.   He was at the same time Canon and
Chanter of York, Archdeacon and Canon of Lich-
field, Archdeacon of Stafford, Canon of London and
Hereford : all which I rehearse not as so many
certificates of his sanctity, but as rewards of his
merits, and pledges of respect and honour from
such chapters, ambitious to have him a member of
the same; and it were to be wished that such were
always in their hands who would use them to their
improvement.

While things were in this course, John de Breton,
a worthy prelate, governed the See of Hereford, one
well seeing both into the canon and common law of
the land, which latter he illustrated with his writings.

This man dying in this interim, left his chair vacant
to a successor, and the care of providing a fit one
to the vigilancy of the chapter. The carriage of
things as to the election, as we find recorded in
the process of his canonization, was after this tenor.
It chanced while the chapter was deliberating about
that point, St. Thomas, a canon of the same, though
his ordinary residence were at London, was acci-
dentally called down thither upon the score of other
affairs. The day, prefixed for the election before
his coming, happened while he was there, and he,
as a member thereof and of great regard both for
his virtue, learning, and nobility, was desired to
preach before the chapter, and so give a happy
entrance to the work. All proceeded canonically
according to method, but yet the result of the votes
was not so clear and absolute that day as to decide
the question and tell them positively this is the
man. The next meeting did it; and all the chapter
by joint decree, saith the process, did conclude,
first that the party to be elected should be a Thomas,
and next that the ambiguity of that name should be
resolved to the individual Thomas Cantilupe : whence
followed an unanimous acclamation of all, desiring
and accepting and voicing him their Bishop. Hence
he was carried to the High Altar, and a *Te Deum*
solemnly intoned by way of thanksgiving, with the

universal applause and good liking of all besides
himself. For he, like one surprised at unawares,
and expecting nothing less than what happened,
broke forth into tears, bemoaned his condition, de-
precated the burthen, alleged his own insufficiency,
and used all the arguments he could devise to reverse
the election. He did as saints used to do, who,
measuring themselves by the ell of their own mean
conceitedness, and poising the burthen which such
a charge draws after it, the eyes of their humility
make them deem themselves weaklings, and the
burthen, like an Etna, insupportable, well knowing
what it is to be accountable for so many souls.
He did like an humble saint, and they like a wise
and sage chapter, who knows those to be fitted for
prelacy that are least ambitious for it, and them
ablest to answer for others who are most careful
over themselves ; for he that is known to neglect
his own soul, how can it be presumed that he will
be vigilant over those of others, since charity begins
at home.

Far was our Saint from those ambitious motives
of preferment which possess even good souls : and
though the Apostle says,[1] ' He that desires a bishopric
desires a good work,' yet great saints find good
reasons why to waive, yea, suppress, such desires,

[1] 1 Tim. iii. 1.

especially when they find them to arise more from
self-seeking than God's honour or the good of souls.
Nobody ought to emulate this honour but he that
is called by God, as Aaron. It is want of interior
light that makes many more forward than considerate
in this kind; who, seeing only by the glimmering of
self-love (a false light issuing from an *ignis fatuus*),
think that often gay which has nothing such but
what it borrows from false reflections. Whereas
saints who are of a more refined sight, as seeing
things by true lights and measuring them accordingly
by the weights of the sanctuary, make a far different
estimate and proceed quite contrary. As we ought
not to censure the former unless their sinister intention and self-endedness condemn them first for mer-
cenaries, so we cannot but admire those others who
prefer an humble security before a splendid danger,
and dread the honour by reason of the burthen.

As the Holy Ghost, the great President of the
Church and its affairs, presides influentially in all
its canonical elections, so we cannot doubt but that
the Finger of the Father's right Hand did here, as
it is His office, inspiringly point out this shepherd,
whom He designed to govern that flock and set up
as a light in the candlestick of the church of Hereford, to shine to all in learning and virtue. That
this was an assured decree of Heaven, not only as

all canonical elections are, but also peculiarly pre-
ordained by a special providence, may be showed
both by the whole steerage of his life, whose actions
and behaviour seemed to be squared and moulded
for such a course, as also by several predictions
and prognostications which intimated the same. The
saying of Walter Cantilupe, Bishop of Worcester,
and his kinsman, uttered in our Saint's childhood
concerning his future state of life, cited in the third
chapter, seems by the event to have been prophetic,
and as such was received by his parents, who thereupon directed the whole education of their child
to a perpetual advance in knowledge and piety, the
two ornaments and supports of prelacy. It was no
less remarkable what passed while he studied the
law at Orleans, and for his excellency in that science
supplied the absence of his professor. When, the
night before he was to read, one of his fellow-students
beheld him, by way of dream, not only in the chair
or pulpit, but also carrying a Bishop's mitre on his
head, the circumference or border whereof was full
of crosses, as ominating that he was to walk by the
way of the Cross, full of hardship and contradiction.
We may add to these a third prediction of his immediate predecessor, who, two years before his own
death and the other's election, foretold he should
succeed him in his charge.

The choice being made and ratified to the satisfaction of all, the day and place of his inauguration
were pitched on. The day was to be the 8th of
September, sacred to the Nativity of the Virgin Mother
of God; nor could any other have fallen more suitable to his desires and the devotion he had for
that glorious Queen, whose nativity, as it brought
a deluge of joy and happiness to all mankind, so
he might hope it would betide no ill presage to
him, who was now to be born, as it were, a new
man; and most willingly did he come into this new
world under her patronage, under which he was to
live and die, as all they do who live and die happily.
When he had resolved who was to consecrate him,
it was easy to conclude on the place of consecration:
the former resolve was easily made according to his
own inclination; for, connaturally speaking, on whom
would he sooner pitch than on him to whom he was
most beholden, after God, for what he had both in
literature and piety?—who, as he had honoured him
in his commencement of Doctor of Divinity, so also
crown and complete all with the character of episcopacy. This was Robert Kilwarby, whom we mentioned in the preceding chapter, installed now Archbishop of Canterbury and Primate of England, who,
though so great, showed an humble readiness to
comply with the desires of his friend in order to a

consecration, whatsoever they were, or wheresoever
to be performed ; sealing up, as it were, with this
concluding act (for shortly afterwards he was called
to Rome) all his former endeavours for the Saint's
advance in spirit and piety; only it is to be noted
in a word that the consecration was made in Christ
Church, Canterbury, in the year 1275, and of his
age about fifty-six.

In testimony of the common content received by
this election, and the happiness as well as honour
accruing thence to his see of Hereford, it was agreed
by all concerned, both chapter and successors and
for an attestation of the general sentiment, that
thenceforward all the Bishops of Hereford should
give his coat of arms as the coat of their see—to
wit, three leopards' heads jessant G, three flower de
luce Or.[2] So true it is, that honour, like a shadow,
follows those that fly it, and 'that no pursuit besides
contempt is the ready way to its purchase. [10.
11. 12.]

[2] The arms of the Bishops of Hereford, since the time of
St. Thomas, have been 'Gules, three leopards' heads, jessant,
reversed, with a fleur de lis issuing from the mouth, Or.' Formerly they were 'Gules, three crowns, Or,' with either a rose or
roundel between them.

CHAPTER XII.

Retirement and Union with God.

THIS new character made him a new man, nor did he look on himself with the same eyes as before; not puffed up, like many, with the fumes of a swelling exaltation, but purely on the score of his new character, beholding himself as one consigned over thereby to the service of God. They are worse than purblind who look only on a man as a mere man, and make no distinction at all of states and callings, being able to penetrate no further than the exterior lineaments, nor distinguish in their levelling humour betwixt a man and a priest, one with a crosier and a sword. Even such themselves, when qualified and raised to honours, look on themselves as somebody, and will not bate an ace of state; why should not the same be done when raised to a state of sanctity? Bishops are in a state of perfection, and set up as lights in the candlestick of the Church to shine to others: 'You are,' said Christ of them, 'the light of the world'[1]—nothing not squaring with perfection

[1] St. Matt. v. 14.

is expected from them. This consideration makes them reflect on their duty: 'Attend to yourselves and your whole flock,'[2] and so did it our blessed Saint, giving him subject enough to busy his thoughts on, in order to a due discharge of his trust. Which the better to perform he recalls all his thoughts home, and as he had now contracted a new espousal, so he wedded all his endeavours to its interest. A shepherd, till he have a flock of his own, may divert himself more freely among his neighbours, and spend some hours in visiting theirs; but when he himself is once master of one, he attends only to that, and may say, as did the man in the Gospel on another occasion, 'I have married a wife, therefore I cannot come.'[3]

When God calls one to a state, He furnishes him with thoughts, desires, affections suitable thereto; He gives him light to consider it, to ponder its weightiness, to see for what he must be answerable, when 'Give an account of thy stewardship' is said to him. All these employ his mind sufficiently, and make him retire within himself, and consequently withdraw from less necessary exterior affairs. He never was in love with the world, nor taken with its fooleries, and therefore easily retired from it as

---

[2] Acts xx. 28.
[3] St. Luke xiv. 20.   [4] St. Luke xvi. 2.

from what he little cared for. He was long ago like
one glutted and surfeited with its delights, even the
choicest of the Court, and saw too clearly its vanities
to be deluded by them. The more he retired into
himself, the more he loved retirement, its sweetness
being not known but by tasting it; and one truth
he discovered thereby, that a gadding spirit will never
make a saint, nor wandering thoughts which go all
day on wool-gathering, bring home much sanctity.
He found all in God, and contented himself with
Him alone, as well he might, Who to a holy soul is
all in all; and it is in solitude that He speaks to
such a heart, where the choicest sort of virtues dwell,
not upon roads or market-places, as lions and eagles
and such generous creatures are not found in common
woods and fields, but solitary wildernesses, where
they may rule and enjoy themselves, uncontrolled by
the vulgar inferior creatures. Hereupon a great
change was observed in him and his conversation;
he was, and was esteemed, a Saint before, but now
more noisedly; he had long ago the world in contempt, now in hatred.

What lay not a little heavy on his heart, and was,
as I may say, the burthen of his thoughts, was his
new charge, or the solicitude of its good discharge.
To comply duly with this was all his care, and to do
it well, a great supply, he knew, of virtues was re-

quisite, and those chiefly which attend such a
function.   Those he conceived to be in the first
place and above others, vigilancy, he being now a
shepherd that was to keep watch and stand sentinel
over his flock : a virtue so proper to one thus intrusted, that on it the whole welfare and safety of
the same flock seem in a manner to depend as to
its preservation and integrity, both for the preventing
of mischief and giving redress when incurred.   A
vigilant pastor withstands the incursions of wolves
and other beasts of prey, not only when they appear
in their proper shape, but also disguised in the dress
of sheep ; nor is it his duty only to prevent and repel
evil, but also to implant good.   It happened when
men were asleep that the enemy found opportunity
to sow tares upon the good wheat and spoil the
harvest.   To recommend this virtue the High Priest
in the Old Law carried an amethyst, enchased in his
Rational,[5] as a symbol of watchfulness, the nature
of that precious stone disposing much thereto ; and
nature inculcates the necessity of it both by the lions
sleeping with open eyes, and the crane with a stone
in her talon, not to oversleep themselves, as the
foolish virgins did, but be ready for the least alarm ;
which lesson is taught us by the Spouse, and may

[5] A stone originally supposed to prevent drunkenness ; hence
the etymology α (privat) μεθύω—to be drunken.

serve for a motto to all: 'I sleep, and my heart watcheth.'[6]   Upon the same score he considered himself not only as the master of a great family, which he was to feed with the bread of the Word of God, and keep in good order as beseemed the house of God; but also (which touched him nearer to the heart) a common father of so many children, whom, as such, he was to embrace with the arms of a fatherly charity, and tender their spiritual welfare as much as any parent, for each one whereof he was to be accountable to Him Who intrusted them in his hands.   This made him 'put on the bowels of mercy, benignity, humility, modesty, patience,'[7] and bear with the faults and frailties of others, becoming all to all that he might win all to Christ.   This humble condescendence gave him a powerful ascendant upon the hearts of the good, to incline them much towards virtue and piety, and gained him so much esteem in their affections, that his words were 'as of one that spoke with an awful authority.'[8] Yet he loved them as his children, and was so beloved by them, and feared accordingly; for that fear is best and most effectual to good which is grounded on and arises from love; when it is otherwise, it is not so much filial as servile, that is, proper to slaves rather than children.

[6] Cant. v. 2.   [7] Coloss. iii. 12.   [8] St. Matt. vii. 29.

This retirement, as it sequestered his heart and thoughts from the world and its affairs, so it gave him a fairer prospect of virtue and its advantages to Christian perfection, and the necessity thereof towards the due ordering of body and soul. To have all well, there must be a right understanding and subordination betwixt these two : the soul must be mistress, and, good reason why! the body hand-maid and subservient. Reason must command, sense obey : this will not be done but by a true subjection of the inferior man to the superior; nor that, but by frequent penance and mortification, interior and ex-terior, both in macerating the flesh and subduing our passions and appetites. To effect this the servants of God make war upon themselves by chas-tising their bodies,[9] lest while they preach to others, themselves become reprobate, and to this purpose embrace the hardships of fasting, watching, hair-cloth, and the like, to further and complete the conquest of themselves. And this was the practice of our holy Saint, as the recorders of his life and gests do testify, and had also been through his former age, wearing a rough· hair-cloth next his body for many years together, penancing his innocent flesh with frequent fasts and watchings. But now he frequented all these in so much greater perfection, as he con-

· i Cor. ix. 27.

ceived the need he had of their present support to be more pressing, though not to suppress any rebellious mutinies, yet to obtain greater supplies of grace. Yea, even in the hour of his death and amidst the encumbrances of a long and tedious journey, he was found shrouded in one of these, as in a coat of mail, against the stings of death; as if he intended, according to the proverb, 'to drive out one nail with another,' or make a cordial for his sickness of that which seemed as ill as the sickness itself. But saints esteem those cordials which we do corrosives. And his fervour in this kind was such, that by these and other the like austerities he incurred great infirmities of body, and was much pestered with most sharp fits of the cholic and pains of the stomach, which with other sicknesses gave him a full exercise of his patience for many years, with no small increase of merit.

But the vigour of his mind mastered all these, which served only to render his body, or inferior part, more pliant and supple in a due subjection, whereby his soul, perfect mistress of the family, yielded a rational obsequiousness to God its Creator, by dilating itself in prayer and meditating the Divine perfections with the repose of so much devotion and sweetness, that he seemed to be then as in his centre. And it is recorded of him peculiarly, that his exterior

composure and recollection in the same were such
that the very sight of him was sufficient to stir up
both faith and fervour in the beholders ; as also that
in celebrating the Holy Sacrifice of Mass, his heart
and eyes were so dissolved into tears, as if he had
actually beheld the bloody mystery of the Cross
represented to them, so lively was his faith, so ardent
his devotion.   He carried a great love to this exercise of prayer, and deservedly, for by it all spiritual
enterprizes are achieved, that being the source from
whence we derive both light to discover, and strength
to act, and courage to attack, and perseverance to
crown our undertakings.   By this a soul converseth
with God, and He with it.   Conversation, we know,
breeds familiarity, and this, friendship or union of
hearts ; and when one is arrived to that *amicorum
omnia communia,* what needs he more by way of
supply than the store-house of God Himself?   Union
is the result of love, that making the lover and beloved one ; and love consists in a mutual communication of goods and talents.   If we give, we need
not doubt but we shall receive, His very essence
being goodness and bounty.   All these are the effects
of prayer, and chiefly this union which, whosoever
has attained, what wants he of perfection?   Perfection consists in charity, which is consummated in
unity ; for then everything is deemed perfect when

it attains its end, and unites itself to that which is
its ultimate consummation. The consummation of
a rational creature is God, and God is in us and we
in Him by charity. Being thus united to God by
charity, or, as St. Bernard calls it, married to His
Word, the sequel is, that as two spouses are two in
one flesh by corporal espousals, so God and a soul
become two in one Spirit by spiritual espousals ; and
all the consequences, advantages, participations of
honours, riches, ennoblements, alliance, &c., which
are communicated by the former, are, after a much
more Divine manner, participated by the latter.
What wonder, then, if our Saint endeavoured so
earnestly for union with God, and took prayer so
much to heart as the begetter of this union. To
maintain and heighten the same was all his endeavour : and he endeavoured it by employing to that
purpose the three powers of his soul—memory, understanding, and will—in a perpetual presence of Him.
His memory, by recounting His great and daily
benefits in a thankfulness of heart ; his understanding,
by meditating His Divine truths, perfections, and
attributes ; his will, by loving Him in all, and con-
forming his to the Divine ; and this is the noblest
employment of a rational soul, and an imitation of
what the saints do in Heaven. The more straitly
he united himself to God, the more he did partake

of His bounties, Who scorns to be outvied by any
body in this kind ; and this participation increased
the flame of his charity, which dilated itself both
towards God and his neighbour, loving God for
Himself, and his neighbour in and for God, and as
himself; and this is the fulness of the Law and
Prophets.   Hence he became so zealous both of the
honour and house of God, which is His Church,
and so sensible of the concerns of his neighbour,
both spiritual and temporal, that he seemed to be
born for their relief, and especially of the poor and
needy : both of which parts of charity we shall treat
more amply in the ensuing chapters.

CHAPTER XIII.

Love to the Poor.

To think that one so groundedly maximed in perfection and the practice of all solid virtue as he was, would rather impair than improve by his exaltation, is a paradox. 'Who is holy let him advance in holiness,'[1] said St. John, and so says every truly virtuous soul, whose glory is to be always mounting with the sun to the top of his meridian. All our Saint's ambition and satisfaction was in a happy progress towards perfection, knowing that as to its pursuit we are, as it were, in a stream where there is no standing still: for the rower not to ascend is to descend, and to go backward not to go forward. Even while he was yet a churchman or canon he was very much devoted to almsdeeds and the relief of the poor; how much was this pious practice advanced when by the imposition of hands he had received the Holy Ghost, Who is Father of the poor, and made him such; but whether before or after

[1] Apoc. xxii. 11.

matters not, the virtue being equally commendable in both states, and we will speak promiscuously of it in both.

Though good words give but barren comfort to an empty stomach, yet still it is true that out of the abundance of the heart the mouth speaks, and then they are only expressions of a willing mind; and however even a compassionate answer is in some sort satisfactory. The poor were sure at least of that from him, if nothing else, though he seldom stinted his charity there; and as he esteemed them the patrimony of Christ, so he spoke with all humility and respect to them, as he would to Christ Himself, knowing that to be done to Him which was done to the least of His members. Upon this account the esteem he had of them was such that he commonly called them 'his brethren,' a name of greatest love, and with his goodwill would have had all his domestics to have called them so too, and chid them that they did not. Whence it is recorded that being set at table with half a dozen such guests, and finding yet place for more, he sent one of the waiters to the palace gate to see whether any of 'his brethren' were there or no; if there were, that he should bring a couple of them along with him. He returning told his lord that there were no brothers of any order whatsoever. 'No,' said the Bishop,

'not of this that sits here by me?' pointing to the
beggars. 'Yes, my lord,' replied he, 'there are at
least a dozen such.' 'Go then,' said the Bishop,
'and bring five of the number along with you'—
which was forthwith done, 'and the marriage was
filled with guests.'[2]

But words be they never so good are still inferior
to deeds, these latter being a better proof of charity
as costing more, and affording more relief. This
was the substantial part of his love to the poor, and
he was not sparing of it : he had, to wit, learned the
great lesson of his Lord and Master, 'It is a more
blessed thing to give than to receive,'[3] and he was
resolved to practise it in this behalf. The recommendation of his own merits and noble descent had
furnished him with a large proportion of Church
revenues even before the access of his bishopric,
which, besides a competency of maintenance beseeming his quality and the discharge of other incumbrances, he knew not how to bestow better than on
the poor. He knew that the goods of the Church
are the patrimony of Christ, and where could he
spend them better than on the living members of
Christ, either to his own content of mind or satisfaction of conscience. This is the way to grow rich
in Heaven, and make friends of the mammon of

<hr>

[2] St. Matt. xxii. 10.   [3] Acts xx. 35.

iniquity, that, when other means fail, these may
receive us into the eternal tabernacles: '⁴ nay, even
procure us temporal commodities, since almsdeeds
laid up in the bosom of the poor (this is the best
way of honouring our Lord by them) fill both the
press with wine and barns with corn, and the alms-
giver with other blessings. He indeed had no great
sins of his own to redeem by them, as having probably never lost his baptismal innocence, but he
aimed at a treasure of merits due to such works of
corporal mercy, and to be laid up in Heaven against
his reception there, out of the reach of rust or moth.
Hence he took this virtue so to heart that it was
very resplendent in his practice, and the poor resorted
to him as to a common parent from whom they
never departed empty handed. He found it no
bad medicine to work by the body upon the soul ;
and true that to gain the one charity must be showed
to the other. An indisposed body is like an indisposed mind, hard to be wrought upon while necessitous ; fill the hand, and you gain the heart, now
flexible to any good impressions. Our corrupt nature
is more sensible of hunger than of devotion, and
resents want of sustenance more than want of virtue
or grace. It is as hard to hammer it to good, as a
piece of iron to a good shape unless it be first made

⁴ St. Luke xvi. 9.

supple by the fire of a subventive charity. This
done, you may form it as you please : works of
corporal mercy must dispose for the spiritual Therefore his custom was to seek admittance to the mind
by relieving the body, and made it a part of his care
to order things so, that while he refreshed the body
the soul should not also want its food, partly by
pious discourses and godly instructions, partly by
causing some good book to be read suitable to the
present exigence.

To this so laudable and holy practice of his former
life, he seems to have superadded this circumstance
after his episcopal instalment, that what he did before
in this kind by others, he would now do by himself,
and with his own hands. This is particularly recorded
of him, and deservedly worth noting, as a great
superaddition to the former virtue; for how could
he employ his hands, now consecrated to God, more
piously than by consecrating them to such an exercise
of charity? What is laudably done by another is
more laudably by ourselves; God does it by Himself, as the Psalmist tells us, 'Thou openest Thy
hand, and fillest each creature with benediction.'[5]
The sun sends not a servant, nor the heavens either,
to divide their influences to this sublunary world.
Besides that thus, not only an act of charity, but

[5] Psalm cxliv. 16.

also of humility, and no mean one, is exercised.
It is good to give alms by others, but much better
to do it by oneself, as more meritorious: one has
the merit both of the alms and of the manner of
giving it, and the manner in some respect even
doubles it; for who thinks not himself more graced
by receiving a gratuity immediately from the Prince's
own hand than from his servant. The more immediate the influence, the more it is prized. For these
reasons it is accounted a praiseworthy practice in
parents when they do it not themselves, to inure
their children, a part of themselves, to be the con-
veyers of their alms, unless other motives impede.
It has not only a more comfortable acceptance both
from God and man, but also it habituates, or
rather seasons, these new vessels, capable as yet
of any tincture, with such a flavour of charity, that
many times it sticks by them their whole life long.
And perchance our blessed Saint took his from such
a rise of devotion, or document of his pious parents,
and grew up with him so palpably, that of him it
might be said without rashness, ' From my infancy
mercy grew up with me.'⁶

However, certain enough it is that the practice is
very Christian, and much to be recommended, due
circumstances being observed; and even while I am

⁶ Job xxxi. 18.

reviewing these papers a fresh example for its confirmation comes from the Emperor's Court at Vienna
with the acclamation, approbation, and also edification of all that hear it. The little daughter of
the present Emperor Léopold (piety being always
hereditary to that Imperial family, which God long
preserve) feasted a competent number of children
of her own age and sex; nor content with this, to
complete the charity, would serve them with her
own hands. To wit, she and her noble parents
deemed it nothing unworthy either of themselves
or her, to serve God in His meanest members, as
being ascertained of the truth of these words,
'What you do to one of these little ones you do
to Me.'[7] This I allege to show that parents need
not be shy or nice in point of apprehending it a
disparagement, since they see it practised by one of
the most illustrious of the world. But it suffices to
have hinted this.

While he was in the Universities (and in them
he spent the greatest part of his years) his charity
vented itself in a particular manner upon the relief of
poor students, thereby to enable them to a prosecution of their studies. This was seen chiefly in
relieving the hungry, clothing the naked, providing
necessaries for those in distress, who must other-

[7] St. Matt. xxv. 40.

wise have interrupted their course, both to their own
undoing and that of many. It is most charity to
help them who probably are like to be most beneficial to the public good, and consequently greatest
promoters of charity, who, having been sustained
by it, have learnt by experience and their own
wants what it is to be charitable to others: *Non
aliena mali miseris succurrere disco.* And what fairer
way toward this enablement than a good foundation
of learning, upon which the superstructures of preferment may be built, both in Church and commonwealth by employment spiritual and temporal; whence
he might say, 'I by my charities have enabled so
many, and put them in a capacity to do the same
to others:' and I think every one will applaud his
placing them so well. Upon this score of love to
the poor he was more ready at all times to hear
their confessions than those of the better sort, who
could never want ghostly Fathers, and those that
would be forward to assist them, while those of a
meaner condition were easily put by, though not
by him who equally beheld Christ in all, and
knew not what acception of persons signified. This
was so remarkable in him, that a person of quality,
who measured all by a worldly ell, objected it as
a discredit to his birth and calling, but received
no other answer than this, 'I must be accountable to

Almighty God, the great Judge, as well for the poor as the rich, ignoble as noble.'

To this he added another, but in another kind, yet still to the poor, and with as much or more demonstration of love and devotion as the former. For who more poor than those who are deeply in distress, and cannot help themselves in the very least, those whom the Holy Ghost calls by the Psalmist, 'The poor and needy,'[8] and gives them not one, but many blessings to those that are sensible of their necessitous condition. I mean the souls in Purgatory, who are a great object of charity, and beg compassion with a *Miseremini mei*, and they must be hard-hearted that are not moved, since it will be one day their own case. It is recorded of him that, even while Bishop, if in travelling he met with a corpse, he presently alighted from his horse, and together with all his train said on his knees a *De profundis* for the soul departed. So true it is that he was a lover of the poor both living and dead.

[8] Psalm xl. 2.

CHAPTER XIV.

Charity to all, and detestation of detraction.

THE former chapter gave us a scantling of his love and charity to the poor, this indifferently to all. Virtues as well as causes, the more universal, they are also the more perfect, as most resembling those of the saints in Heaven. Charity is a fire whose activity is still dilating itself where it finds fuel to feed on : it knows no bound but discretion, and many times scarce that, though it ought always to be orderly ; but it uses as little to keep a mean, as it is of its own nature much communicative. St. Thomas's heart was in Heaven, and the sun of this Heaven was charity, as influential as any Heaven, and as pure and simple as fire from all self-ended composition; like the sun, it regarded all equally, without acception of persons, having latitude of heart to embrace all, and each one in their proper quality, both noble and ignoble, rich . and poor. This sun, like our material one, rises equally to the good and bad, just and unjust : to

the former for their improvement, to the latter for
their amendment, beneficial to all, affording both
light and heat, by word and example; and as he
loved all, so was he beloved generally by all, love
as naturally exciting love, as benefits do gratitude.

It might truly be verified of him what the Apostle
so earnestly recommended to the Corinthians, 'that
all their devoirs should be done in charity,'[1] and so
were all his actions, all his words, and proceedings,
as if issuing from a heart all made of charity they
carried its relish and perfume, like the plants of
Arabia Felix, because rooted in that perfumed soil,
they did partake thence of the same fragrant odours.
And to this purpose it was deposed in the process
of his canonization that his daily conversation was
such, that not the least excess, either in word or
gesture, yea though highly provoked thereto, could
be discovered or forced from him contrary to charity.
Causes are known by their effects and trees by their
fruits: the fruits of charity and the Holy Ghost,
Whose prime issue it is, are recounted by the
Apostle[2] among others to be, patience, benignity,
meekness, a peaceful disposition; and that he was
eminently practised in all these, we shall make
evident by examples. He looked on patience as
the virtue in which he was to possess his soul, and

[1] 1 Cor. xvi. 14.   [2] Galat. v. 22.

for that reason was so deeply rooted in it, that no
wind or weather, by word or deed, could shake its
constancy, or render him the least impatient; yea,
all the retaliation he used to make was to pray for
them, heaping thus the hot coals of charity upon
their head and overcoming evil in good, as most
beseeming a Christian. He had divers controversies
relating to his Church with Friar John Peccham,
then Archbishop of Canterbury, which cost our Saint
afterwards a journey to Rome; and whatever passed
in fact, he had but hard measure in words, being
treated with contumelious language and in a high
degree; yet he did not so much as repine thereat,
nor suffer any of his to recriminate in the least.
These three properties of charity, patience, meekness, and benignity, are so nearly allied and linked
together, that, for brevity sake, we may treat them
all under one, they being, as it were, twins of the
same mother, most like as in nature so in features,
and consequently what commends the one commends
the other.

I have already exemplified in the seventh chapter
how patiently, while yet Chancellor of the University,
he carried himself in that bustle betwixt the southern
and northern scholars in an affront as contemptuous
as could be put upon him ; yet he never complained
of the insolency, much less sought revenge, con-

tenting himself with the merit of his patience; and this not out of any pusillanimity or want of courage, for he, as being of a vigorous spirit, had enough of that, but merely overswayed with motives of virtue, he put all up, fulfilling what God bid him, 'Leave revenge to Me, and I will see it repaid.'[3] He had a great suit-at-law with the Earl of Gloucester and his officers, from whom in the open court he received many unhandsome and reviling speeches little beseeming him or them; all he said by way of reply was this, and he did it with much meekness: ' My lord, say what you please of me, you shall never provoke me to say anything against you misbeseeming; that's not the thing I come for, but to recover the rights of my Church.' Yea, this virtue of a patient meekness was so remarkable in him, that if any of his servants, no just cause being given, fretted impatiently at his commands, his custom was to humble himself first to them towards a reconcilement, as if he, not they, had been in fault, giving them sweet and mollifying words, to show thereby that all was forgot and forgiven, as not proceeding from passion or spleen. While he lived at Paris, four years before he was Bishop, he had a clerk in his retinue who had this custom, that taking his afternoon nap, whoever awaked him out of it, he would, half asleep as

[3] Heb. x. 30.

he yet was, thank him with his fist and that very liberally with many a blow. It chanced one day, no other being at hand, that his master, unacquainted with this ill habit, went himself to be his caller, nor did he fare better than others used to do; to wit, the man, not fully himself, fell on his master, and among others gave him a shrewd blow on the side. The Saint, nothing moved or offended, herewith made only this short reply : 'Take heed, child, what you do, it is a priest whom you beat.' Other examples of this nature might be alleged to show the absolute mastery he had over his passions, standing lord paramount to their control whenever there was danger of overlashing; and what greater sign of an eminent sanctity?

Charity is always both peaceful and a peacemaker, inasmuch as it cements up all breaches, and concludes all in unity; and he took this much to heart, as knowing that a beatitude was annexed to it : 'Blessed are the peacemakers.'[4] He not only had no enmity with any one living, but made it his endeavour to piece up all discords wherever he found them, and reconcile parties to a true understanding of mutual charity. As to himself, or his own person, it was impossible to fix a quarrel upon him, he esteeming no loss greater than that of charity, and would part

---

[4] St. Matt. v. 9.

with anything rather than infringe it. He knew not
what it was to bear hatred or ill-will; and to prevent
all grounds of mistake in this kind which might be
occasioned by ill-management of affairs, he used
always to have able lawyers and discreet counsellors
about him; but every day, as soon as Divine Office
was ended, he called them to consult, and scanned
every cause which was to be decided. This must
needs contribute much to peace, and such an upright
prudential proceeding to the maintaining of charity;
nor was he content with this care, but over and above
he burthened their consciences, and taxed them with
it, if he found any false-dealing among them. All the
controversies he had with others were not on his own
score, but on the behalf of his Church, and consequently not to be deemed his own but hers;
though in other respects he were a lamb, yet in
her defence he was a lion, and feared no colours
or opposition whatsoever, nor refused either labour
or danger for the preservation of her immunities.
Upon this account he undertook a journey to Rome,
which cost him his life, nor could any temporal
power, how formidable soever, appal him when he
found justice his abettor: in this a true imitator of
his glorious patron, St. Thomas of Canterbury. Of
his magnanimity, since it is to be the subject of the

next chapter, I will say no more here than only to refer the reader to it.

Now as charity had made him her victim, and as such, a perfect holocaust of love, no wonder if loving it so entirely he hated as heartily its opposite rival, detraction. The horror he bore to that vice was so signal that all the writers of his life take notice of it, and in such expressions of aversion that greater can hardly be invented. And indeed how could these bowels all made of love do otherwise than abhor its destructive, a compound made up of malice and envy. It is a murderer of its neighbour's good name, a robber of his merit and praise, a thief that's always pilfering something, a poisonous breath that seeks to blast what's not its own, a mere lump of self-love repining at another's prosperity. He learned this lesson of the great St. Augustine, who as he was charitably hospitable so he excluded none from his table besides the detractor, as the noted distich[5] which he put to that purpose doth testify. Our Saint, as he perfectly detested this vice in himself, so he could not endure it in any of his domestics;

---

[5] *Quisquis amat dictis absentûm rodere vitam,*
Hanc mensam indignam noverit esse sibi.

This board allows no vile detractor place,
Whose tongue shall charge the absent with disgrace.
                    Butler's *Lives of Saints*, August 28th.

nor did he omit, when he found them faulty, to give à severe reprehension. One of his chaplains having been present at a passage betwixt the Archbishop Peccham and him, wherein the Saint seemed to receive hard dealing both as to words and deeds; the chaplain in time of table complaining of it, began to inveigh against the Court of Rome for its negligence in not providing able and fit prelates to govern their flocks, with much more than needed to that purpose. His lord was presently moved thereat, and giving him a check, wished him to speak more reverently and charitably of all, and chiefly of his superiors and betters.

It may be expected that treating of his charity to all, something should be said of it in order to God, Whom it regards in the first place. It is this love chiefly which is the fulfilling of the Law and Prophets, by which we love God above all, and our neighbour as ourself in and for God; so that this latter part of the Law cannot subsist without the former, on which it depends. As his whole life was, as I may say, one continual or uninterrupted act of charity towards God, by which he was incessantly not only tending towards Him, but also united to Him in His Divine grace, as will appear by the review of his virtues; so an ample scope of matter cannot fail him that would dilate himself on this subject

(for what are all moral virtues but so many issues
or shoots of charity their root?), yet at present we
will rather suppose this virtue of virtues, than go
about to prove it, and leave it to be drawn by the
reader rather from his other perfections than make
a formal draft of it; praising it perchance as much
or more by an admiring silence than extenuating
expressions: for what are the commendations of our
words, to the lively colours of his virtues? Besides,
we shall have occasion to say something of it when
we treat of his piety and devotion, true genuine
children of this mother.

CHAPTER XV.

Courage in defence of Ecclesiastical Liberties.

THE Church is the Bride of Christ, espoused at the
expense of His Precious Blood, dearer to Him than
His life, and whoever touches her to wrong her
touches the apple of His eye. For her defence
and propagation He settled a Hierarchy, in which
He gave 'some apostles, some doctors, others pastors,
for the work of the ministry and edification of this
His mystical body.'[1] In this Hierarchy, ministry,
edification, bishops as the immediate successors of
the Apostles carry the first rank both in governing
and feeding: in feeding is regarded the wholesome-
ness of the fodder and pasturage; in governing,
direction and protection; and both these require
that he be a true shepherd, not a hireling, and seek
the good of his flock, not himself. If the hireling
see a wolf coming, saith the best of Shepherds, he
runs away, because he is a hireling; while the good
shepherd exposes his life for his sheep, shunning
neither pains nor danger for their safety and behoof;[2]

---

[1] Ephes. iv. 11.   [2] St. John x. 12.

and so did our blessed Saint, proving himself a good shepherd indeed. His love to his espoused Church was as tender as ought to be to his own Spouse, now a spiritual part of himself and the Spouse of Christ, and he embraced her as such, and together with her espoused all her concerns whatsoever, and this is no more than is ordinarily done even in corporal marriages. It was his devoir to prove himself a faithful manager (steward) of the family he was intrusted withal, and a valiant maintainer of all its possessions, privileges, liberties, immunities, that in none of them it might suffer prejudice. This he took to heart exceedingly, as deeming it the prime part of his charge, resolved to expose and oppose himself as a wall for the house of God; and what we are to relate will show that he failed not in his resolution, sealing it even with the loss of his life; and what greater pledge of his fidelity?

It had been the deplorable misfortune of our poor country that for many years, successively and by fits, it had been involved in an unnatural intestine war, which as it caused great confusion in the civil state, so did it no little in the ecclesiastical. In such times of liberty, abuses easily creep in, an unjust invasion being much sooner committed than redressed; for when the sword gives law, it is in vain for the crozier to plead conscience, or preach restitution, a language

little understood in civil garboils. The weakest, they
say, go always to the wall, and so does the Church,
as least able in such occasions to defend itself, since
it cannot, nor must not, repel force by force; and
so to redeem vexation is compelled to part with her
right, especially when the invaders are powerful.
This was the case of the see of Hereford when our
Saint entered upon it: it had been unjustly ousted
of divers large possessions, and, what made the
recovery harder, the possessors had quietly enjoyed
them divers years, even in time of peace, when the
laws had their course: his two predecessors knowing
well the equity of their cause, but despairing to
prevail against such potent adversaries, one whereof
was the King's son-in-law, Gilbert, Earl of Gloucester,
another, Llewellyn, Prince of Wales, and a third,
Roger, Lord Clifford, besides the Archbishop of
Canterbury and others.

Our holy Saint having maturely considered all this,
though he found the task very hard, yet relying on
the equity of his plea, deemed himself bound, unless
he would betray his trust, to attempt the recovery of
these lands. His courage was such that in God's
cause he feared no colour of greatness, nor multitude
of opposers; and why should he, since he was armed
with the armour of the just, a true armour of proof?
Having justice or a good conscience for his breast-

plate, sincere judgment for his helmet, and equity for an invincible shield. Courage and magnanimity is never better seconded than by virtue and sanctity, and a good cause ; when these make the onset, be the opposition what it will, they carry all before them. Of his own nature he was so averse from suits or contests, that he would sooner have yielded up his private right to an adversary than seek to regain it by law ; in what belonged to his Church he could not, it being not his own but God's, Who required it at his hands. But to moderate and facilitate all, the best he could, the first essay he made was a modest and peaceful claim of his right, proposing an agreement on reasonable terms, and in case it were refused, a ready offer of a reference ; if that were rejected too, then he left the matter to a trial-at-law, in which he played the solicitor so well, and was so diligently watchful, that he would be present at the decision, though he were carried in a litter. This conscientious proceeding, grounded on an equitable right, driven on by a studious attendance, made him never fail to win his plea.

Hence such was the opinion which every one conceived of his zeal and courage in behalf of his Spouse or Church, that, during the time of seven years which he sat in its chair, nobody durst presume to offer the least encroachment on its immunities, knowing well that to offer such a thing were to awake a sleeping lion. But this was not enough, his love and magnanimity aimed at a recovery of what was unjustly invaded and detained : in which behalf, though the endeavours of his immediate predecessors Peter and John had been little successful, being overpowered with might, he also would try his chance, and began with the greatest first. Wherefore, after a legal claim laid to Malvern Chase and other lands and woods thereto adjoining, wrongfully withheld by Gilbert de Clare, Earl of Gloucester, nor receiving any satisfactory answer towards a restitution, he commenced a suit against him, and followed it so close, that notwithstanding all his opponent's greatness and countenance from the King, clear justice was ready to give verdict in the Saint's behalf. The court was held near or upon the place controverted, and the Earl had armed men, together with his foresters, in case of being cast, to keep possession by force; and seeing things brought to this pass besought the King for a suspension of the final sentence, which was granted. All this nothing abashed the holy Bishop, who going aside together with his clergy into the wood, put himself in his episcopal robes and them in theirs, with lighted tapers; thus going before them, he came to the place where the judges, together with the Earl, made

their abode; where the candles being put out, he
solemnly pronounced a sentence of excommunication
against all and every one who that day hindered and
molested his and the Church of Hereford's right in
the said woods and forests. This done, the Earl
perceived whom he had to deal withal, and presently,
taking horse departed; nor was he sooner gone than
the judges proceeded to give sentence, and that given,
the Bishop caused his servants to hunt as in his own
liberties through the same Chase to regain possession;
and he himself for the same purpose walked over the
bounds, unarmed as he was, though it were not done
without danger of his life. For divers of the Earl's
men obstinately persisting to maintain the quarrel,
shot at random very near his person, without any
respect or reverence had thereto : one of whom more
injurious than the rest, he threatened with the Divine
revenge; and the same person shortly after, saith the
record, was miserably drowned, the common voice
of all going that it was a just punishment for his contemptuous carriage towards the Saint, and well for
him if only a temporal.

He proceeded much after the same fashion with
Llewellyn, Prince of Wales, and to excommunication
also, for unjustly detaining three villages situated near
Montgomery, belonging to the said his see. Who
lying thus under the censure came with the King,

as fearing nothing under his shadow, into a church
where the Saint was going to say Mass. He espied
the excommunicated person, and without further
compliment warned him as such out of the church :
the King himself interposed for his stay, but all would
not do, nor he begin till the other had absented
himself, nor could he be admitted into communion
before the satisfaction was performed. He was in
like manner forced to use the same rigour, both
spiritual and temporal, against some Welshmen who
had usurped three villages of his territory and
defended them by strong hand, till proceeding to
the like censures he frighted them into a restitution.
Roger, Lord Clifford, a neighbour upon his diocese,
had trenched so far upon the same in time of war as
to drive booties of cattle and use extortions upon some
of the diocesans. He was too noble minded to deny
the fact, or put the holy Bishop to the proof of it, but
now willing to restore, all his endeavour was to make
satisfaction in private by some composition without
undergoing the confusion of a public penance, and
to obtain this he offered underhand no small sum of
money. He knew not with whom he had to do, nor
the principle, it seems, that a public fault must have
a public penance : the offence being notorious, a
private atonement could not be admitted, nor the
scandal taken away till he in person in the church

of Hereford appearing in a penitential weed, bare-
headed and barefoot, went in procession up to the
high altar itself, the Bishop following with a rod in
his hand and according to the canons striking him.

CHAPTER XVI.

*Journey of Thomas to Rome, and entertainment
there.*

THE last contest he had, and which cost him dearer
than the rest, as going more against the grain (for
he loved not debates with superiors), was with his
Metropolitan, John Peccham, Archbishop of Canterbury, a man of great learning and ability, and a
worthy prelate, as grave authors do testify of him.
Nor is either he or our Saint to be the worse thought
of for this their variance, since good and wise men
may be of a different judgment as to matters of right
or fact until a just umpire decide the controversy;
till then both the plaintiff and defendant may in-
culpably, by course of law, seek their right.

This John Peccham succeeded Robert Kilwarby
in the chair of Canterbury, with whom he bore
this resemblance, that as the other had been Pro-

vincial of the holy Order of St. Dominic, and thence
chosen to that see, so this of St. Francis: both
signally eminent in knowledge and virtue, both great
lights of their respective bodies. This John, his
years of government being expired, travelled through
the Universities of Italy to his great improvement,
and lastly to Rome, where the forerunning fame
having given a large character of his eminent parts,
he was in short time made by the Pope then sitting
Auditor, or Chief Judge of his Palace, in which
employment he continued till, upon the promotion
of Robert to his Cardinalship, he succeeded him in
his Archbishopric.

No record that I could meet withal give us any
further account of this controversy than that it was
ecclesiastical, and relating to the privileges and
immunities of private sees, on which the Archbishop
was thought to trench. A Council was held by him
at Reading, in the which he is said to have laid
some injunction on the particular sees under his
jurisdiction prejudicial to their liberties and beyond
the verge of his power, as was conceived; nor were
they peculiar to that of Hereford, but jointly common
to all that acknowledged him their Metropolitan.
And though they were equally concerned, yet no
one besides our Saint had the courage to undergo
both the labour and expenses and hazards that were

annexed to such an undertaking. They were sure to have a very powerful adversary, the cause was to be tried in the Court of Rome; for that end a journey thither was necessary, and a good purse to defray its charges; all which considered, and the doubtfulness of success, made the rest of the bishops hold off, and rather be content to sit still, losers in what they deemed their right, than to incur such incumbrances in seeking redress. This was the state of the question and in this posture things stood when St. Thomas, weighing maturely the encroachment on their privileges and its consequences òn one side, and the justice of the cause, of which he was thoroughly satisfied, on the other, resolved to lend his best endeavours, and spare neither pains nor cost for rectifying what was amiss, though it should cost him a journey to Rome.

Those very motives which daunted the other bishops were to him so many incentives; he undervalued all labours, he contemned all dangers, and for what end were the revenues of the Church allowed him, but for his own and the maintenance of the Church and her prerogatives? All this arose from the zealous love he had for his Spouse, much dearer to him than Rachel to Jacob, for whose preservation he neither feared to die nor refused to live and serve through heats and colds, night and

day another seven years, if so it pleased Almighty
God. And finding that for the good management
of his suit a journey to Rome was necessary, since
it could neither be determined elsewhere nor there
well without a personal attendance, which is the life
and vigour of such dependences, he resolved upon
the same, though now well struck into years, and
often encumbered with great fits of sickness, both
the one and the other whereof might justly have
pleaded his excuse, could his charity have admitted
any. As in this he discharged his own conscience,
so was his resolution accompanied with the acclama-
tions of all sorts of people, extolling his courage
and zeal now, as afterwards they doubted not to
ascribe to it all the miracles which God was pleased
to work by him, styling him a martyr like St. Thomas
of Canterbury, as losing his life in defence of his
Church, as shall be more fully shown in the next
chapter.

He took his journey from England through Normandy, and making some stay in the Abbey of Lira,
in the diocese of Evreux. What I am about to
recount happened during that interim, nor must be
omitted as being a testimony of his present sanctity.
A child of three years old, wont to play with other
children before the abbey gates, falling into a brook
which ran thereby, was drowned. The child's parents,

I 30

well known to the Saint, gave him to understand the misfortune that had befallen them, to whom he said no more than these few words: 'The child, by God's assistance, will live,' and stretching forth his hand towards the place, made thereon the sign of the Cross. In the meanwhile the father of the child, taking it out of the brook, found it stark dead, full of water and sand, no sign of life or motion remaining in it. He opened the mouth with a knife, and letting the water out to a great quantity, to omit no endeavour, he chafed the body, though hopeless of life, before the fire. His endeavour found effect, life returned, and motion appeared, and in a competency of time all came to its natural pass, to the great astonishment of all present. The recovery was held even then miraculous, but to whom to ascribe the miracle they knew not, and to St. Thomas they durst not, though even then venerable for his sanctity, yet his humility could not brook such extraordinaries. But afterwards, when the fame and number of his wonders were divulged through France itself, the father of the child, before the Lords Commissioners, upon the Saint's making the sign of the Cross, and uttering the aforesaid words, deposed that he verily believed life was restored by his merits and intercession.

He began his journey in or about the sixtieth

year of his age, and notwithstanding his bodily infirmities, arrived there safe and well, Nicholas IV.
sitting then in the Chair of St. Peter. How welcome both the quality of his person and character
of degree made him is needless to insist upon,
besides the fame of sanctity, as well as knowledge,
which accompanied him; nor must we omit the
superaddition of being Chaplain to His Holiness,
conferred heretofore upon him in the Council of
Lyons. Saints carry always with them letters-patent
of a grateful reception, and it is one of the temporal
rewards of sanctity, especially where it is in vogue,
and has its due respect, which if it be not regarded
in the Holy City, where will it? The Court of Rome
is the great patronizer and promoter of sanctity,
where it is as in its centre, which, though trampled
upon elsewhere, here finds its redress, where it has
as many asserters as it has persons of eminency,
such as have an aim to rise by its commendatories.
Virtue is praiseworthy even in an enemy, its own
native beams and intrinsical worth rendering it so,
how much more when it shines in its proper hemi-
sphere, environed with lights, to set it off—not as
foils, but like the moon among the stars. Nobody
prizes virtue more highly than the virtuous, its worth
being best known to such, and none commends it
more than those that practise it, its commendation

consisting not so much in words as in deeds. It is
ignorance that makes the world contemn it, who, if
they knew its priceless value, would sell all to purchase it. This present Pope was a Frenchman by
birth, who besides other great parts wherewith nature
had endowed him, was so far favoured by grace, as
to be eminent in sanctity of life, in attestation
whereof after death his sepulchre was graced with
so many miracles, the blind, lame, and dumb finding
there a present cure. Now, what wonder if one
saint gives another an honourable reception? This
is no more than to give virtue its due, and from
whom may that more justly be expected than from
saints?

The legality of appeals to Rome in Church affairs,
when a decision cannot be had in an inferior Court,
is ratified by the custom and practice of all nations
and ages; to her all fly as to a common and disinterested mother, who holds the weights of the
sanctuary, and without bias and partiality, divides
a distributive justice according to equity. This is no
more than to appeal from an inferior court to a
superior, which the course of justice deems lawful;
nor, indeed, in our present controversy, which was
betwixt a Bishop and his Primate, could any other
Court give a final verdict. To it, therefore, our Saint
appealed, and in prosecution of it made his long

journey, and as he was always happy in this that he undertook nothing but upon mature advice and circumspection, grounded on the sound judgment of wise counsellors, so he seldom or never miscarried in any cause, but all being well digested, the very laying it open proved its decision. Yet a legal course of law was to be observed, and things by degrees brought to an issue, and his was such as he desired, that is, an enjoyment of the rights he was invested in by the decrees of former Popes, without suffering any infringement therein by his Metropolitan, who had not power to explicate Papal constitutions, as our Saint objected to him in the fore-mentioned Council of Reading, and upon his own explication to lay a claim. Where all proceeds according to the rigour of justice, favour pretends no place, nor did it here further than to obtain a quick despatch and removal of those delays, which render law suits both costly and tedious. This was all the favour that was or could be shown him, and he took it for no mean one, longing, as he did, after speedy return, his heart being at home, where was also the chiefest of his concerns, while the rest of his body was at Rome. He did, it is true, by an interior union of mind enjoy God everywhere, having long habituated himself in the same, but yet his content was in recollection; he loved not the cere-

monious visits of Courts, nor the loss of time that
is made in them, they being toilsomely fruitless and
fruitlessly toilsome. While he was Lord Chancellor
he felt the smart of that, and the surfeit caused
then made him less able to digest them all his life
after. Yet to omit them would have been deemed
a solecism against civility, and argued at the best a
stoical sanctity ; therefore who can blame a servant of
God if he endeavour to withdraw himself out of the
concourse of such courtships : ' He that touches
pitch shall be defiled by it.' [18.]

CHAPTER XVII.

Return towards home, and death on the way.

HAVING thus obtained a favourable despatch, and taken leave of that great Court, he put himself with joy upon the way as to himself, though he left it in a kind of regret for his departure, and the privation of the sweet odour of its sanctity caused thereby : what is admired as present, is regretted as absent, nor do we ordinarily know the worth of things better than by their privation. It cannot be prudently doubted but that according to his settled practice of piety, during the space of his abode there, he left many monuments both of his wisdom and sanctity most richly worth recounting had they come to our knowledge. But since they do not, we must rather content ourselves with a patient silence than discourse upon groundless conjectures, contenting ourselves that all is registered in the book of life, or annals of Heaven, to be published at the day of judgment. Nor can I doubt but according to the usual strain of sanctity, which has for its motto, *ama nesciri*, 'love concealment,' he played the silent eagle, not the talkative parrot, and that the course of his virtuous actions the more profound they were the more silent, like deep rivers, and with less noise, did they imperceptibly flow, and therefore no wonder if they escaped the record.

Having put himself on his journey as soon as the heats would permit, all his endeavours now, after Almighty God, were to render it as speedy as he could, much rejoicing in the success of his negotiation, and longing earnestly to make the concerned neighbouring churches at home, as well as his own, partake of the same. Thus do the wisest many times project according to human reasons and motives, while reckoning, as I may say, without their host; they propose and God disposes. Little did he dream that his journey was destined to a better home, and himself designed not for new labours, but a fruition of the past, the evening being at hand when the Master of the Vineyard was to call his workman to receive his hire, and invite him into the joys of our Lord; a thing if not sought for, yet always welcome, as being the much better home. He was resigned for life and death, putting both in the hands of God; and having learned to possess his soul in patience, he was not solicitous to die soon or live long, but to live and die well; which latter can be done but once, and gives the upshot to all.

He was now in the climacterical year of his age, sixty-three, and his crazy body was worn out with former labours, and not only what he now did, but what he had done these divers years, was more by the vigour of his spirit than corporal strength. This is a thing proper to holy souls, who measure their ability, as indeed they ought, rather by the spirit than the flesh, make this against its will keep pace with that, as hath been observed in St. Basil, St. Gregory, and others; and either by communicating a new force, or rejecting the sleeveless excuses of self-love, or by a special blessing of God, they do wonders in this kind. This vigorous resolution had now brought him as far as the State of Florence, and in it to a place known by the name of Monte Fiascone; but its stock, or viaticum, being spent, could carry him no further. Here his debility, destitute of victuals for a reinforcement, caused a distemper, that was heightened to a fever; this in its accesses, as a certain forerunner of death by its symptoms, told him that the days and ways of his pilgrimage would shortly be ended, and so they were, in not very many hours' compass; all its periods concluding in one point, to wit, Almighty God, in Whose sight the death of saints is precious. Now we must look on him awhile as death's victim, and learn of him how to die well, which is one of the most important arts in the world, for what avails it if

we gain the whole universe, and suffer shipwreck of
our own souls. This maxim was the study of his
whole life, and on it all his principles were grounded,
and so well, that he was not afraid to look death in
the face; he regarding it not otherwise than as a
passage to a better life : and therefore, amidst all its
appalments, he sat upon its couch, as the phœnix on
her pile of spices, expecting that the same flames
which consumed his body should renew his soul to a
better and immortal life.

Of this his passage I shall say no more than I find
upon authentic record, the process of his canonization,
reflecting on two things—first, his preparation to it :
secondly, the sequels of it. And as to the former,
when he perceived that the evening of life was in a
great decline, and its sun near upon setting, though
his whole life had been nothing else but a preparation
for death, or disposition to the sleep of saints, by
which they rest in our Lord; yet the nearer it
approached, the more it awaked him to a discharge of
his last duties. And therefore, with heart and eyes
fixed on Heaven, the first of his desires, according to
the rites of Holy Church, were the Last Sacraments,
or Viaticum of that great journey, doing himself as
he had taught others to do in that passage. These
are Confession, Communion, and Extreme Unction,
which as no good Christian doth omit, so no good

servant of God, but has them in esteem and veneration, and the greater, the better insight they have into
the concerns of their soul and its happy passage.
Having thus provided for the substantial part, all the
rest of his minutes were let out at the highest exchange, and he, unmindful of all worldly things,
invoked the Spirit both of light and life, by a *Veni
Creator Spiritus*, to be assistant to him in this last
conflict against the spirits of darkness, when both
light and life lie at the stake.   This done, he armed
himself with the sign of the Cross, or ensign of
Christianity, as formidable to the infernal powers as
comfortable to a parting soul; who whilst he consigned himself by it over to Almighty God, he added
these devout expressions, taught him probably in his
childhood, *Per signum Crucis de inimicis nostris libera
nos Deus noster;* and again, *Per Crucis hoc signum
fugiat procul omne malignum;* and lastly, *Per idem
signum salvetur omne benignum.*"[1]   All these are put
down verbatim in the record, and teach us how to
arm ourselves in our last conflict towards a victory
over our enemies.   This done, he called his retinue
about him, and imparting to each, saith the lessons of
his Office, the kiss of peace, together with the wholesome instructions for a pious life, amidst these

---

[1] 'Through the sign of the Cross deliver us, O God, from our
enemies.'   ' By this sign of the Cross may all evil be put to flight.'
' By this same sign may all good be preserved.'

embracements he took and gave the last adieu. And
now by this time, the stock of life being quite spent,
the pangs of death came stronger upon him, and
these increasing, he betook himself more earnestly to
his refuge of prayer, making use of that verse of the
Psalmist proper in such a passage,[2] *In manus tuas
Domine, commendo spiritum meum,* which words, whilst
he repeated thrice with his hands elevated towards
Heaven, he rendered his sweet soul most acceptable
to Heaven, to be received, according to its merits,
into the eternal tabernacles. This was the setting of
this sweet sun, showing much not only of the
Christian but the Saint, and verifying the old saying,
Ut vixit sic morixit, teaching us that general rule
without exception, He that lives well dies well. Which
sun, though he went down in a strange horizon, yet
found a welcome in the ocean of bliss, or a blessed
eternity: the true Christian deems that his hemi-
sphere where God places him, we being all citizens
of the world, and like beggars, never out of our way
while we are tending to Paradise. Happy they that
can make a happy conclusion of so important an affair,
which when thus concluded, our work is done; and if
not happily, all is undone, and that without redress.
That is a moment of greatest moment whereon
depends eternity.

[2] Psalm xxx. 6.

Though his festivity were kept on the 2nd of October, yet the day of his death happened on the 25th of August, or the morrow to the Apostle St. Bartholomew. And since all authors that I can find unanimously agree as to the place, to wit, that it was Monte Fiascone, one would wonder why Bishop Godwin, in contradiction hereof, without alleging any ground of his assertion, should maintain that he died at Civita Vecchia, and on his way to Rome, whereas there are undeniable proofs both of his arrival there, and obtaining his pretensions, return by land, and holy death at the place aforesaid. To say the least, this cannot but argue a spirit of contradiction proper to one of his coat, and little beseeming the name of a Bishop (nor had he more besides the revenues); only it is a known trick of such (I can call it no better) to render the clearest truths disputable, and thence doubtful, and so by degrees enervate all faith, both human and Divine, by undermining the authority which is their basis.

It happened the night after his decease that one of his officers whom he had left behind him in England, his name was Robert of Gloucester, then his secretary, afterwards Chancellor of Hereford, being at that time at London, and lodging in the Bishop's own chamber, had this dream or vision, call it as you please. He thought himself to be at Lyons in France,

where in the great street of the city which leads to
the cathedral, he seemed to behold his lord and
master going towards that church whither himself
was also bound. Both being entered, his lord, he
thought, went into the sacristy, where putting off the
upper garment which he wore, he vested himself with
white pontifical robes, and those most rich, and
carrying in his hand the Body of our Lord, or most
Blessed Sacrament, in form of a consecrated Host,
he appeared suddenly in the midst of a most solemn
and stately procession, both of clergy and religious,
and those likewise clad all in white. The procession
seemed to move towards the cloister of the cathedral,
while others of that choir intoned and prosecuted
with delicate music, that part of the Capitulum
proper to the Office of St. Peter ad Vincula, *Occidit*
autem Jacobum fratrem Joannis gladio. But before all
were entered the gate which led into the said cloister,
it on a sudden was shut, and Robert, who with many
others desired also to enter, were excluded, to their
no small defeatment, and left to consider the dream,
of which he, as then ignorant of the Saint's death,
could look upon no otherwise than a dream. But
when, immediately after, certain tidings both of his
death and the precise time of it came to be known,
and that it and his dream jumped so pat together, he
could not but think it more than a fancy, and that

Almighty God would intimate thereby that as he died, though not in persecution, yet in prosecution of the rights of his Church, and in some sort lost his life for the same, the Saint had not only deserved, but received the reward of a martyr.

This relation I have copied out of the Process of his Canonization, where it was juridically deposed before the examinants, and approved, as suiting well with what I said above of the common apprehension of all, that God wrought miracles by him for his actings and sufferings for His Church. And the same relation adds yet further, to let us know it was more a vision than dream, or rather a vision by way of dream (as is not unusual in Holy Scripture, both Old and New), that after this first apparition the blessed Saint was seen often to the same party, not indeed, saith it, as one in glory, but yet such as that his joyful contentedness spoke him to be in a most happy condition.

CHAPTER XVIII.

The remains of St. Thomas.

THUS much as to his sacred death and other circumstances which' accompanied or related thereto. Now we must pass to the other part, to wit, the sequels that followed thereupon. He died a passenger in this life's pilgrimage, and in a common inn; and, indeed, what other are all the lodgings in this world? We take them up, we bespeak supper, we forecast our future journey, we go to bed and rest, promising ourselves, like the man in the Gospel, many days of life, when, called fools for our pains, we are surprised with a fever, and all the journey we make afterwards is only to our grave. Our blessed Saint was too watchful to be stolen upon by that night thief; they only are so surprised who are found unprepared, that is, keep no watch and ward, and consequently are unprovided for the assault: and therefore we pray together with the Church to be delivered, not from death, nor from sudden death, but from sudden and unprovided death; for indeed, to one that is provided, no death is properly sudden.

The records tell us that his sacred corpse lay
exposed in the same place for six days together;
and this is but suitable to what is done to persons
of his extraction and quality, according to the respect
everywhere given them. Though here another reason
occurred which might more than probably authorize
the same : for no sooner was the sweet soul departed
like the extinct flame of a stick of perfume, but such
a heavenly fragrancy filled the whole room, that it
was most delicious to the scent and recreation to
all that were present. This, to wit, was a blessing
redounding to the body for the joint concurrence
that copartner afforded it in his virtuous exercises
in the service of God and His Church, and a testimonial of the odour of sanctity of that holy guest
which lodged therein. Such sensible witnesses of
an innocent integrity in His servants doth Almighty
God sometimes impart for their glory and our incitement, we being not easily moved but by our senses
either to conceive highly of them, or be egged on
to imitation, though the odour of virtue and sanctity
in itself far surpass whatever is of sense. In the
meantime the fame hereof, together with his death
being bruited abroad, as virtue and nobility is ever
in esteem with the noble and virtuous, it made many
great personages resort thither, and some Cardinals
among the rest, who acquainted with him during his

abode at Rome, or the opinion that went of him, had been no strangers either to him or his perfections. By their concurrence chiefly an honourable funeral was prepared for his interment the Sunday following, when he was buried in the Church of St. Severus, belonging to an abbey of that name situate near the old city of Florence, at what time a funeral sermon was preached by one of the Cardinals, who could not want matter to dilate upon, while he commended him for his noble descent, exquisite learning, and eminent sanctity.

All these particulars are thus far minutely specified in the record, but its warrant carries us no farther, nor any other that I could meet with as to the sequels of his interment. And consequently we are at a loss both as to that present and future times how to know whether any or what public veneration was there given at any time to his sacred corpse, or whether graces and miracles were wrought thereat, as in England at his sacred bones, what memory remained of him, and how long: all this must be left to Doomsday book and its register, when all will be published to the glory of God and the Saint, and satisfaction of all. In the interim we may know, that in the Catholic Church not every one that dies with opinion of sanctity is forthwith honoured as a saint. The public declaration of the Church, to prevent abuses and regulate all in an orderly way, is thereto requisite, and nothing permitted but under this warrant. He died, it is true, a saint, but his sanctity was not authorized. He died a stranger and an alien, and how little notice is taken of such ; five years elapsed before any miracles were noised abroad even in England itself, and twenty-five before his canonization. ' What wonder if the memory of him, not preserved by any special graces or signs, grew cold, and in that coldness vanished to oblivion. Though God were pleased at his mediation for the comfort of the people, incitement of their devotion, and other reasons best known to Himself, to work such wonders at his sacred bones ; yet He does this when and where and how long He thinks good, and nobody must presume to ask, Why do You so? All these are the secrets of His dispensations, and He says to us as He did to the Apostles, 'It is not for you to know the times or moments which the Father has put in His own power.'[1]

The news of his death, we may imagine, brought heavy tidings to his flock at Hereford, who, as it was most happy in his government during life, so sustained an incomparable loss by his death, the sorrow of the privation answering proportionably to the joy of the possession. . But these are blows

Acts . 7.

which all must be content to suffer when God inflicts
them, nor is there any redress besides a humble
acquiescence in His holy will. When we have paid
a little tribute to nature, all the rest is a submissive
resignation. Who dare say to Him, Why do You
so? Yet though his people could not have him
alive, it would have been some comfort to have had
him dead, that is, him in his corpse, to the end they
might have enjoyed him in his relics, which even
then, for the great opinion they had of his sanctity,
were esteemed for such.   In the present circumstances that could not be conveniently done, but
care was thus far taken, that the bones being separated from the fleshy parts, they, together with his
head and heart, were transported into England, and
deposited as a most precious treasure in the church
of Hereford.   These were received with much
devotion by the people, who went forth together
with the chapter and clergy to meet them, and were
enshrined in the chapel of our Blessed Lady in the
same cathedral, that they might repose in her bosom
after death to whom living and dying he was so
singularly devoted.   And where could his heart rest
better than in her hands to whose honour he had
sacrificed both heart and hands?

Among others whom either devotion or curiosity
moved to meet this welcome pledge, was one Gilbert,

Lord Clare, Earl of Gloucester, betwixt whom and our Saint, as we insinuated heretofore, there was no good understanding upon the account of some lands which the Earl detained and the Saint claimed as due to his Church, and recovered from him by force of law with much both cost and pains. He now, approaching to the sacred pledge, it was very remarkable, and looked on as a miracle by all the company, that the dry bones in his presence began to bleed afresh, and in such a quantity that he and all might see the cask in which they were carried imbrued with the same. The Earl, much amazed hereat, was struck with compunction, and acknowledging his fault, made a full restitution of all to the Church, expiating by penance what he had rashly committed, as the only way to make the best of an ill bargain.

In the retinue of the deceased Bishop the chief manager of affairs was Richard Swinfield, his secretary, first in authority above the rest. He was a priest of great parts and virtuous conversation, for which he was afterwards promoted to succeed in that vacant see, and in process of time chief solicitor and informer in order to the Saint's canonization. To him, as such, belonged the charge of conveying the sacred depositum, and he tells us in his deposition before the Commissaries Apostolical, what happened to himself the night before he with it arrived at

Hereford. To the end all things might be the next morning in a better readiness, he cast his journey so as to lodge with his company that night in a village two miles distant from the city: where, weary with journeying and going late to bed, he overslept himself beyond his time the next morning. His chamber was remote from all company, and so high, that without a ladder there was no access to the windows: and yet three knocks were given as with the knuckle of a bended finger on the same, and so loud that they served for an alarm to awake and tell him it was time to rise. And in that sense he understood them, and thereupon called up his company; concluding within himself, that this was a favour done him by the Saint towards the pursuit and furtherance of what they had in hand, to wit, the solemn reception and placing of the same bones. And what indeed could it be else, since humanly speaking, nobody without a ladder could come there, and looking curiously about he saw there was none: therefore he ascribed it to the merits of the Saint, and very thankful for such an extraordinary favour, to his honour he recorded it to posterity; making thence a conjecture that this piece of service, the conveyance of his bones, was acceptable to him, since he had been pleased to give it such an unusual concurrence.

While St. Thomas was yet alive, nobody seemed to carry a greater respect and veneration for his sanctity than Edmund, Earl of Cornwall, son to Richard, King of the Romans. He it was that invited the Saint to keep his Whitsuntide with him at his Castle of Wallingford: where, whilst he sung the *Veni Creator Spiritus*, the strange miracle of the birds happened, which we shall relate hereafter in the twenty-third chapter. However it was procured, this great devotist made means to get his heart, a treasure he esteemed above any jewels; and to testify this esteem, thought he could not honour it sufficiently any other way than by inclosing it in a most costly shrine together with a parcel of our Blessed Saviour's Blood, and founding a monastery of Bonshommes at Ashridge, in Buckinghamshire to its honour, where it might daily and duly be venerated to the praise and glory of Almighty God, Who had raised His servant to such an eminency of perfection. This devout Earl had such a confidence in his patronage and intercession, that he was wont to profess he had not greater in those of our glorious apostle, St. Austin. [14. 15.]

CHAPTER XIX.

The translation of his holy bones into a more eminent place.

THE near approach of the most welcome treasure being known at Hereford, stirred up the citizens, both ecclesiastics and laymen, to join, as we said, in a solemn procession to fetch it in; so showing by their veneration to the dead how much deeply they resented their incomparable loss. It was done with as much splendour as the shortness of the time would permit; and so amidst all the festivities of devotion it was brought into the cathedral, a small parcel, God wot, of what they desired, yet even as such most welcome. They wished him such in his return home as they sent him abroad, alive and governing as their Pastor: they wished, if dead, not only his bones but whole body; for a treasure the greater it is the better and more precious: but as it was, content with what necessity imposed, they lent their concurrence towards a solemn interring it in the chapel of our Blessed Lady, the place designed for its reception. Here it was laid in a coffin of stone, and a fair gravestone, such as beseemed his quality, placed for a cover to the orifice, cemented, on all sides as close and handsomely as art could make it.

Here it lay five years amidst the private veneration of devout persons, partaking of no more honour than their devotion gave it, each one according to the opinion they had of his sanctity. For though divers things more than ordinary, and such as beget much wonder and veneration were related on several passages, as, the fragrant odour it exhaled, the blood it sweat, morning call, &c., yet formal miracles none were wrought nor pretended to; and the Catholic Church hath always used a special wariness to prevent disorders of this nature, that nothing may be publicly ascribed before attested by legal authority; and we need not doubt but the Saint himself among so many decrees as he made, had left this enacted. During this interval of time the vacant chair was provided of a successor; the party elected was Richard Swinfield, of whom we said something in the precedent chapter; the same that accompanied our Saint to Rome, and by his good services there on his Church's behalf, as also by the safe conveyance of his relics had much improved himself in the opinion and esteem of that chapter. And the providence of God, as to this, seems remarkable in the election, both that none could have concurred more to the

glory and illustration of our Saint, none knowing him
and his merits better than he, and consequently could
be more zealous in that behalf; as, also, because he
was both a great preacher, truly virtuous, and
thoroughly versed in the affairs of that bishopric, as
bred up under the Saint. The profound respect and
zeal he had for his holy predecessor took little
content to see his bones, so worthy of greater
veneration, lie so obscurely beneath their desert,
even as he was a Bishop, not only a Saint. Whereupon he determined a solemn translation of the same
to a more eminent and conspicuous place of the
cathedral ; where he resolved to erect a stately
monument of marble, and have the action solemnized
with the greatest magnificence he possibly could.

The time pitched on for this purpose was Mandate
Thursday in Holy Week ; the report whereof blazed
abroad invited both Court and country to honour it
with their presence, nor needed many motives, the
opinion they had of him was sufficient. It was made
in the year 1287, the 6th of April, the Bishop and
chapter jointly concurring thereto : and the place to
which it was translated, saith Godwin, was the east
wall of the north cross aisle where yet is to be seen,
saith he, a tomb of marble. King Edward III., in
whose reign it was made, was then at Calais, which
he had not long before taken from the French King;

but purposely came over out of his devotion to the Saint, and to grace the solemnity with his presence. He and his nobles, saith John 'Stow, were entertained at the charges of Nicholas Cantilupe, Baron, cousin to St. Thomas : nor did the King miss of a due reward from the said Saint in recompense of his religiousness. For while he was attending to that action he received private intelligence of a design on foot for the delivery of that town to the King of France by a Genoese, Emericus of Padua, who lived there and was a private pensioner of the French King : he played lack on both sides being also in fee in King Edward, who suspecting nothing less kept him and his men there for the defence of the town. Nor was here an end of the blessing ; for the King hastening to its succour, not only forestalled the other's treachery, but with a handful of men repulsed the numerous enemy, took many prisoners, and put all in a posture of safety.

The sacred depositum, as we hinted before, was put into a stone coffin shut up under a fair great gravestone, which was to be removed ere the coffin could be taken out, and how to remove it, so great and massy as it was, gave no small difficulty, naturally speaking, in that narrowness and situation of place. While their wits were thus contriving, two of the Bishop's pages who stood by, put their hands to it

as it were in sport to try their strength, where four
of the ablest could have done nothing. And here
behold a strange accident : at the slender impulse of
these two alone, the massy stone yielded and gave
place as far as was necessary for the present purpose,
as if it had been a thin board, not what it was. All
the company cried out, a miracle (for they could
ascribe it to nothing else) wrought by the Saint to
attest his sanctity, and show how grateful the translation was to him. But here was not an end of their
amazement ; yea, it was much increased, when after
the Mass of Requiem and solemnity ended, trial was
made again in the same manner to put the same stone
into its former posture, which now, though they had
the advantage of the ground much more than before,
not these two but neither ten more joined with them,
endeavouring with all their might and main, were
scarce able to set it in its place.

This was an essay or prelude to the manifold
miracles which immediately followed : for such was
the working power of Almighty God to evidence the
glory of his servant, St. Thomas, that that very day
of his translation five miracles were wrought at his
tomb, and as many each ensuing day for divers
together. Nay, there was a perpetual continued
stream, the source being once opened, without surcease
for many years, of which we shall speak more in the

insuing chapter. Great was the devotion of the
people in this solemnity, heightened we may imagine
not a little by these fresh foregoing wonders : and
where there is devotion, God is never sparing of His
graces and mercies; that His sovereign oil ceases
not still to run, so long as there are such fresh pots
disposed to receive it. Why He reserved these extraordinary blessings for this feast, let us not curiously
inquire of Him in Whose hands is the free disposal
of times and moments; but let us take His dispensations when they come, humbly and thankfully,
being assured that He knows better what and when
things are to be done than we can tell Him.

In the translation itself and time of Mass of
Requiem said at the new tomb for the dead (for as
yet the Saint was neither beatified nor canonized),
a man who had been two years blind, and a woman
eight, both of them received their sight in the presence of all the people who were spectators, admirers,
and witnesses of the miracle. To give a particular
account of all the rest that were wrought (though
they be all upon record and attested) would be too
tedious, and especially all that were wrought during
the octave of the solemnity (forty in number); but
as Easter Day, by reason of its glorious festival,
claimed to itself a peculiar splendour above the rest,
so Almighty God seems to have kept a noted and

particular cure for it, much redounding to the honour
of our Saint, as wrought upon one both noble of
himself and well known to all the nobility of the
land, and consequently more famed abroad and
divulged than many others. This was one Miles,
a famous warrior, renowned far and near for his
exploits in tilting. With frequent falls and bruises
and other misfortunes, such a weakness came upon
him that he became contracted in his limbs, and
they all useless to him. And thus he remained six
whole years, all art of physicians labouring in vain,
now an object of compassion as much as he had
been before of congratulation. This man, familiarly
known to Bishop Richard, was by name invited to
the translation, and particularly on Easter Day, when
celebrated with greater solemnity: the good Bishop
intimating withal that divers great miracles were then
daily wrought at the Saint's tomb, and who knew
but he might have a blessing in store for him. He,
like one in misery, hearkened willingly to any advice
that relished of redress. He made himself be carried
to the tomb on Easter Eve; he prayed there de-
voutly the whole night, beseeching the Saint that as
he was noble himself, he would be propitious to a
noble knight, commiserating his present pitiful condition, and vouchsafing him the gracious favour of
a cure. To render himself better disposed, like a

good Christian he frequented the holy sacraments of confession and communion ; and at the time when in the said church the Mystery of the Resurrection, saith the record, was that morning represented, he found himself so perfectly cured at the said tomb, that the same day, exulting in our Lord, whole and sound, he played the serving-man at the Bishop's table, waiting on him and his other guests.

For a conclusion of this chapter I must insert a remarkable cure which was wrought while the sacred relics remained yet in our Lady's Chapel, six days before the translation, that is, the day before Palm Sunday, and therefore may deservedly claim to be here inserted. It is thus recorded in the fore-mentioned process. One Edith, wife to a citizen of Hereford, in the beginning of that same Lent was seized with a furious frenzy, and, all human means falling short, so she continued till the day before Palm Sunday. The recourse to St. Thomas not being as then famed by any miracles, her husband caused her to be measured to a relic of the Holy Cross, much venerated in that cathedral, at whose altar she was kept night and day, bound, and attended by two of her sex ; though at the same time she was advised by a priest of the church to have recourse to St. Thomas, and to be measured to him, giving her great hopes of a recovery by his intercession. All this was done at his suggestion, and a candle was made of the thread that measured her, and set at her head as she lay bound, hand and foot, her ordinary station being all this while at the altar of the Holy Cross. The Friday before Palm Sunday, as she was there hearing Mass, not only the candles on the altar, but all through the church, were on a sudden put out, nobody knew how, and a great noise, like the murmur of a great river, was heard at the same time. This lasting the space of ten *Paters* and *Aves,* visibly before them all fire came from Heaven and lighted the candle standing at her head, whose wick was made of the thread that measured her to the Saint. At the lighting of this she recovered her senses and became well, the Saint at that instant appearing to her and bidding her be well; at the same time also the cords which bound her of themselves became loose, and she, in the presence and hearing of all, repeating it over and over again, said aloud, 'Where is this St. Thomas that bids me be well?' She went to our Lady's Chapel, prayed before his relics, a *Te Deum* was sung in thanksgiving for the cure: she continued as well and sensible as ever before; and this was the first miracle which the Saint wrought in the Church of Hereford.

Upon the relation of this miracle it occurs to me

that some peruser of the same may check, perchance
(as it is always easy to find fault), at one or two
passages mentioned therein: the which to clear up
by way of prevention will haply not be unacceptable.
One may be, her leaving the Holy Cross and its
altar to betake herself to St. Thomas, in which, if
there were any fault, it was the priest's who advised
her to it; which could not be great, it being
warranted by the good miraculous effect immediately
ensuing. Neither did he dissuade her from the Holy
Cross, whose efficacious virtue is venerable to all
Christians, but only persuaded her (whether by divine
instinct or the impulse of his devotion matters not
much) to make her recourse to God and it, by the
mediation of the Saint. His devotion to St. Thomas
moved him to urge this recourse, which, if upon the
opinion had of his sanctity, he advised, where is
the error? Nay, it is glorious to the Holy Cross,
as it is also to honour God in His Saints (so far is
it from disparagement to see its servants honoured
and invoked); besides that a new star may many
times, and without prejudice to the sun, draw more
eyes to it than the sun itself, and have its influences
more cried up. Both devotions were compatible and
good, nor doth the latter derogate from the former.

Another, perhaps, will be dissatisfied, yea, even
a little scandalized, at this measuring to the Saint,

and ask what it means? Truly, I do not remember
to have read it elsewhere, nor is it any ecclesiastical
ceremony of any Church, much less of the Catholic:
it seems to have been taken up by the devotion of
the people thereabouts, and as an innocent, harmless
expression of their devotion and recourse to the
Saint, approved by custom; and though frequently
used, yet not so of necessity, but that it was, and
with equal success, as frequently omitted, at least
not mentioned. This their recourse and application
to the Saint was twofold, and the miraculous effects
as to both show its acceptableness to him, either
by bending a piece of silver coin over the patient's
head who sought redress to the honour of the Saint,
appropriating the party by this expression to him
and his peculiar patronage for redress; or else by
measuring the said client by a thread, or some such
thing, that is, by taking his length and breadth with
the same intention as in the former, and depositing
them at his altar or to his honour. The manifold
miraculous effects ensuing hereupon vindicate the
fact from all suspicion of irreligiosity and superstition; and if the Saint was pleased to accept it, let
not us harbour a prejudice against it. When we see
the candle whose wick was made of this measure,
miraculously, and before all the rest, lighted from
Heaven, let us take that miracle for an approvement

of its innocency: ' All's well, when all's meant well '
—*Alius quidem sic alius autem sic.*[1] Thus much I
thought good to premit for the scandal of the weak.

CHAPTER XX.

The multitude of miracles wrought by the Saint.

WE may indeed call them a multitude, and of the
greatest size, for few saints perchance in God's
Church have wrought more, and therefore he was
not undeservedly called in the Preface the Thaumaturgus of that age. And their quality is no less
remarkable than their quantity, it being such as
renders them unquestionable in their kind, that is,
evident and patent, like those of the Gospel, and
such as our Blessed Saviour both wrought and
alleged for testimonials of His reception as Messias,
by giving sight to the blind, healing the lame,
raising the dead, &c., and these, as well as others
in great abundance. For the reader's satisfaction,
and the Saint's greater glory, I will summarily put
down here what the several authors of his Life say in

[1] 1 Cor. vii. 7.

this behalf, that the authority of his miracles may
remain as questionless as they are numerous.   Which
authors, when they have consigned his virtues
over to us with this seal of deeds, and delivered
them under this consignment (they having before
signalized them with words), it cannot be denied
but all legal formalities are observed, and that they
ought to stand in force as a deed signed, sealed, and
delivered, according to the tenor of our courts of
justice ; and why should not saints in Heaven partake
thereof as well as sinners on earth ?   To deny it
them were a great inconsequence.

These miracles took their rise or source from his
translation, and continued their stream some ages
together.   In treating of them we will not launch
forth into their main of all particulars, for so we ,
should lose ourselves without end, but only cruising
near the shore, pass both swiftly and safely through
such an ocean.   The first I cite in this behalf is
Laurentius Surius, a grave and exact author, who, out
of one anonymous or concealed ancient writer, but
judicious, testifies that among the miracles which
stand upon record, our blessed Saint is found to have
restored from death to life sixty-six ; sight to the blind,
forty-one ; use of their limbs to the contracted or
sinew-shrunk, fifty-two ; palsy-struck, twenty-one. And
he recounts only what came to his knowledge not

that he professes to know all. Dr. Nicholas Harpsfield, Prebend of Canterbury, and a diligent collector of the gests of our saints, makes such a like relation ; who, speaking of our glorious Saint and his eminent virtues, tells us they were recommended to us and future posterity under the attestation of frequent miracles, one hundred and sixty-three whereof were wrought, saith he, in the compass of a few years, and rendered his merits famous far and near for the same. John Capgrave expresses himself in this sort as to the Saint and this point of his miracles, where he saith, ' The miracles which after his death Almighty God was pleased to show to us sinners in evidence of his sanctity, and to the honour of His own name (for God is honoured in His saints) I saw,' saith he, ' at his tomb, registered in divers volumes, and they were in a manner infinite.' ' In one whereof,' saith the same, ' I counted four hundred and twenty-five wrought by St. Thomas at his shrine, all miraculous effects, many whereof were in the cure of different diseases,' and even Bishop Godwin himself, a mere pickpocket in this kind, filching away whatever he can, grants that many miracles are said to have been wrought at the place of his burial, in regard whereof it pleased the Pope to make him a Saint. Thus doth he mince the matter, which he dares not deny nor yet confess without a clear condemnation of himself and his brethren, who pulled down a Church and faith, so stored and confirmed with miracles, to set up a chapel of their own building, to verify the old proverb, ' Where God has a church, the devil will have a chapel.'

The last confirmation which I bring of his miracles and their multitude is beyond all exception to any unprejudiced judgment, for I know it from ·the very authentic acts and records juridically proved and approved in the process of his canonization. A copy of these same acts and records, taken by a friend of mine of unquestionable sincerity, out of the original, which is kept in the Vatican Library, I have at this present lying by me, and whatsoever I have or shall say concerning his miracles, is all, or in greatest part, borrowed from thence. There I find upon record in all four hundred and twenty-nine, and them examined and approved partly by the Lords Commissioners deputed by His Holiness then living for that end, and partly by four authorized notaries. The Lords were the Bishop of London and Bishop of Miniat, who sat sometimes at St. Catharine's, London, sometimes at Hereford, to avoid charges in the citation of witnesses. They were commissioned only for four months, and in that time they could examine no more than thirty-nine miracles, all which they subscribed. The four notaries were a kind of

standing committee for that purpose, whose power
stood good without limit of time or stint of authority,
and all the force of approbation which the rest have
is derived from them. And thus much in general is
sufficient to ascertain us both of the creditableness
of what we allege, and to show how highly he was
in favour with Almighty God; for all these being
things above the ordinary course of nature, they
require a special and supernatural concurrence, a
thing merely of grace, and not granted but upon
extraordinary exigencies, for the illustration of the
power of God in His saints, and to let the world
know how wonderful He is in them: *Mirabilis Deus
in sanctis suis.*[1]

Miracles, when frequent, are an evident conviction
of true sanctity, as being the seal not to be counterfeited, which God Himself sets upon it for its mani-
festation and authorizement to the world, which seal
whosoever can exhibit under test, his virtue needs no
other touchstone to prove it current or genuine. Not
that all that doth not carry them is spurious, or that
all saints to be such must work miracles, or that
they are of the essence of sanctity, it being of itself
too nobly divine to need any such support besides
itself. And many great saints, as the holy Baptist,
St. Joseph, and others, have during life wrought

[1] Psalm lxvii. 36.

none at all, and yet were held for such, unless we will say the whole tenor of their life was a continual miracle. Yet still, where found, they are deservedly esteemed so many pledges of God's favour to the worker, and infallible attestations of his sanctity, it being against the Divine goodness to permit hypocrisy to be accompanied and authorized by those distinctive marks with which He has signalized the true faith and sanctity. But it is not in point of faith as it is in point of sanctity as to this ; that true sanctity may be found without miracles, though the true Church or faith cannot, Christ having entailed them upon it : insomuch that that Church which cannot show miracles cannot be the Church of Christ. But he has not annexed miracles to true sanctity, nor are they of its essence, and consequently though they grace it extremely when present, yet it may be as perfect and grateful to God when absent, because not an intrinsical commendatory, but merely extrinsical, and as to us by way of testimonial, a grace gratis given by Almighty God.

Now, to satisfy the devotion of the reader, or rather to inflame it the more, we will descend in particular to relate some few of so many miracles, and give a little scantling thereof, which, as they are particular pledges of God's special favour towards His servant, so they cannot but be special incentives to us of a peculiar reverence towards the same.

One Juliana, living not far from Hereford in her childbed, fell into such a contraction of all her limbs, that she became wholly destitute of their use, and this for the space of nine years together. All human remedies proved unuseful to her cure, and how to obtain Divine she knew not. The fame and name of St. Thomas was then not blazed abroad, though it happened after his death, and while his sacred bones lay buried in our Lady's Chapel. Yet the charitable Saint had a kindness for the poor creature, and appearing six several times to her, wished her to go to the tomb of Bishop Thomas, which was in our Lady's Chapel at Hereford, and there she should be cured. She neither knew what Bishop Thomas nor Lady's Chapel meant, but upon so many warnings, resolved to send her husband to Hereford to learn by inquiry what they might mean. He went, he informed himself, he returned, yet the disabled wretch lay languishing a whole year before she could resolve to be carried thither. The bruit of the solemn translation quickened her devotion a little, and being carried in a basket was placed in our Lady's Chapel at the Saint's relics. There falling into a slumber, he appeared to her again, bidding her rise and go to the new tomb. She made what shift she could to get to it, nor had she sooner touched it, and said a few prayers, but by leaning on it, she rose, found herself well, and walked thrice about it, and the next day home without any help. The basket in which she was brought she left behind her at the tomb, but it being borrowed of a poor neighbour, who demanded her basket again, Juliana the next morning sent for it, and restored it to the owner. But what much heightened the miracle was this : the basket was no sooner taken away, but the woman relapsed into her former contraction. It seems the Saint required it for a monument of his charitable redress. What remedy now ? She is carried again to his tomb, and in the same basket, remaining so amidst tears and prayers a whole day and night. The next morning her good benefactor, mindful of his patient, restored her limbs once more to a full and perfect use of them, and lest she might incur a second forfeiture, she presumed no more to take away the basket.

A public incendiary was taken *in flagranti*, and deservedly by the Lord of the Manor, who had legal power, sentenced to the gallows, which was executed, and he lay there a sad spectacle of justice, with all the certain signs of a dead man, insomuch that now they thought of nothing more but his burial. The lady of the Manor, a very virtuous matron, and her daughter, like herself, having their charity not tied to merit, much beyond his deserts, had a great mind to have him, thus, as he was, measured to St. Thomas, in hopes of a revival, confiding surely that the latter part of his life would be more edificative than the former. In fine, she did it, and not once or twice, but thrice, with much devotion, seconded with the fervent prayers of all that were present. Her faith was equal to her hope and charity, and all three so acceptable to the Saint, that upon this devout petition, as a prelude to what would follow, the dead body moved first one foot, then began to breathe, the eyes which hung ghastily upon his cheeks fell back of themselves to their proper place, and so did his tongue to its—in fine, there was a perfect recovery from death to life, and he is said (and no great wonder it should be so) to have mended his manners very much, and behaved himself through all like a good Christian. It is not granted every one to die twice.

The palpablest of miracles, or the raising the dead, was so ordinary with our glorious Saint that forty such like resuscitations stand upon a juridical record. Our Lord and Saviour has the sole dominion of life and death, keeping in His own hands the keys of both without control; yet so, as that He lends them sometimes to His servants, who, what they do, is by

His power and dispensation, as are also all the miracles which they work, not done by their proper virtue but His concurrence Who communicates it : and thus He wrought with our Saint, who will say, as did St. Peter to the Jews : 'Ye men of Israel, why marvel you at this? or why look you upon us as though by our power or holiness we have made this man to walk? the God of Abraham,'[2] &c. In this kind, a little child scarce three years old playing with another of the same age on the bank of a fish-pond, the other to frighten her, made as if she would thrust her in, and she out of fear fell in indeed, and was actually drowned before the mischance known, or help could be given. This pond belonged and was near to an alehouse, where store of company was at the time making merry, and among the rest the parents of the child : so close many times and un-pectedly doth sorrow follow mirth at the heels, dashing the wine of comfort with the water of tears, suitable to that of the Wise Man : 'Mourning taketh hold of the end of joy;'[3] and thus many times is all the sport spoiled. The child is taken out life-less, and while they are all lamenting over it, the father, who had heard much of the miracles wrought by St. Thomas, together with all the company re-commended the matter with much devotion to the

---

[2] Acts iii. 12.　　　　[3] Prov. xiv. 13.

Saint, and with his girdle measured her to him according to custom. Thus they all persevered praying and on their bare knees, saith the records, till next morning without any sign of life: in the morning natural heat came into her body, motion of her limbs followed that, and speech motion, and so by degrees came perfectly to herself. This miracle was among the first which Almighty God wrought by His Saint, and it being noised abroad people came far and near to behold the child: it was also the first which was solemnly examined and approved by the Lords Commissioners. She lived till she came to woman's estate, but could never be persuaded by her parents to marry, though much urged thereto; and therefore was commonly called by the name of St. Thomas's Virgin.

A poor man, by an unjust oppression of his landlord, was cast into prison, and so loaded with irons that the weight of them broke his left arm. In this sad condition, both of want and torment, all human means failing him he sought Divine, and had recourse to our Saint; making a vow that if he cured his arm and restored him to liberty, himself would make a pilgrimage to his tomb. He found a propitious patron; his arm was forthwith cured, and he ere long released from hold. But, alas! a good purpose is sooner made than kept; he that said *Vovete* said also *Reddite*,

which latter part was wholly neglected by this ungrateful client, who now having obtained what he
desired thought no more of what he promised, and
so it fares with a great many. The Saint sent him
a remembrance, and he fell into a grievous fit of
sickness, and in it into phrensy, in a raving transport
whereof his arm is broken again, and in the same
place. Being fallen asleep he seemed to see the
most glorious Mother of God, and hear her saying to
St. Thomas who stood by her : 'Friend, help this
poor caitiff.' 'Help him!' replied he ; 'he made a
vow to visit me before this, and has not been so good
as his word.' 'Ah,' said the sweet Mother of Mercy,
'he will come to you, help him, I pray.' 'Let him
then come,' replied the Saint, 'on Whit Sunday and
he shall be cured in the name of our Lord.' Which
said, they both disappeared, and the sick man related
the vision to the bystanders, was carried by them on
that day to the Saint's shrine, where he found redress
of both his maladies by the intercession of the Most
Glorious Virgin and the merits of the Saint.

One of Staines, not far from London, became so
infirm that all present judged he could not live one
hour to an end. This extremity or infirmity was the
least part of his misery : for he found himself haunted
and obsessed over and above with multitudes of devils
in most hideous shapes, which not only beset him,

but some taking him by the head, others by the feet, they hauled and pulled him almost to pieces. The poor sick man, half distracted, had recourse as well as he could to Almighty God, beseeching Him by the merits of His devout servant, St. Thomas of Hereford, to afford some assistance in this dreadful agony. And behold, while he silently thus recommended himself, he saw the man of God approaching him, and clasping his head betwixt his hands stood in his defence against these wicked spirits the greatest part of that night. About break of day, put to flight they all vanished, the Saint still holding the sick man's head as before; who suddenly awaking out of his sleep, and his aid or helper withdrawing at the same instant, he found himself perfectly restored to health, both of body and mind, by the powerful mediation of his heavenly champion who came so seasonably to his rescue. To whose tomb therefore by way of thanksgiving he with his neighbours undertook barefoot a long pilgrimage, and there in each one's hearing attested the cure.

To let us know how dangerous it is to meddle with edged tools, that is, to jest profanely with the proceedings of saints, making a piece of drollery of what we ought humbly to venerate, if we do not understand; a young man, Fleming by nation, and servant to an English lady of quality (he was better fed than

taught), being in a citizen's house in Hereford, among
other raillery, began to speak scurrilously of our
blessed Saint, saying, that while he lived he was
certainly of a covetous humour, since after his death
he receives so many precious gifts, refusing nothing
that was offered him.   While he presumed to go thus
on, one of his hands suddenly shrunk up with such
violence of pain, that acknowledging his fault, he was
forced before all present to invoke the Saint for
redress : which no sooner desired than obtained, so
charitable was he towards him, the hand being
presently restored, and all as well as before.   But see
the inveterateness of an ill custom !   Shaken off, it
recurs again and again, and clings to us like a second
nature.   The ungrateful wretch thus cured, attributes
both the pain and cure to a natural cause, and
neither the latter to his benefactor, nor the former
to a punishment of his profane scurrility.   While he
was uttering these words, so violent a pain and
contraction seized the same hand a second time, that
no stroke but one from Heaven could cause it.
Affliction gives understanding, and so did it him ;
he acknowledged the hand of God upon him for
his ingratitude, and now heartily penitent called
upon the Saint, and desired all the standers-by to
do the same.   Their prayers were presently heard,
his hand restored, and he learned more wit than to

relapse a third time. Let us learn hence to detest atheistical drollery, and serve God and reverence His saints, in whom He is so admirably admirable.

The next I will relate happened in the person of Bishop Richard, the so-often mentioned successor to our Saint. He, in the first years of his Episcopacy, was so ill of the stone, that both physicians and others looked on him as a dying man, nor for the space of five or six weeks did he stir out of his chamber. His chamberlain, who deposed this cure, sleeping one night in his lord's chamber to be ready on all exigencies, seemed in his sleep to hear one say to him, 'Arise, take the relic which thou hast of St. Thomas (it was the first joint of his right thumb, and nobody besides himself knew of it), wash it in the wine which, in a silver cruet, stands in the window; give thy master to drink of it, and he shall be cured.' The chamberlain, either mistrusting the call and its effects, or fearful that the wine might not be good for his lord, dissembled the matter, nor took notice of it, chiefly indeed for fear of losing his precious relic, which he deemed too precious for him to keep were it once known to others. The next night he heard the same call, with a menace for his former neglect; yet he, out of the precedent motives forbore also the second time: the night following, or third, he seemed to behold our Blessed Lady accompanied with many virgins, all which were clad in white and environed with great brightness, entering the chamber in which the Bishop and his chamberlain reposed, and coming near to the latter's bed, who for some days before had with much devotion sought her assistance by the merits of St. Thomas for his master's recovery, said to him in French, saith the process, 'Denis (that was the chamberlain's name), art thou asleep?' He answered, 'No.' 'Rise, then,' said she, 'take the wine above mentioned, and if thou doest it not, at thy peril be it.' This last threat made a deeper impression, and as soon as it was light he communicated the matter with the Bishop's confessor and physician to know their judgment upon the matter. With their approbation and in their presence he washed the foresaid relic, and the physician gave three spoonfuls of the said wine to the Bishop, wishing him to drink it: he, making the sign of the cross, did so, rose immediately, went down to the chapel, which he could not do for so many weeks, heard Mass, and remained all that ensuing year as free as if he had never been molested therewith.

I will conclude this present narrative with another, deposed juridically before the Lords Commissioners by the party concerned then living, who in his younger days had once been a menial servant of the Saint, but marrying afterwards, lived at London, and by trade was a barber. This man, upon the sudden, without any visible occasion, lost first one eye, then the other, and both with such excess of pain, that it made him seek all human redress, though in vain, and try the skill of chirurgery, which notwithstanding, he remained three years stark blind, fain to be led whithersoever he went, and he daily did to St. Paul's Church to hear Mass. Much discomforted with this accident, he called to mind his old patron and great well-wisher, St. Thomas, now canonized a saint and working miracles. He recommends himself most earnestly to him and our Blessed Lady, beseeching her by the devotion he had to her to obtain of Almighty God a cure of his misery and restorement of sight, that he might again to his comfort behold her Son in the Consecrated Host, while it is elevated for all to adore. For this end he caused himself to be measured, according to custom, to St. Thomas, and sent the measure and two eyes of wax with it to Hamelden in Buckinghamshire, the place where our Saint was born and christened. Two days after he found some glimmerings of light, so as to distinguish imperfectly motion and colour, and thereupon caused himself to be measured the second time, and that measure he

sent to Hereford, to the Saint's shrine; and thereupon found such help that within eight days' space
he could walk any whither without a leader, and
could discern, as he desired, the elevated Host at
a competent distance. The cure he ascribed to the
Saint, as also in this respect the cause of his blindness; for that he in his youth, when he served
St. Thomas, being of a loose life and wanton behaviour, and chid therefore frequently by him for his
amendment, the Saint obtained of Almighty God
this temporal affliction (it many times gives understanding and such blindness light to see ourselves)
towards an amendment of his spiritual: and he
acknowledged that he had reaped great benefit
thereby, and heartily thanked Almighty God and
the Saint for the same.

It were as easy for me to cite some hundreds as
these few, were it any part of my design to swell
this little summary into a great volume. It doth
not aim at a rehearsal of his miracles, but of his
virtues, which are the noblest kind of miracles; for
in this corrupt nature of ours, so prone to vice, I
esteem every soul eminent in sanctity so many miracles of God's grace working in it. And these miracles
are more for our purpose, that is, for our imitation,
to which purpose if we do not apply them, we
swerve from the purpose; the greatest honour and

devotion we can show towards a saint being to imitate his virtues, as also the most beneficial to us. Miracles are good witnesses of sanctity, ascertaining us how high the Saint stands in the favour of God, and they stir us up also to a due recourse towards him in our necessities; but to profit otherwise than by imitation we cannot pretend, since, being above the course of nature, they are objects rather to be admired than imitated. Set yourself to a glorious imitation of their virtues, and you may probably work miracles yourself. [16—21.]

CHAPTER XXI.

Canonization of St. Thomas, and general devotion of all unto him, both Prince and people, till this unhappy breach.

THE multitude of extraordinary graces and favours which Almighty God imparted to all sorts of people by the merits of His glorious servant and bishop, St. Thomas, was the reason why the whole kingdom solicited the then Pope for his canonization. Now twenty-five years or thereabouts were elapsed since the translation of his sacred bones into his new sepulchre, since which time the current of miracles never ceased, and the daily monuments thereof hanging at the same were so many remembrancers minding them as much to glorify him as he was beneficial toward them. One good turn requires another: if saints obtain us temporal blessings, let us give them the glory thereof. Glory is a cele-brious knowledge with praise; nor can this be better had in this world than from the mouth of the Church, whose words in this matter are oracles, and her public declaration in point of sanctity a canonization. Hence it was that prince and people, clergy, religious, secular, all interested alike in his favours (yet above others the Bishop and Chapter of Hereford), became joint solicitors, that as Heaven had owned his piety by so many prodigies, the Church would authentically declare it, authorizing them to honour him as a saint who had exhibited so many undeniable proofs of sanctity. The generality of the bishops of our nation concurred to this, and I find a transcript in the process itself exhibited by the Procurator of the Chapter of Hereford to the Lords Commissioners, which transcript was subscribed by the Lords Bishops, John, Archbishop of York, Antony of Durham, Godfrey of Worcester, John of Llandaff, John of Winchester, Ralph of Norwich, Walter of Bath, Alvian of Bangor, John of Carlisle, Thomas of Exeter, and was directed by them to His Holiness, containing their esteem and sentiment both of his life and virtues and the wonders daily wrought at his shrine.

Upon this and other such solicitations it was that a public process of the Saint's life and miracles was instituted, and Commissaries Apostolical deputed thereto, the two Bishops and Archdeacon specified in the precedent chapter. The Procurator for the Chapter of Hereford was one Henricus a Schorna, and Bishop Richard, who best knew the Saint living

and dying, as one that was bred under him, con-
scious to all his secrets, was the first and chief
deponent. The Commission took date the 13th of
July, 1307, and was to continue but four months,
which limitation of time, and multiplicity both of
witnesses and miracles, was the reason why they
could not insist upon or pass through all; but as
many as were examined by them, in order to his
virtues or miracles, all depositions passed under
oath, the Holy Gospels lying open before them,
and they swearing to speak nothing but truth.
Which depositions were duly registered by appointed
notaries, reviewed by the Commissioners, and by
them consigned up to His Holiness, and kept to
posterity in the Vatican library; the perusal of an
authentical copy whereof, by the favour of a special
friend and diligent searcher into the gests and
legends of saints was communicated to me, and
therefore I can aver much for the undoubted truth
of what I say. The information being taken as
above and a due return made to the Congregation
of Rites, whom such matters concern, all being ad-
justed according to form, His Holiness John XXII.,
at the instance of our King and prelates, proceeded
to a canonization, which was solemnized both at
Rome with the usual festivals, and to the universal joy
of the whole kingdom, much more in England, and

chiefly in the Church of Hereford. Though the
day of its solemnization be not specified, yet we
may credibly think it was on the 2nd of October,
on which day the Church celebrates his yearly
memory, though it be otherwise certainly known, as
we said above, that the day of his deposition or
death were on the 25th of August.

The fame of his sanctity attested so many years
by a world of miraculous cures of all kinds, to all
sorts of people, did not bind itself within our own
island, but working at sea as well as at land, and
passing our straits, it filled both France and Italy,
as well as Scotland and Ireland; and as all received
a new access of joy by this new access of honour,
so every one strove to put on a new fervour of
devotion suitable to his merits and their obligation.
A new declared saint is like a new star in the fir-
mament; he draws as many hearts as that doth
eyes, and if the influences of the latter be more
visible, the communications of the former are more
benign and obliging. A flame of devotion which is
continually nourished with the oil and fuel of successive blessings did not fear a decrease of heat,
and such was the peoples towards our Saint. One
King and two Queens have been seen prostrate
pilgrims before his tomb; nor was their majesty
ever more gloriously great than when thus humble

before God's servant : there is no truer greatness
than that which accrues from a profound humility.
All the princes and nobles of the land imitated
their example with votaries in their hands : the
greatest prelates and their clergy were the first in
this religious worship ; nor was it then accounted
superstition or idolatry to honour God in His saints.
How happy was the people of this kingdom in such
a propitious patron where, in their greatest plunges
of necessity, they needed only as it were to ask
and have, if the grace were fit to be imparted and
they disposed to receive it, his shrine alone being
a pharmacopœia or dispensatory of receipts for the
cure of all maladies, even death itself. And thus
it continued many years to the common comfort of
all, and doubtless would longer, had we remained
still in the union of God's Church and communion
of His saints, members of that mystical body which
only partakes of the Divine influences of its Head,
Christ Jesus. The breach of which union broke all
our happiness and us into division from our Mother
the Church, from whom to be divided is an utter
disinheriting from the birthright of the children of
God, since he shall not have God for his Father
who has not the Church for his Mother, as witness
St. Augustine and St. Cyprian. A most unfortunate
breach, which, as it unsainted saints and demolished

the shrines their forefathers' devotion had erected
to their sacred memory, what wonder if it obstructed
thereby the stream of their favours, it being not fit
to give holy things to dogs, or cast such pearls to
swine to feed on.

Yet to show that the Saint is still in Heaven and
powerful with Almighty God, if we were but worthy
to deserve His favours, even in our time, not many
years ago, a furious plague, sweeping all before it
in the town of Hereford, and threatening utter destruction to the inhabitants, that pestilential contagion
received such a check from our Saint's relics carried
in a private procession, that it gave a total surcease
to the same, and so suddenly that it was ascribed
to miracle. Such reserves of His ancient bounties
Almighty God is pleased now and then to communicate, to keep our devotion on foot, and give us
hereby a pledge that when He sees time He will
restore both our distracted country to unity of faith,
and the current of His graces to their wonted channel.

The generality of devotion had to this Saint may
in part also be showed by the numberless number
of donaries offered at his tomb: nor can I give
my reader a more satisfactory account of them than
by relating what I find specified in the register of
the Lords Commissioners. As they were exact in
all, so in this particular also; and what they found

extant they caused to be listed in a schedule; and
to give here a review of it will perchance not be
ungrateful.   Thus, then, it specifies : In primo, a
hundred and seventy votive ships in silver; and in
wax forty-one.   Item, divers images of silver, some
of the whole body, others of several parts, in all
one hundred and twenty-nine.   Of the whole body
in wax, four hundred and thirty-six; of several parts,
very near upon a thousand ; and among them figures
of horses ; other beasts and birds, seventy-seven,
besides innumerable of eyes, ears, teeth, breasts, &c.
Item, children's coats, some of silk, some of linen,
to the number of ninety-five.   Three little carts of
wood which the lame upon their cure left for a
monument of the same, and one of wax.   Crutches,
one hundred and eight.   Great waxen tapers, ten.
Webs of silk and cloth of gold, thirty-eight.   They
found also many pendants, ear-rings, bracelets, and
other ornaments belonging to women, many pearls
and other jewels which were said to have been
offered out of devotion ; among which there were
four hundred and fifty gold rings, seventy silver
rings, sixty-five necklaces of gold, thirty-one of silver,
and divers precious stones.   Nor must we omit
other chains, though of iron, anchors, pikes, arrows,
swords, falchions, &c., instruments of hurts received
and now monuments of miraculous cures.

And all these within the space of little more than the first twenty years after his translation and before his canonization. What may we conceive of the whole age or two next ensuing? To what a mass would they probably swell in two centuries, when, by his canonizatian and consequently increase of devotion, he came to be better known and more religiously worshipped, and consequently more profuse of his graces. Those to whom the forfeiture of all did escheat, when of Catholic worship all became Protestant profanation, those, I say, could have informed us more exactly if they pleased; for though they love not saints nor their shrines, yet they can both finger and devour all the donaries which hang at them, of what metal soever they be, without the least scruple of conscience or indigestion.

According to the drift of my first design, here should my narrative make an end, it being no part of my intention to bulk it further with his miracles; and we have touched upon all the chief passages of his life which have come to our knowledge. But because divers particulars relating to his virtues could not be inserted in the said former passages, and that part of his life—his virtues I mean—imports us most for our instruction and imitation (for why do we write or read the lives of saints, but that we may imitate them ?), therefore I will make a brief but fuller review of some of the said his virtues, and illustrate and confirm them with such examples as I find upon record, with which I am furnished by the forementioned process, it being great pity to deprive them of light.

CHAPTER XXII.

Humility and abstinence of St. Thomas.

I WILL begin with his humility as the foundation and preserver of all virtue and sanctity, the groundwork on which all spiritual edification, that is, the house of perfection, is to be raised.   Nor is it only the foundation, but also the cement or mortar of this building, which gives a combinement and both unity and union to all the parts by making it one house; and this union is both the order and beauty of the structure or whole.   And in this it squares very properly ; for as the mortar not only combines, but lies concealed and is not seen, so humility, though it give lustre to other virtues, yet it conceals itself, carrying for its motto, *Ama nesciri*—'Love to lie concealed.'   What charity is in theologicals, the same is humility in morals : as that perfects the former, so this the latter; insomuch that neither the virtue of penance, nor mortification, nor obedience, of which St. Leo saith, that nothing is hard to the humble, nor poverty, nor patience, nay, nor even charity itself, can subsist without humility, since this alone can cement up the breaches of charity, according to St. Bernard, *Sola humilitas læsæ charitatis est reparatio.* To build without this foundation is to build to ruin, since no other without this can sustain the stress of such a machine as is spiritual perfection: who builds not on it, builds on the superficial sands of self-conceit or some such like; and consequently when a storm comes, and the winds blow, and the rains fall, great will be the ruins of that house,[1] as our Saviour said, because it is not built on this rock or groundwork.

It is proper to this virtue to empty ourselves of ourselves, that is, of self-love and self-ease, a lazy humour which sews a pillow to every elbow, and is always leaning homewards, that is, not to seek God and His greater glory, but itself, hating to take pains and use diligence, which is called the mother of good success, and good issue seldom failing the diligent. And humility is always such, nor, indeed, can it be otherwise, since the care and solicitude of the humble man is not bent upon himself, whom he deems unworthy of any good, but on God, Whose

---

[1] St. Luke vi. 49.

beneplacitum is his sole joy, and to be accounted a good servant his only happiness.   Pride, on the contrary, always seeks itself, as prizing nothing but itself, it being a mere lump of self-love ; and proceeds towards God as did that man towards Jupiter, who, giving him half of all he had, eat the kernels of his nuts, and gave him the shells.   As humility empties us of ourselves, so doth it replenish us with God and His graces : for when we put off ourselves we put on Almighty God, and where the creature ceases to be, there succeeds the Creator by a sequel morally necessary in the order of grace, as in that of nature, the air connaturally succeeds the substraction of another body to hinder a vacuity.   For God, Who is everywhere, by His immensity, has His proper mansion-house, saith St. Austin, in the heart of the humble ; but then He will have no inmate besides Himself, He will not share lodgings with any one ; no, not even with the landlord himself.

I make this short eulogium of humility to give the less acquainted reader a little knowledge of its worth.   It was one of the glories of our Saint, rendering him as acceptable to men as grateful to God, and it is expressly noted in his life that it got him the love of all.   And no wonder ; for the humble man incurs nobody's displeasure, since he trencheth neither on their profit nor credit ; he contents himself with what he is, and deeming himself a mere nothing, he rests in that, and consequently is beneath envy; whereas the proud self-lover is ungrateful, as contemning all and caring for nobody but himself, while the humble all besides himself; and to love is the way to be beloved. All his comportment was seasoned with this ingredient, and carried a strong relish of it in his words, his actions, and behaviour, so that it was a virtue, as it ought, transcendental through all. This gave him that candour of an ingenuous simplicity so proper to Christian conversation and the spirit of God, inherited from these ancient Patriarchs, Jacob, Job, and the rest; praised by God, in the first place, for this, a virtue so opposite to all duplicity or double-dealing, and consequently the mother of integrity and uprightness, as well as all happiness, making his tongue and his heart go both together. There is great difference betwixt simplicity and simpleness as the world takes it, which is so ignorant of this virtue, that it cannot distinguish betwixt it and folly; whereas it doth not exclude prudence, but craft and duplicity. Prudence is its individual companion, and therefore our Blessed Saviour wished His Apostles to join the prudence of the serpent with the simplicity of the dove; and how eminently prudent our Saint was shall be showed in the last chapter. This humble simplicity made him so obsequious to all just commands; for what teaches obedience but tractability, and tractability but humility, the only disposition to subjection and subordination, as pride on the contrary is its opponent. We have showed already in the thirteenth chapter what a love and respect he had for the poor, how he called them his brethren, heard their confessions before the rich, made his table so open and common to them that it entertained sometimes thirty, sometimes forty, fifty, yea, a hundred, together, who, as he was as poor of spirit as the most, so he loved like birds of a feather to sort with them ; and all this was a result of his humility, which naturally branches into charity, seeking others more than itself. From this also was sourced his singular contempt both of himself and all that is specious in point of employment or preferment: hence he rejoiced so much at his deposing the office of Lord Chancellor, as much, to wit, as others at its attainment, and was the cause that his promotion to the Bishopric of Hereford, cost him so many tears, desirous rather to lie hid under a bushel than be set in the candlestick of the Church. Hence he was ever ready to pardon any delinquent upon point of due submission and pardon demanded ; and many times, though the fault were theirs, he would prevent them, by way of example, seeking friendship when they had broken it ; but to the stubborn and incorrigible he was not easily reconciled.

This virtue taught him also patience, which is soon lost amidst the crosses of this world, if it be not supported by humility, which fits our shoulders for every burthen, and persuades us we bear no more than our due; whence it was that without repining he readily received all the personal affronts above mentioned in the fourteenth chapter, without so much as offering at a retaliation even in word.

To his humility we may join his mortification, and these two suit well together, and lend a mutual hand to each other. For it is the humble man that is mortified, and the mortified humble; humility by self-contempt making way for mortification, and mortification advancing humility. No man that is a self-lover will set upon mortification unless it be to destroy self-love, and who aims at that besides the humble self-denier? The advantages of this virtue in order to sanctity, as it makes one truly master of himself and all his passions, appetites, inclinations, &c., are very great; for it is this unruly and mutinous populace which gives us all our disturbances and conflicts betwixt the spirit and the flesh, while these servants will needs be masters, and domineer over and against reason, putting all into a combustion. The Royal Prophet bids us bind fast their cheeks in bridle and bit, and this bit or curb is mortification: they must either be hampered thus, or there is no ruling them. They are like fire and water, good servants, but ill masters; give them an inch, and they will take an ell; but keep them short, close to their task, within their bounds, and they will do you good service. Our blessed Saint, in his light and experience, found all this true, and therefore resolved to keep a strict hand and watchful eye over them and all their motions, ready to suppress any insurrections in this kind. And by internal mortification, which is much the nobler, he preserved his mind in such a peaceful calm that one could scarce discover any commotion to the contrary; insomuch that he might seem to live in a region above flesh and blood, where neither winds nor tempests have access. And this is a thing feasible enough to the servant of God, if he make it is business and take it to heart, grace willingly seconding such endeavours; and our Saint profited so much in this kind, that, considering the equal tenor of his conversation, one might say he either never had passions, which is impossible in such a liveliness of nature, or else kept them in a perfect subjection to reason and virtue, which is no more than truth.

To this interior mortification he joined exterior, as much facilitating the former, and rendering the flesh duly subordinate to the spirit: a thing necessary for those who aim at a perfect conquest over themselves; and this he practised in a triple kind. First, by hair-cloth and other austerities to which he accustomed himself many years, and even at his death, not contenting himself with the incident sufferances of so long a journey, he was found with a hair-shirt next his body, and that of the rougher size. Second, by watching, and subtraction of sleep even necessary, stinting himself to a very short pittance, which was much felt by those about him as cutting theirs too short also; yet he made this a daily custom, spending the remnant of the night in prayer and reading of Holy Scripture, or other such like pious exercises. Third, by a wonderful abstemiousness and sobriety of diet, the proper food of sanctity and refection of virtuous souls, by which they gather more strength and vigour than by the choicest dainties. Experience teaches too truly what an enemy gluttony and full feeding is to devotion; how it indisposes the mind while it overcharges the body, and makes it think more on the fleshpots of Egypt than the Manna of Angels. A refection is necessary for the recruit of our decaying forces; a repletion, which rather oppresses than refreshes, never: he must content himself with necessaries, and even retrench them a little, who will avoid super-fluities. This was the prayer of the Wise Man, and must be ours.[1]

[1] Prov. xxx. 8.

St. Thomas knew well all the advantages of a
sober abstinence, and therefore his diet was so spare
that his familiars did wonder how it could give a
competent sustenance to maintain life, and this
usually. And thus much Bishop Richard deposed
in his Process upon oath, assevering withal that his
abstinence was such that one might truly say his
whole life was a continual fast. He made but one
meal the day, and that with these short commons,
not for want of an appetite, but to curb and mortify
it ; for being asked that question by the said his
successor, who then sat next him, he confessed in-
genuously that his stomach served him for much
more ; and taking a good piece of a loaf in his hand,
said he could eat all that, and with gust. To this
rigour of quantity he added another of quality. If
he tasted of any curious or costly dish, that was all,
then made it be carried either to the sick or poor.
His ordinary fare was of the homelier sort, such as
would satisfy nature, not please the palate, and his
drink suitable, to wit, small beer. He seldom drank
wine, unless in a very small quantity or much tem-
pered with water ; he never willingly drank betwixt
meals ; and when the quality of the persons was
such that it required such a civility from him, he
used pretty sleights and artifices to evade it, by
seeming to drink when he scarce touched the cup.

In his younger days and better health he was wont
to fast Good Friday and all the eves of our Blessèd
Lady, with bread and water; but afterwards, when
his stock of strength would not bear that rigour, by
the prescript of his physician he was forbid that, and
appointed to take a little broth. In confirmation of
this his temperance, a pretty passage is related by
the aforesaid Bishop Richard, who then was present.
A kinsman of our Saint, and his companion for
twenty years and upwards, William of Albenac, sitting
once at table with him, when all had done and it
was taking away, St. Thomas espied him still eating
some bread, with which a little surprised, he said
merrily to him: 'Old man, what art thou doing?'
'I am eating,' quoth he. 'Why now?' replied the
Saint. 'Because,' said the other, 'I find an appetite.' 'What,' said St. Thomas, 'and are you wont
to eat as long as you find an appetite?' 'Yes, I
profess,' said William, 'and all do so that I know.'
'All do so?' said the Saint in a chiding tone,
'marry, God forbid. I can assure you in very truth
that for thirty years till this day I have not risen
from table with a less appetite than when I sat
down.' But this latter part he whispered in his
ear, forbidding him to speak of it while he lived.
Another story, much to the same purpose, stands
upon authentic record, and both are a great testimonial of his abstemiousness and sobriety.

CHAPTER XXIII.

St. Thomas's discharge of duty towards God and his neighbour.

His humility and abstemiousness fitted and disposed him rightly towards this discharge, the former by withdrawing him from self-love, the latter from worldly, and those are the great obstructers of the love of God and cause of our slackness in His service, it being certainly certain that nobody can serve two masters. This religious discharge is the work of our whole life, and consequently of greatest concern, implying both parts of Christian duty, to decline from evil and do good; and do good, not howsoever, but after a good manner and as beseems such a Majesty; for God loves not slobbered services, but will have them done as well with the heart as hand and tongue, or else they will find a cold acceptance. By a due compliance in this kind we show our love to Him, and this compliance in our spiritual functions is called devotion, which is esteemed greater or less as our performance is more fervorous or remiss. Devotion is an effect of love and an issue of Divine grace which, if not sourced from these two, is not esteemed genuine and current, but to want of its grains of weight; and this may be counterfeited as well as other virtues.

The subject of his devotion, or his spiritual exercises relating immediately to Almighty God, were chiefly prayer, the Holy Sacrifice of Mass, his Canonical Hours or Divine Office; and in the discharge of these he was not only, saith the Record, devout, but most devout, performing them with a most profound attention and reverence. Prayer is called an incense, and this incense he was, I may say, continually offering according to the advice of St. Paul: 'Be always praying,'[1] not only as each good work, in the opinion of St. Basil, is a good prayer, but also by a more near, interior, and familiar conversation with Almighty God by the powers of our soul, employing them not only in a consideration of His attributes, but an union of will. And what could a pious heart, nursed up in its baptismal grace, and consequently the Throne and Altar of the Holy Ghost, sacrifice to so Divine a Guest besides prayers and praises? The former to beg new blessings, the latter in thanksgiving for them received. To attend the more freely to this was the chief reason why he cut his sleep so short, and rose by night that he might

1 Thess. v. 17.

watch and pray, and offer early a morning oblation
to God and His Saints in an odour of sweetness,
killing, as the royal Prophet did, in the fervour of
his prayer, all the sinners of the earth.[2] He knew
that in a spiritual life no great matter could be
achieved, or advance made, without this, and therefore he made it his daily bread, and was much more
frequently feeding his soul with it than his body with
corporal, deeming it the life which was to animate
all his actions. We treated in the twelfth chaper of
his retirement and union with God, and this union
was chiefly effected by prayer, and intimates a frequent and constant practice of the same, even to an
intimate familiarity whose result it is.

Even before he was Bishop he was particularly
noted for his singular reverence and devotion in
reciting the Divine Office, which argues a true feeling
of spirit and the presence of Almighty God : in which
his exterior composure of body and attention of mind
was such that it was of great edification to the beholders. Thus he begun, thus he persevered until
the end, fulfilling exactly what our holy mother the
Church requires of us for a due discharge of that
great function, and it were to be wished all those
to whom this obligation is incumbent were imitators
of the same. He was most exact in the administra-

[2] Psalm c. 8.

tion of the sacraments and performance of ecclesiastical ceremonies, so mixing piety with a majestic
gravity, that both the one and the other begot a
reverential esteem towards those sacred rites in them
that were present. But above all, he was most
singularly devoted to the Holy Sacrifice of Mass;
here his devotion seemed to triumph, and he at the
altar to be in his centre, so full was his heart fraught
with pious affections, with such a spirit of humility
and contrition did he approach it, such an ample
testimony hereof did he give by his abundance of
tears, that one would have thought he had rather,
saith the Record, actually beheld the bloody Sacrifice
itself, and his Lord and Saviour therein immolated,
than an unbloody and mystical representation of the
same—an argument both of his lively faith and
ardent charity. To indulge the more to these pious
affections, he gave here ample scope to his devotion,
much beyond the ordinary stint of half an hour,
letting his soul feed at leisure on these sweet
mysteries ; and Almighty God did so concur, that
he was frequently alienated from his senses, and, as
it were, in a rapture, so that it was necessary for the
server (who deposed this upon oath) to cough and
make a noise to bring him to himself and make an
end of his Mass ; and this, saith the same, happened
frequently while he lived at Rouen, from the feast

of St. Peter ad Vincula till the feast of St. Michael
next ensuing.

To show how acceptable this his piety in the Holy
Sacrifice and other spiritual devotions was to Almighty God, it pleased His Divine Majesty to grace
him particularly at the same time with a favour which
all that were present attributed to miracle, and as
such it was approved by the Lords Commissioners
and those that beheld it. On the feast of Pentecost,
or Whit Sunday, he was invited by Edmund, Earl
of Cornwall, a great admirer of his sanctity, to cele-
brate the feast and say Mass at his Castle of Wallingford, and it happened in the second or third year of
his Pontificate. While he was preparing and disposing himself thereto, by singing the hymn *Veni
Creator Spiritus*, upon the intonement of the first
verse a flock of birds, in the sight and hearing of all,
with musical notes, and beating their wings against
the chapel windows, seemed to applaud the Saint
while he sung, and he having ended, they retired
while the choir prosecuted what he had intoned till
the end of the strophe. But he intoning the first
verse of the second, they returned again, and while
he sung, both with voice and wing they accompanied
him and applauded as before ; and so strophe after
strophe till the hymn was ended. This seemed a
great novelty to the said Earl and all that beheld it,

which were many; and to satisfy themselves the better, they went out of the chapel abroad, and had a full sight of them, judging them to be about forty, and beheld them coming and going as before, nor could interpret such an unusual thing, never observed before nor after, otherwise than as ordered by God to witness the sanctity of our Saint and the acceptableness of the great work he was about. Then it was that the Earl, in the hearing of all, Bishop Richard, then Chancellor of Hereford, being present, made that expression cited in the end of the eighteenth chapter, of his singular confidence in the prayers and patronage of St. Thomas, no less than in those of our great Apostle St. Austin.

The lively faith and high esteem he had of the dignity of this Divine Sacrifice, as it made him recollect all his powers and attention for its better performance, so it made him waive all human respects when he was about it, not admitting any interruption whatsoever, not even from the King himself, though otherwise most observant and submissive to his commands. It happened once that, while he was ready to vest, a messenger came in all haste from the King, to call him to Council without delay upon matters of great importance (and it was his office to attend, he being of the Privy Council). What must he do? After a short pause he calls the messenger,

who was a priest, wishing him to tell his Majesty, if
he pleased, in these terms : that he was now engaged
in the service of One greater than himself, Who
required his present attendance; but 'when I have,'
said he, 'discharged my duty to Him, I will not fail
to wait on his Majesty. After all done and his
devotions ended, he repaired immediately to Court,
then kept at the Palace at Westminster, and receiving
a gentle rebuke for his delay, the matter was proposed
and discussed : in the handling whereof he delivered
his advice so pertinently, and suggested beyond the
rest such expedients so pat and feasible, that all
without reply embraced them as sent from Heaven.
And the King, overjoyed herewith, is said to have
spoken to him in these words : ' Many blessings, my
lord, light upon you, and ever praised and magnified
be that highest Master Whom you serve, and long
may you serve both Him and us.' So true it is, that
if we seek in the first place the Kingdom of Heaven
and His justice, not failing of our duty in that, all
these secondaries will be cast into the bargain.

I will conclude the love he showed to God by the
religious performance of these his spiritual obligations,
with the devotion he carried to His saints, and chiefly
to the Queen of Saints, the Virgin Mother. The
proverb saith, ' Love me, and love my friends ; ' and
God saith, ' Love Me, and love My saints, My dearest

friends;' and deservedly, for how can they be said
to love Him who love not those that are one with
Him? In his love to our Blessed Lady I will com-
prise all the rest, and although this were notedly
great, that is, so great that he was publicly noted for
it, yet we have not much left upon record whereby
to illustrate and amplify it. This notwithstanding, if
we may measure the lion by his claw, and guess at
Hercules by his foot, we have sufficient hints or
grounds both to inform and inflame us to his imitation in this particular. I have showed above out of
authentic records, that in his younger days he was
wont to fast the vigils of her feasts, with bread and
water, which custom he continued till want of health
disabled him thereto; and what greater expression
of a tender devotion could he exhibit? The expression is as extraordinary as is the fast, and the fast
speaks as much devotion as a fast can do, and ranks
it with the tenderest. He chose her Nativity, as I
noted above, for his episcopal consecration, receiving
that sacred character under her patronage; and divers
apparitions of her with him after death in a joint
concurrence of both to the cure of many, show how
dear he was to her during life. And I find that
abroad he carried the common esteem of one singularly devoted to her, and was pointed at as her
particular client; and this persuasion wrought so far

with some that they used it for motive of mediation
to obtain what they desired, beseeching him for the
love and devotion he bore her to grant their request.
And to this purpose it is recounted of one who before
had been of his household, and falling into a great
fit of sickness for ten weeks' space, three whereof
he passed sleepless, turning himself to the Saint, he
earnestly besought him for the love he bore to the
Mother of God, that he would obtain for him the
benefit of sleeping.   This said, he fell into a slumber,
and in it thought he saw two men bring into his
chamber a very fine bed, in which being laid by them
he slept soundly and quietly till the morning, when
being awaked, and missing the bed, though he was
more than a little concerned that it should be carried
away, yet nevertheless he found himself quite cured
of his infirmity, and upon the score of the Saint's
devotion to our Blessed Lady.

As for his love towards his neighbour, I had rather
waive than mention it, as not able to treat of it in
that due manner I ought and it deserves; not but
that it was mainly great in itself, but time and records
have been so injurious as not to convey the particulars to our knowledge; and in these things we must
not go by guess, but certain relation.   Who can
rationally doubt but that he who was a flaming
furnace of love towards God, was enkindled with

the same towards his neighbour for love of God? Or he that played the Good Shepherd for seven years together in feeding his flock, had not a tender love for the same flock, without which he had proved himself rather a mercenary hireling than good shepherd? Or if he were so zealously courageous for the maintenance and recovery of his church lands and liberties, would he not be much more solicitous for her children's souls and salvation? If he took her dead concerns so much to heart, how much more would he her living? If he were so charitably charitable after death in the cure of their bodies, how much more while he lived in curing their souls? We know that he was assiduous in preaching and teaching, in reconciling enmities, in hindering debates, in administering justice, in promoting piety, in depressing vice, in redressing abuses, in administering the sacraments, &c.; but what is all this to his boundless zeal, which not contenting itself with obligatories, would branch into supererogatories; and none of these latter are come to our knowledge besides what is already specified. I cannot satisfy myself as to what I would and ought to say on this point, and therefore I pass to the next.

CHAPTER XXIV.

Purity of body and mind.

AMONG all the virtues which like so many stars embellished our Saint, three seem conspicuously eminent above the rest, and, as I may say, of the first magnitude. One was his zeal and courage in the vindication and maintenance of his Church's liberties; and of this we have treated in the fifteenth chapter. The second, his parsimony and sobriety of diet, to such a degree of spareness and mortification of his appetite that he might be said, as we mentioned a little before, to have observed for many years of his life a strict ecclesiastical fast; and of this in the twenty-second chapter. The third was a wonderful innocency of life, by which he is thought to have preserved the baptismal garment of his soul pure and unspotted all his life long, at least from any mortal stain; a privilege granted not to many; and this I call his purity of body and mind, and shall be the subject of this chapter.

This purity is that cleanness of heart to which our Blessed Saviour affixed a beatitude, and in its beams our blessed Saint saw God so present in all his actions that he was ashamed as well as reverentially afraid to offend Him: whence it made him solicitous to walk like a child of light, and the Apostle tells us that their journey and progress is 'in all goodness and justice and truth.'[1] Whence it was that the Royal Prophet,[2] desired so much to have a clean heart created in him; for such as is the heart, such is the whole man, and God, Who so earnestly covets our hearts, will either have a pure one or none. This is the eye of man, which if it be simple the whole body will be lightsome; if troubled and obscure, darksome; and if the light that is in us, saith our Saviour,[3] be darkness, how great and lamentable must that needs be. This is the reason why the Wise Man advises us to guard our heart with all diligence, because it is the original house of life as well spiritual as corporal, the chief seat of life and the Holy Ghost, Whose throne it is. What is engendered here must be like that of pearls by the pure dew of heaven, without speck or blemish, one drop of salt water causes a miscarriage; and as the Spouse feeds and lies not but among lilies, so if we covet His company at bed and board, this must be His entertainment: even a discomposed cast of an eye will make Him quit the company; for Divine Wisdom will not enter

[1] Ephes. v. 9. [2] Psalm l. 12. [3] St. Matt. vi. 23.

into a malevolous soul, nor dwell in a body subject
to sin.[4]

To this due preservation of the heart and maintenance of purity, there must be a joint concurrence of
both the parts of man, body and soul, nor will the
one be able to effect it without the other, it being
a result of both.   One flaw spoils the worth of a
jewel, one distorted limb of even a beautiful body ;
perfection consists in an integrity of the parts and
and whole ; and this was the care and solicitude of
our Saint to combine both his in this respect into a
common interest ; nor did he endeavour it by fits and
spurts, but was the constant practice of his life, and
whoever aims at it his solid resolution must be like
that of the ermine, *Malo mori quam fœdari*—rather
die than suffer a blemish.   To effect this was the
grand work of our blessed Saint, as it is of all those
who intend to serve God in sincerity and purity ; and
to compass it the better he kept a strict eye upon
both and their proceedings, by a due inquiry into
them, and set for that end watch and ward upon all
the avenues which lead thereto, securing himself thus
against all surprises, by a due intelligence of all that
passed, admitting the good, rejecting the bad.   By
this diligence he enjoyed a perfect peace both at
home and abroad, nor in his interior did he find

[4] Wisdom i. 4.

either mutiny or insurrection; and whoever will imitate this his management of such affairs shall experience the same. By this wary watchfulness, and the assistance of a good spiritual director in his beginnings or younger days, he preserved himself so undefiled both in body and soul, the grace of Almighty God cooperating, that he deserved from the same his director in his now declining age that public eulogium of his integrity which I mentioned in the tenth chapter, which by advancing from virtue to virtue he was still consummating even till death.

This was one reason why he treated his crazy body so severely, both by abstinence and other chastisements, knowing right well that to have it a dutiful servant it must be kept under and at task, lest through idleness getting head it become unruly and play the wanton, debauching the soul to its licentiousness, to which our corrupt nature too much inclines it. This flesh of ours is the worst natured creature upon earth, a mere devil, to our and its own undoing; it cares for nobody but itself, and that's the property of self-love, never regarding what woe it work the soul, so it can compass its desires and please its appetites; it is little concerned either for Heaven or Hell, credit or discredit, friend or foe; and what do we in pampering such a one, but make much of a churlish cur which will one day do his best to pull

out our throat, that is, undo us. The way to cast
out this devil is that which our Saviour prescribes—
'by fasting and prayer.'[5] He added to this, by way
of prevention, a shunning of conversation with women
(occasion, they say, makes a thief, and he that
touches pitch shall be defiled by it), even his own
sisters, as much as could stand with common civility,
not permitting them to lodge above one night in his
palace, and then his custom was to leave it himself
and divert to some of his manor-houses. He had a
horror of all speeches glancing at levity, nor durst
any in his presence scatter such smutty jests, much
less utter broad ribaldry, without the penalty of a
sound check : a language much unbeseeming Christian
conversation, as made up only of the dregs of wit, fit
only indeed for the mouth of a bargeman, though not
a little in vogue among many worldlings. The love
of this virtue made him conceive a perfect hatred and
horror of the contrary vice, and as both the impious
and his impiety is abominable to God, so had he not
only a loathing of the latter, but also an aversion
from the former, and those he knew to be given to
the same, nor could he affect them further than
Christian charity commanded, though otherwise his
nearest allies. This he made evident by his carriage
towards a nephew of his, one for whom he had a

[5] St. Matt. xvii. 20.

great kindness so long as he did well, maintaining
him in the University, making him his confidant, and
would certainly have done very much for him. But
understanding that he was become loose of behaviour
and not so chaste in his ways, he totally withdrew
his affection, and though much pressed to take him
along in his journey to Rome, no persuasion could
prevail; on which subject he expressed himself to
this effect—'These young men,' said he, 'are not
now-a-days so bashful and modest as heretofore; for
when I was such a one, if a handsome woman had
looked me in the face, I should presently have been
put to the blush, turned my eyes from her,' (they are
words of the Records), 'or pulled my hat over them,
that either I should not have seen her, or she me;
but now things go far otherwise.' Nor could he ever
be induced to receive him into favour or familiarity.
This virtue of angelical purity was so conspicuous in
him that the prayer used in the Office of his feast
petitions by it graces from God, and that by its merits
we may deserve to be associated to the choirs of
angels, and the first Lesson of the same Office calls
him *angelicus homo*—an angelical man.

And the love and esteem he had for this virtue
was not only verbal, or from the teeth outwards, but
he made good indeed what he professed in word;
and Almighty God was pleased to permit some trials

of this kind, and to give him a strong combat for the greater glory of his victory.　While he lived at Paris, he like another chaste Joseph was assaulted in the same as dangerously as impudently, and he like him forced to flee and leave his cloak behind him, nor can that flight be deemed disgraceful when by it we get the victory.　He got it, and in this was more happy than Joseph, that he won not only the combat but also the tempter into the bargain, reclaiming her to a chaste life from her impudent lubricity, and so deserved a double reward.　Such a chaste body was fit to be the consort of so pure a soul to make up an angelical compound ; and it is but meet that such a jewel of purity should be kept in a suitable cabinet : that both parts might bear proportion, and mutually correspond.　A Christian ought to train up his body to immortality, and labour to leave it, such in life and death, as he desires to find it in the resurrection ; such that it may be acknowledged and owned for a member of Christ, as indeed it is, and what a shame then is it, as the Apostle argues, to make it the member of a harlot.　Our blessed Saint understood this right well, both as to proportion, decency, and other advantages which thence accrued, and therefore he made it always his business to procure and maintain a good correspondence betwixt both.

Now he that was so industrious in the cultivating and preservation of his body, what would he be for his soul and conscience? The body is but the servant, the soul the mistress; the one but the shell, the other the pearl; and he knew very well how to give every one its due. All he was to do in this kind was to keep it to Christian duty according to his state, to cultivate it in piety and the service of God, sowing in it the seeds of all virtues; and how he did this even in his youth, and in what a nice and delicate temper he kept it, may be known by what we related in the end of the fifth chapter, of the vine prop taken out of another's vineyard, and the seven years' penance he did for the same.

Whence we may gather how angelically pure that delicate soul was, which checked so feelingly at so small a matter, and how far it was from harbouring any great offence which deemed the least to be so great. Nor yet was it one of those which flee a gnat and swallow a camel, according to the expression of our blessed Saviour, or stumbles at a straw and leaps over a block; but pure illuminated souls in their quick-sightedness can espy a blemish, where a dim eye of a grosser complexion makes no discovery at all. This was the constitution of his mind and tenor of proceeding when he was now in the flower of his youth, and nature pronest to lubricity, where nothing but the special grace of God in an eminent sanctity, could work such effects, so opposite to nature and above it.   And as he went always advancing to sanctity even till death, so did he also in purity; sanctity, as St. Anselm defines out of St. Denis, being a most perfect and unspotted purity, free and entire from all blemish, and to what a pitch of eminency must he needs arrive! I shall conclude all in this, that he lived and died a pure virgin both in body and mind.

CHAPTER XXV.

St. Thomas's justice and prudence.

BOTH these are cardinal virtues, and when I have showed with what a rich stock our Saint traded in them, I shall have made him conspicuous in all four.   As for his temperance and fortitude I have already given a character of them; the former, while I treated of his abstinence, the latter, of his courage and magnanimity in defence of his Church.   As to what we treat of at present, he had great practice of the former, to wit, justice, in both his chancellorships, and discharged his trust with such integrity, that all parties concerned were abundantly satisfied.   And he took the true way to do it, for he sought it, not himself, and made its advance his end, not his own,

nor the enrichment of his estate ; while others per-
versely invert true order by taking the quite contrary
course. The ordering of this depends much upon
the will or ill-ordering of their own conscience, which
must be the beam of the balance, and to be right ;
stands always perpendicular, inclining neither to one
side or other, but as the scales sway it ; in the one
whereof must be justice, in the other the thing controverted, to the end an even and impartial hand may
be kept. It were much to be wished that all dis-
tributors of justice did this, more indeed to be wished
than hoped for, while so many make a trade of selling
what they ought to give, and gratis ; their honesty
becoming venal to avarice, and themselves imitators
of Judas, who as he sold his Master, so they their
mistress, for what are all in office but her servants
and ministers ; that which captivated the other captivates them, perverts their sense, and misleads them
from the paths of equity. This proceeds from being
not so well principled in point of conscience and
justice, which go always hand in hand together,
and are attended by uprightness and sincerity, and
thus our blessed Saint walked in them with the common approbation of all, guided not by the dictamens
of this world, but Divine wisdom, by whose direction
all, both lawgivers and administers of justice, decree
and execute just things.

Thus he purchased that vogue of integrity which everywhere accompanied his proceedings, growing up with him even from his youth, and so habitually rooted and relucent in all his carriage, that it is noted as the prime motive why he was chosen first to the Chancellorship of the University, and then of the whole kingdom. And certainly such an integrity of justice is an excellent commendatory to preferment, as giving great advantage to a full discharge of trust, and strange it is that men do not take this way to compass it, when they seek so greedily after it. If natural abilities be so much regarded, how much more in all reason ought supernatural? If wit, how much more virtue? Wit without virtue and grace degenerates for the most part into craft, and turns public justice into private ends and self-seeking. Even those that are not virtuous are great admirers of it in others, as being praiseworthy in a very enemy; and since nobody but loves to have their things well done, and nothing contributes more than it to their well-doing, as they willingly covet the former, so they are forward in preferring the latter. Besides that honours and offices are commonly at the disposal of the honourable, or persons of honour and integrity, and who stand more clear in their eye, or are deemed better deserving, or lastly, whom are they like to have more credit and satisfaction than by the uprightly

just and virtuous? This virtue is particularly specified
in the ancient lessons of his Office, where he is said
to have been 'always much devoted to the practice
of justice,' and elsewhere in the same, 'he courageously
defended the rights of his Church, armed with justice
as a breastplate.' And this repute purchased him such
a name that it set him as it were out of the reach of
temptation, and he in reality so abhorred anything
in its administration which looked like a bribe, that
he was afraid even of its shadow. It is particularly
recounted that certain religious men, who had a suit
depending at law, applied themselves to him for his
favour and furtherance in the despatch of the same,
and thereto presented him with a jewel of value,
which he rejected not without indignation, asking
them whether they thought him to be won with gifts.
Their intention questionless was good, and aimed at
no more than a redeeming of the delays of the law,
not a buying of it, which they knew could not be
sold; but a judge must avoid even suspicions in this
kind, choosing rather to sit without a lawful gain
than have it with hazard of dishonesty. 'Better is a
good name,' saith the Wise Man, 'than great riches.'[1]
One in that office who carries himself so religiously,
where so many eyes are upon him, as not to be taxed
by any, it is a great evidence that he discharges his

[1] Prov. xxii. 1.

trust uprightly.   In the University he had the same
character, and that was a step to the other promotion
where he gave as ample satisfaction by a just performance of his office in promoting learning, advancing
virtue, exacting discipline, redressing abuses, punishing
offenders, maintaining privileges, complying in fine
with all points of duty, so that he also might carry
for his discharge or motto: ' He did all well.'[2]   It
was chiefly for the esteem they had of his justice and
piety that he was made Chancellor of the University,
and for these particularly was he praised publicly in
the same by Robert, Archbishop of Canterbury,
affirming that in all his judicial acts relating to the
students, he was neither swayed by favour or fear,
but regulated himself merely by justice and the
merits of the cause.

In administering justice, what he did by himself,
the dictates of a good conscience inviolably kept
would not let him swerve from a virtuous reason ;
and in what he was forced to intrust others withal,
he burthened their consciences (the only tie to him
that owns one) to a faithful discharge, as they would
answer it at God's tribunal.   When complaints were
made against his bailiff or other officers, he took the
matter to his own scanning, and if he found them
faulty, he was not content with punishing them, but

[2] St. Mark vii. 37.

revoked and annulled what they had unjustly done, causing satisfaction to be made to the injured parties. Whenever he apprehended a concern of justice, in any cause, he was so resolute for its vindication and maintenance, that he waived all other considerations; whence it was that in his lawsuits for the recovery of his Church lands, mentioned above in the fifteenth chapter, though the power of his adversaries were formidable enough, and the issue on that respect doubtful, yet he could never be brought to hearken to any underhand composition, though more per-chance for his private interest. The Earl of Gloucester, when he perceived himself cast in law, offered round sums of money to let the suit fall; Peter Corbett did the same on a like occasion; and Roger, Lord Clifford, as knowing himself more liable to the law, for he in time of war had taken the then Bishop of Hereford prisoner, merely to extort a ransom from him, laboured to redeem his public penance with a hundred sterling (a great sum in those days), but the Saint was inflexible to all such motions, resolved to leave all to the court of justice. In the public interest he as councillor had in affairs, he observed that the Jews, permitted then to live promiscuously, were very pernicious to the State, not only for counter-feiting falsecoin, but also by reason of their usurious extortions by which they eat out the estates of their

debtors to their utter undoing. Whereupon he pre-
vailed with the King that some fit men might be
appointed to preach to them, and if they would still
remain obstinate, that then they should quit the
realm. They understood what was doing, and five
hundred of them, saith the Record, came in a body
to him, offering large sums of money if he would
desist; but they missed much of their mark, nor
found him like some others capable of a bribe.
His answer was, they were enemies to God and
rebels to faith, nor could ever gain his goodwill but
by becoming good Christians.

I will conclude this corollary of our Saint's virtues
and narrative of his life with that which consummated all into perfection, his prudence: this
deservedly accompanies justice and is its associate,
since this orders what that executes. Prudence is
styled by the Wise Man, 'the science of saints,'[3] a
a science without which the greatest learning is
ignorance, and wisdom folly; and it consists, saith
the prince of divines, in a due election of mediums
and ordering them to our final end, the compassing
whereof is our final beatitude, and consequently
consummate wisdom. This is its great act or master-
piece, and from hence imparts its influence into the
common concerns and management of all our pro-

[3] Prov. ix. 10.

ceedings, giving them weight, and squaring them according to Christian virtue. This part of Divine wisdom grew up with our Saint from his childhood; and that it might not degenerate into craft (a hand-maid issue that will needs like Ismael stand in competition with the legitimate Isaac), he joined simplicity with it to exclude all duplicity or double-dealing, the only art by which craft thrives; knowing right well the truth of that common saying: *Prudens simplicitas densa felicitas*—'Prudent simplicity fertile felicity,' and what a rich crop is to be reaped thence! It is recorded of him that he was of an eminent prudence and had a deep insight into all sorts of affairs, as well temporal as spiritual: and why not? The light of grace doth neither dazzle nor overcast, but rather clear up the sight of our judgment, and and when supernatural light is added to natural it must needs perfect and improve, since an inferior can never suffer an alloy by mixing with a superior, as brass or silver with gold. Whence I conclude that the greatest saints are fittest to make the greatest statesmen, not only because they are freest from corruption, and least swayed with passion and interest (two great blunders of judgment), but also for the singular advantage their natural abilities receive from the light and assistance of Divine grace. Whence it is observable in our histories that in Catholic times learned bishops and virtuous prelates were employed ordinarily both at home and abroad in the management of weightiest affairs: and who, I pray, more knowing than they, or ought to be of greater integrity?

As a general opinion acquired by his just and upright carriage preferred him to the Chancellorship of the University, so his prudent demeanment in the same, made King Henry III. prefer him to that of the kingdom. And though upon that good King's death at his own earnest request he were licensed by his son, Edward, to relinquish it, yet he kept him still of his Privy Council; and how much he esteemed his advice is seen by what we recounted in the twenty-third chapter. He that could wade through the deep affairs of two Chancellorships and a bishopric, and keep still above the waters of any dislike or dissatisfaction, where so many sink, must needs have been supported with a great prudence. The means he used for this support was to have knowing and conscientious men about him, who understood both what in prudence was to be done and would execute it honestly: and when, all circumstances duly weighed, he found that according to the dictates of prudence and conscience this was to be effected or that omitted, he stuck so close to his principles that neither fear nor respect could move him in the least; and this we confirmed with an example in the eighth chapter. We must also consider the times in which he bore the aforesaid offices, most unquiet and turbulent, and to keep sure footing on such slippery ground argues a great prudence and wisdom : it argues that he could master both the times and himself, not they him.

And now having given as good a character of this virtue in our Saint as my brevity and informations will allow, it is time to make an end : and though I have said little in regard of what might be said, yet I think I say much to its and his commendation, when I show that by it he ordered both his spiritual and temporal concerns, so as to prove himself a great saint in the former, and a great statesman in the latter. In his declining age, especially after he was made Bishop, he withdrew himself as much as he could from all worldly employments, the more to apply himself to heavenly, and that was the greatest point of prudence which ever he exercised, teaching him that the Kingdom of Heaven was to be sought in the first place and above all. For what will it avail one to gain the whole world if he lose Heaven and his own soul? or with what exchange will he be able to redeem that loss? What matters it if one enjoy all the pleasures of the world, all the treasures of the world, and all its highest preferments, if he have not Heaven

at the end of them ? That is to say, what matters
it to enjoy here a seeming momentary happiness, and
be most unhappy hereafter for all eternity? To
be truly prudent is to be prudent to eternity, and
so was our Saint, and whoever is not thus prudent
proves himself a very fool.

True prudence guides to true happiness ; as there
is no true happiness but eternal, so neither true
prudence but that which leads to this eternity.   This
is true prudence indeed, its great act and master-
piece ; at which all our practical prudence in this
great management must level as at its final scope,
and the purchase of all our endeavours in this life's
commerce.   As nothing less than eternity will do
our work, that is, make us eternally happy, so must
we acquiesce in no other, none but that being truly
satiative, and all the rest an empty shadow.   'The
prudence of the flesh,' saith the Apostle, 'is death,'[4]
and operates it: 'The wisdom of this world,' saith
the same, 'is folly with God.'[5]   Such cannot be a
guide of our proceedings.   Ours must be refined
above the world and death, the issue of Divine
wisdom, and therefore is called by it, 'the science
of saints'[6]—*Scientia sanctorum prudentia.*   This
science our blessed Saint studied all his life long,

---

[4] Romans viii. 6.
[5] I Cor. iii. 19.   [6] Prov. ix. 10.

and learned more true knowledge out of it than he
did out of the Philosophy of Aristotle, or Ideas of
Plato. He learned to be virtuous, to keep a good
conscience, his duty towards God, his neighbour, and
himself; to subdue sense to reason, and the whole
man to the obedience of the Divine law. He learned
to prefer a solid happiness before a seeming one,
eternity before time, the soul before the body, and
God and His service above all. Christ our Blessed
Saviour sends us to the serpent to learn this prudence, and it teaches us a twofold lesson : to expose
the whole body to save the head, the seat of life ;
and so must we all our external goods, body and all,
for the preservation of our faith and safety of our
souls. The serpent, say naturalists, stops one ear
with its tail, the other it claps close to the ground,
so to become deaf to charms and enchantments ;
and prudence bids us imitate this amidst the enchantments of sinful pleasures (according to that of the
fifty-seventh Psalm), to which our corrupt nature
inclines ; common errors lead the way, custom like
a torrent carries us along, and engulfs us in a sea
of spiritual miseries. To these two we may add a
third, and it is, that the serpent by forcing her
passage through a narrow cranny strips herself of
her old coat and altogether of her old age, and so
becomes young. We, by endeavouring, as our

Saviour advises, to enter by the narrow gate, may effect the same, and, stripping ourselves of inveterate habits, put on a newness of life. Let us learn at least to avoid gross mistakes against prudence, if we cannot all. Even common prudence bids us secure the main concern when we cannot all particulars, it being accounted no indiscretion to hazard something to save the whole. What is our main concern but our soul? If we lose that we lose all: to venture a limb to save our life is a dictate of nature; and to expose both body and estate to save our soul, is a certain maxim of grace. If we must quit either a lease for life or an inheritance, it would be deemed madness to part with the latter to secure the former, this being as much in its kind as to exchange pearls for pebbles, and gold for clinkers; and is the same whenever soul and body, time and eternity, Heaven and this world come into competition. To make here a right election is the part of prudence; and our glorious St. Thomas both did it and teaches us to do it, and of all the virtuous lessons of his whole life none than this is more important, none more prudent. God in His grace and light give us strength to make the same resolves, and execute them with an equal fidelity. Amen.

CHAPTER XXVI.

Supplement to the Life of St. Thomas of Hereford.

1. THE exact date of St. Thomas's birth cannot be fixed with certainty, as the witnesses were not agreed as to his age when he died. Bishop Swinfield, the one most likely to know, said that he was sixty-three and more; so that, dying as he did in August, 1282, his birth was in 1218 or 1219. Hambleden, in Bucks, but in the Lincoln diocese, not far from Great Marlow, was the place of his birth. The manor was then in possession of the Crown, and probably held by the father or grandfather of St. Thomas. He was baptized in the parish church, of which nothing remains except, possibly, the old font. The right of patronage to this church was the subject of a lawsuit, after St. Thomas's death, between the Earls of Cornwall and Gloucester. An oratory, or chantry, was added to the church by Edmund, Earl of Cornwall, in honour of St. Thomas.

2. As to the Cantilupe family, it was the grandfather of St. Thomas, who was so distinguished for his loyalty to King John and his bravery in the siege of Montsorel, in Leicestershire. He was Sheriff

of Warwickshire, Leicestershire, Worcestershire, and
Herefordshire.   His chief residence was Kenilworth
Castle.   He built and founded a hospital at Studley,
and his name is perpetuated in Aston-Cantelow.
His son, the father of our Saint, succeeded to most
of his honours, and was one of the English Envoys
at the First Council of Lyons.   The mother of
St. Thomas was first married to Almaric V., Count
of Evreux, and this explains the close alliance there
was between the Cantilupes and the Montforts.
Neither was our Saint her first or only child by her
second marriage.   Her sons were William, Hugh,
Thomas, John, and Nicholas.   Of these Hugh and
Thomas were devoted to the Church ; the others
were soldiers.   William and John died comparatively
young.   John left a son, named William, to the care
of our Saint, to whose retinue he was afterwards
attached.   The father of St. Thomas died in 1251,
and his eldest brother, William, four years after.
Thus it happened that within a few years three
generations of this family passed away.   Walter
Cantilupe, the uncle of St. Thomas and Bishop of
Worcester, was a prominent figure in the history of
that period.   He was the friend of Grostête, Adam
de Moresio, and Simon de Montfort.   He died
shortly after the battle of Evesham, not without the
reputation of sanctity and miracles, and was buried

in his Cathedral of Worcester, where his tomb and certain relics extracted from it may be seen. St. Thomas had three sisters. Juliana, the eldest, married to Baron Tregoz; Agnes, who married Lord St. John; and a third, married to Baron Gregonet. A witness relates that they used to visit their saintly brother every year, but that he did not converse much with them, for he said that women's talk was foolish; nor would he allow them to stay a night in his house.

3. The early or home education of St. Thomas was conducted by a noble matron remarkable for her piety. When seven years old, good and pious masters were engaged for St. Thomas and his brother Hugh. One witness says that they used to hear Mass daily and be present at the recitation of Canonical Hours, which, when old enough, they recited daily. Their uncle, Walter, then a priest and a royal justiciary, it is said, watched over their education, and used his interest to obtain benefices for their support. It is not unlikely that Robert Kilwarby, who had not yet joined the Dominicans, had a hand in their bringing up.

4. Our Saint, and probably his brother Hugh, went to Oxford in 1237, two years before their uncle was consecrated Bishop of Worcester. He studied in the house of the Black Friars, 'renowned for its famous men,' says Antony à Wood. There his chief

lector was Robert Kilwarby, who had become a Dominican seven years before. He did not remain long in Oxford at this time, but the reason for his leaving is not stated. Perhaps it was the confusion which befell the University on the occasion of the Legate Cardinal Otho's visit. The Legate's brother, acting as the cook to the Cardinal, who was staying at Osney Abbey, lost his temper through the importunities of an Irish mendicant student, and threw hot soup in his face. A Welsh student, filled with anger, drew his bow and shot the Legate's brother. Public opinion in Oxford defended the act and shielded the guilty party. The Cardinal left precipitately, threatening excommunication and interdict against the University. And it was with great difficulty that the Bishop of Lincoln, the Father and Protector of the University, brought about reconciliation, on condition of a public penitential procession.

5. Following Chaucer's maxim, that 'sundry schools make subtil clerks,' it was not uncommon at that time for students to pass from Oxford to Paris or *vice versâ.* So to Paris our Saint went with his brother. Here they lived in some style as young noblemen of wealth and position, and here they both 'proceeded in arts,' or, to use the modern phrase, took their degree. In 1245 the First Council of Lyons was held. Thither their father, the Seneschal

of Aquitaine and one of the English' Envoys to the Council, took his two sons, and presented them to Pope Innocent IV., by whom they were made Papal Chaplains or 'Monsignori.' It is probable that they were then ordained priests. It is certain that from this Pontiff St. Thomas received two special dispensations; one permitting him to hold a plurality of benefices; the other allowing him to study civil law. Acting on the second, he betook himself 'to Orleans, attracted probably by the form of some special professor. The University of Orleans was not established till more than fifty years later. Thence he came back to Paris to study canon law, where his elder brother Hugh, the future Archdeacon of Gloucester, was devoting himself to theology. The brothers now lived apart and kept separate establishments. Hugh, the barber, the servant of St. Thomas, gives an outline of his master's life at that time. He had one chaplain constantly with him, whose early Mass he heard before going to the schools. At least five, and sometimes thirteen, poor were fed at his table. Two poor scholars were supported by him, and for others he often begged help from his rich friends. Charity to poor scholars seems to have been his special devotion throughout his university life, both here and at Oxford. At this time, or on a later occasion, he

had the honour of receiving a visit from the sainted
King Louis.   After he had obtained his licentiate,
he left Paris for Oxford, there to teach canon law.

6. It is not possible to ascertain the exact date
of St. Thomas's return to Oxford.   About this time
he lost both his father and eldest brother.   The
latter was buried at Studley in 1255, 'there being
present divers abbots and priors, also sundry great
earls, Simon, Earl of Leicester, and Humphrey, Earl
of Hereford.'[1]   Probably St. Thomas returned to
Oxford soon after this event.   The year 1257 was
memorable as the great famine year,—a wet summer, fruit did not ripen, and corn remained uncut
till November.   The bishops gave permission that,
weather permitting, people might work at harvesting
on Sundays and holydays.   Wheat rose from 2s.
a quarter to 20s. or 24s.; horse-flesh and the bark
of trees were eaten.   In the following year, during
Lent, that season wherein 'quarrels are easily begun
and not without much labour allayed,' Oxford was
disturbed by quarrels and fighting between the
Southern and Northern students.

> Mark the Chronicles aright,
> When Oxford scholars fall to fight
> Before many months expired
> England will with war be fired.[2]

---

[1] Dugdale's *Baronage*, vol. i. p. 731.
[2] Ant. à Wood's *Annals*, bk. i. an. 1258.

7. This was soon to be proved true. In 1262 St. Thomas was chosen by the Master and Doctors to be Chancellor of the University, and their election was confirmed by the Bishop of Lincoln, Grostête's successor. The office was then commonly held for two years. In the exercise of this office witnesses commend his justice and firmness. The number of students under his charge was probably about twenty thousand. In 1230 the number of students at Oxford was thirty thousand; but on the disbanding of the University in 1264, only fifteen thousand. They were allowed to carry arms, which were subject to confiscation for bad behaviour. Hugh the barber says that St. Thomas sometimes had quite a small armoury of confiscated swords and bows. The disturbance, which occurred on the occasion of Prince Edward's approach to the city in 1263, will give an idea of a Chancellor's difficulties. The Mayor and his officers kept the city gates fast, to prevent the students going to Prince Edward's camp. At dinner time the big bell of St. Mary's was tolled. 'All left their meat and ran to their swords, bows, slings, and bills: gathering together in a body, they fought most courageously, wounded many of the townspeople, and forced the rest to fly. The Provost's house was burnt; William the espycer's was broken up, with all the spicery itself, from one den

to the other, and most of the goods therein spoiled. At the house of the Mayor, who was a vintner, they drank as much wine as they could and wasted the rest.' An inquiry was ordered by the King, but many of the scholars fled.

8. At the close of the year 1263 an attempt was made to ward off the threatened civil war between the King and his barons by an appeal to the arbitration of St. Louis, the King of France. The *mise* of Amiens was held in January, 1264, and St. Thomas was one of the proxies to plead the cause of the barons. The Tewksbury annalist gives the following account of the result: 'The King (Louis), hearing of the King and his faithful barons, was much moved and disturbed in the bowels of his compassion with grief and affliction. At first he formed a favourable judgment and approved the doings of the barons, saying that as a ship at sea would run great risk except for the guidance of the mariners, so neither could any king rule his kingdom in prosperity or defend it in adversity without the cooperation of his own country, affirming that every kingdom should be ruled by its king and faithful subjects, and not by foreigners. At the words of the Lord King all were rejoiced, and the envoys returned with joy, praising and glorifying God. At the same time, however, the King of France was deceived by the

serpent-like cunning and address of a woman, the Queen of England; as it is written, *Non est fraus super fraudem mulieris*, for by it were deceived Adam, and King Solomon, and David the King, and others too. The heart of this same King was changed from bad to worse, from worse to worst.' The arbitration failed. In March, 1264, the King summoned his forces to meet at Oxford and sent home the students, lest they see 'the chieftains, many of whom were fierce and untamed.' Many of the students went to Northampton, and were so prominent in defending that city against the Royal forces, that when the city was taken, the King could hardly be dissuaded from hanging his young Oxford prisoners. Then followed the battle of Lewes and the victory of the barons under Simon de Montfort. The sympathies of our Saint were with the popular and national party, of which his uncle, the Bishop of Worcester, was one of the leading spirits. The first English Parliament was summoned in January, 1265, and St. Thomas was chosen to be Chancellor of the Exchequer. The entry on record is : ' On Wednesday next, after the feast of St. Peter in Cathedra, Master John de Chishull, Archdeacon of London (who had been sigillifer), restored ·to the King his seal, and he on the same day committed the custody of it to Master Thomas de Cantilupe, who immediately sealed

with it.' A later entry says: 'As our beloved in
Christ, Mr. Thomas de Cantilupe, has been chosen
by us and our barons, who form our Council, to be
Chancellor of our kingdom, and we have willingly
admitted him to that office, wishing to provide for
his support and that of the clerks of our chancellery,
we grant to him 500 marks a year, &c. And be it
known that with his own hand the Lord King folded
this brief and in his presence caused it to be sealed.'
Thomas did not hold the office more than a few
months. Prince Edward made his escape from
Hereford to Wigmore Castle in May. As our
Saint's help was needed to assist in opposing him
at a distance from London, the great seal was transferred to Ralph de Sanduril, Keeper of the Wardrobe,
to be kept by him till Thomas de Cantilupe should
return, under the superintendence and to be used
with the concurrence of Peter de Montfort, Roger
St. John and Giles de Argentine.[3] The battle, or
as one chronicler terms it, the massacre of Evesham
took place in August. St. Thomas was at once
despatched from office, and in 1266 a pardon was
granted to him.[4] He seems to have remained a
member of the Privy Council both of King
Henry III. and of Edward I.

[3] Campbell's *Lives of Chancellors*, vol. i. p. 137.
[4] Bloow's *Barons' War*, p. 257.

9. St. Thomas withdrew to Paris, where he studied theology. After a year or more he returned to Oxford, and was a second time Chancellor of the University. In 1267 the fight between North and South occurred, when St. Thomas separated the combatants, as our author describes. In 1273 he became Doctor of Divinity, and received very exalted testimony to his virtue from his old friend, confessor, and master, Robert Kilwarby, then Archbishop-Elect of Canterbury. In the following year he was present at the Second Council of Lyons, accompanied by his nephew William as his chaplain. Pope Gregory X. made him one of his chaplains. About this time probably he received many of the benefices, of which the author gives a list. Many witnesses give evidence of the scrupulous care he took to fulfil the obligations attaching thereto and the charitable use he made of the revenues. The Prebend and Canonry of Preston Wynne, in Herefordshire, which he received from Bishop Breton, entailed upon him a ruinous and lifelong lawsuit in the Papal Court.[5]

10. St. Thomas was chosen Bishop of Hereford, 1275, and consecrated at Canterbury by Archbishop Kilwarby and the Bishop of London and Rochester. There is a document extant, printed by Haddon and Stubbs, which expresses 'the Archbishop's annoyance

[5] *Swinfield's Roll.* Camden Society, clxxix.

P 30

that other Bishops, and especially the neighbouring Bishops of Wales were not present.[6] The diocese of Hereford was extensive. On the north it stretched where the Severn enters Shropshire to where that river is joined in the south by the influx of the Wye. It embraced portions of the counties of Radnor, Montgomery, Salop, Worcester, and Gloucester, and touched upon that of Brecon. It included the town of Monmouth with four parishes in its neighbourhood. The Bishop's manors were Boston, Bishop's Castle (Salop), Bishop's Frome, Bosbury, Bromyard, Colwall, Cradly, Coddington, Eastnor, Eaton, Grendon, Hompton, Hereford, Ledbury, Ledbury North (Salop), Ross, Ross Foreign, Shelwich, Sugwas, Tupsley, Upton, Whitborne, and Prestbury near Cheltenham. Also he had house in Worcester and in London. The total revenue is given at about £520 per annum, or about fifteen times that amount in the present money. It was not only a diocese, but an episcopal barony, which the Bishop held of the King in chief, with a list of tenants, including some of the principal families in the county, who did homage to him and performed suit and service when required. He was answerable for fifteen knights' fees. So vast a charge necessitated a large number of dependents of all sorts

---

[6] *Councils and Ecclesiastical Documents*, vol. i. p. 506. Haddon and Stubbs.

and degrees : proctors in the Papal Court, advocate in London, clerk to the chapel, and bailiffs, larderers, falconers, porters, stable-grooms, farriers, butlers, chamberlains, huntsmen, and messengers. In addition to these, the Bishop had to keep a champion, ever ready for the wager of battle, a mode of trial not then extinct. Thomas de Bruges held the office at the yearly income of six shillings and eightpence, and the terms of the agreement are preserved in the Cantilupe Register.[7]

11. The diocese was in a sad condition when St. Thomas became its Bishop. The violence of the civil war and the weakness of the two preceding Bishops had worked great mischief with both its spiritual and temporal affairs. Encroached on and plundered in all directions by the neighbouring barons, the Church of Hereford needed a strong and zealous pastor, and found one in St. Thomas. Clifford, Corbit, Llewellyn, Prince of Wales, and even Clare, Earl of Gloucester, the most powerful men in the kingdom were made to feel that right was stronger than might. The trench dug along the Malvern Hills is a monument to St. Thomas's memory, which neither Iconoclast can destroy nor time efface.

---

[7] Webb's *Note on the Swinfield Roll*, p. xxxv. from which all these facts are taken. The fosse was made by the Earl of Gloucester in 1287 to prevent his deer straying into the Bishop's preserves.

12. Difficulties about jurisdiction arose with some of the neighbouring bishops. He had a long suit with Anianus II., Bishop of St. Asaph, ending in an appeal to Rome, which was ultimately given in favour of the Church of Hereford after St. Thomas's death. The right of consecrating the Church of Abbey Dore led to a contest with the Bishop of Menevia, who was supported by Baron Tregos and his armed retainers. St. Thomas consecrated the church at the risk of his life. So successful was he in all these undertakings, that one of his opponents said to him, 'Either you are full of the devil, or you are over familiar (*nimis secretarius*) with God;' which latter was the true explanation, coupled with the fact that he never entered upon such conflicts without being sure of his ground both in law and equity.

13. St. Thomas's most serious contest, which cost him his life, was with his own Metropolitan Archbishop Peccham. It is not easy to get at the facts of the case and to hear both sides. While Peccham's case may be clearly seen from his letter to his Proctors printed in Wilkins' *Concilia*, there is very little preserved to show what St. Thomas's contention was. It is clear that there were certain general complaints against the Archbishop which St. Thomas maintained in common with the other suffragans of Canterbury, and also certain special

gravamina of his own. The grievances of the bishops are summed up in a document of twenty-one points, printed by Wilkins, with Peccham's not very courteous replies. This document is also in the Cantilupe Register, and very little else besides to throw light on the controversy. In the Council of Reading St. Thomas disputed the Archbishop's claim to interpret certain Papal Constitutions, and, in common with his fellow-bishops, protested against certain innovations. These related to questions of appeal from the Bishops' Courts to the Court of Arches, and to alleged interference with their jurisdiction. On these general points it is pretty clear the bishops had the right of it, for in May, 1282, after St. Thomas had appealed in person to the Holy See, a Committee of Inquiry was appointed. In accordance with the Report of this Committee, the Archbishop published certain Articles remedying the evils complained of. But the personal controversy between St. Thomas and the Archbishop was occasioned by the officials of their respective courts. First a marriage, and then later a probate case, led to what the official of Hereford thought an uncalled for interference with the rights of his court. He was accused of disobedience and contempt to the higher court, and forestalled the threatened sentence of excommunication by an appeal to the Holy Father. The quarrel of the officials was taken up by their principals.   The contention of St. Thomas was, that the Canterbury official intervened too quickly, and thus prevented the proper course of appeal which should lay from the official of Hereford to the Bishop of Hereford, and after that to the Court of Arches.   Also he disputed the right of the Archbishop or his official to punish the subjects of the Hereford diocese, except through him as their bishop.   To defend his rights, St. Thomas appealed to Rome.   At first he prosecuted his appeal through his proctors, and in, order the more easily to communicate with them by messenger, he crossed over into Normandy.   There he abode for a year and a half, residing for a portion of the time at the Benedictine Abbey of Lyra.   He returned in 1281, and was present at the Synod of Lambeth.   In January of 1282, an ineffectual reconciliation was made with the Archbishop.   Every inducement was offered to St. Thomas to persuade him to give in. Then the controversy broke out more bitterly than ever, and was brought to a final and prompt issue. Robert of Gloucester, the official of Hereford, was excommunicated, and St. Thomas was called upon to publish the sentence against his own official, under penalty of major excommunication to himself and interdict to his chapel.   This he refused to do, on the ground that the sentence against his official was in-

validated by that official's previous appeal to Rome.
To protect himself, St. Thomas appealed to Rome on
this fresh issue, and certified the Court of Arches of
his appeal. Yet, ignoring this, the official of Canterbury, with the consent, though not in the presence of
the Archbishop, pronounced sentence of major excommunication against the Bishop of Hereford, and
interdicted his chapel, saving in the possible presence
of the King or royal family. This sentence was
ordered to be published throughout the different
dioceses. Some bishops refused to do this, and St.
Thomas caused the fact of appeal to be made known
everywhere. This appeal he made haste to prosecute
in person. He paused on his journey to make a
pilgrimage to Pontigny, where the body of St.
Edmund lay. Archbishop Peccham's proctors were
instructed to throw every obstacle in his way, and if
possible, to prevent his reception at the Papal Court.
Pope Martin IV. held his Court at Orvieto, and
thither St. Thomas repaired. After a short preliminary
examination as to his status, he was most honourably
received by the Holy Father and the whole Court
of Cardinals. He retired to Montefiascone, there to
await the full hearing of his suit. But this never
took place, for not long after he fell sick and died.

14. Even death did not disarm Archbishop Peccham's resentment, and when St. Thomas's bones

were brought to England, he forbade them Christian burial until he was shown the absolution given by the Papal Penitentiary. Then did he desist, and even joined the other bishops in offering Indulgences to those who prayed for the repose of the soul of the sainted Cantilupe. And some years later, when the fame of his miracles was noised abroad, and his own infirmities were multiplied, the Archbishop had himself measured to St. Thomas, and sent a priest to the tomb of his former pupil and excommunicated suffragan, to pray for the poor Archbishop who had wronged him. Some of the chroniclers are hard upon the memory of Peccham, saying that in punishment for his injustice he lost his senses and died in his dotage. His official happened to be in Hereford when the first miracle took place, and was so indignant that the merit of it should be imputed to St. Thomas, that he suspended Gilbert, the Hereford proctor, for publishing the fact, and caused it to be given out that it was due to Robert Betun, a former Bishop of Hereford, who died a century before with a reputation for sanctity. This he did despite of the constant assertion of the woman who had been cured, and could best know who cured her, that it was St. Thomas Cantilupe who had appeared to her, and that she knew him in his lifetime; so that there could be no mistake.

15. But all doubt was soon removed by the number and magnitude of the miracles that everywhere followed the invocation of St. Thomas.   In 1288 Bishop Swinfield, the executor and successor to St. Thomas, erected to his memory the handsome tomb in the north transept of Hereford.   Thither his bones were translated, and on the fifth anniversary of his death Requiem Mass was sung for the repose of his soul, and a sum of money paid over by the executors to the Hereford Chapter to establish his yearly obit, but with a special reservation in the event of his future canonization.   This was the first intimation of the possibility of such a thing ; but it was not till two years later that Bishop Swinfield first wrote to Pope Nicholas IV., who when Cardinal had preached the funeral panegyric at St. Sevres.   In this letter Bishop Swinfield makes known to His Holiness that the whole English Church rejoices that she hath brought forth so wise a son in the Lord ; that the Lord God of His abiding goodness and infinite power had confirmed with multitudinous miracles the Pope's commendations of St. Thomas in his eloquent discourse.   'Nor is it surprising,' he says, 'that he who when living adorned the Church of God with his exalted merits, and in defence of the rights of his Church underwent with all patience very great toils, preferring to be afflicted in a foreign land for the

people of God committed to him, rather than to
enjoy temporal happiness with his noble kinsfolk and
friends, should not cease now to adorn the same
Church with the splendour of a brighter light, showing
that though departed from this life he liveth more
really than he ever lived to promote the honour and
glory of His name, Who permitteth not that the
merits and rewards of so great a man should be
obscured ; in so much as of old he forbade the light
to be hid under the bushel. These things, most Holy
Father, I write to you with the safer conscience
because for about eighteen years I was in the household of the aforesaid servant of God, a frequent
witness of his virtues.' And he begs that this great
servant of God may be lifted up upon the Church's
candlestick, that all who enter may behold his light
and glorify 'Our Father Who is in Heaven.'[8]

16. No answer was received to this petition. About
four years later the Bishops of Durham, Ely, and Bath
and Wells, addressed fresh petitions to Pope Clement V. In 1299 Swinfield wrote what he called his
'last letter' on the subject. But no real advance was
made till King Edward I. took up the affair in earnest, and sent a personal petition to Pope Clement V.
The barons, and amongst them even Gilbert, Earl

---

[8] This letter, extracted from the Swinfield Register, is printed in
full by Mr. Webb in his Notes and Appendix to the *Roll*.

of Gloucester, forgiving the loss of Malvern Chase, petitioned.[9] In answer to these petitions, Pope Clement appointed three Commissioners to examine and report to him. The great Durandus, Bishop of Mende, was one. They held their Court of Inquiry for some months at St. Paul's, in London, and afterwards at Hereford, in St. Catharine's Chapel, now destroyed. Sixty-two witnesses were examined on oath, who gave evidence from personal knowledge of the life, virtues, and miracles of St. Thomas, whose depositions are still preserved. Ten years passed away, during which King Edward and Bishop Swinfield died without obtaining their request. Edward II. renewed the petition, sending to Avignon the Bishop of Hereford and a royal justiciary; and at length, to the great joy of the English Church, Pope John XXII. issued the Bull of Canonization in 1320. Thus it came to pass that the canonization of the last canonized saint of Catholic England was a great national event, brought about by the prayers of two Kings, one Archbishop, fifteen bishops, eleven earls, many lords and nobles, to the centre of Catholic unity, for the canonization of a bishop who died appealing to Rome to defend him against the injustice of the Metropolitan of Canterbury.

[9] Some of these petitions and other documents relating to the canonization are among the MSS. of R. J. Ormsby Gore, M.P. of Brogyntyn.

17. Thirty years afterwards Bishop Trilleck translated the relics from the tomb erected by Swinfield to
a shrine in the centre of the Lady Chapel.   At the
ceremony the King, Edward III., was present with
many nobles, and the memory of it was kept every
year in the Hereford Use on the 25th of October.
The author confuses this translation in Bishop Trilleck's time with that which occurred in 1288, and it
was the third Edward who was the hero in the
conflict with Ribaumont at Calais.   It is clear for
many reasons that the shrine of St. Thomas stood
in the Lady Chapel.   Sir Peter Grandison, whose
beautiful monument is there, was the grandnephew of
St. Thomas, and he prayed to be buried near his
shrine.   The chapel of St. Anne was in the crypt
beneath, and is described as under the feretrum of
St. Thomas.   Bishop Audley, at the close of the
fifteenth century, built his chantry there, that he
might pay his devotion at the shrine of St. Thomas;
a silver feretrum in the form of a church is mentioned in the book of Obits as his gift.   And when
the cathedral was restored, the old stones which
formed the basement of the shrine were found *in situ*,
much worn by the knees of pilgrims.   But the shrine,
with its silver feretrum and precious jewels, was
destroyed when Henry VIII. gave command 'to
take away, utterly extract, and destroy all shrines,

coverings of shrines, and all monuments of feigned miracles, pilgrimages, idolatry, and superstition.' Yet Bishop Swinfield's tomb, the former resting-place of the relics, and the scene of countless miracles, still stands in the north transept, with its stone-cut Templars guarding the honour of their sainted Provincial master. It is not unlikely that the large stone which forms the base of the structure, and which Mr. Havergal, in the *Fasti Herefordienses* describes as carved with a curious cross, is the very stone which was over the first grave in the Lady Chapel, and was lifted by the two acolytes, as our author relates. As the identity of this tomb has been questioned, it may be well to quote the testimony of John of Iregoz, a kinsman of St. Thomas, who when praying beside the tomb, describes a vision and cure granted to him in a way which clearly identifies the present tomb in the north transept with that beside which he was kneeling. He deposes that the figure of a mitred bishop seemed to come forth from beneath the brass which was upon the 'sarcophagus' of the man of God. This brass, which was a half-length, has disappeared, but the matrix may be easily traced. Dingley, who visited Hereford Cathedral about the close of the seventeenth century, thus describes in his *History of Marble* what he saw: 'In the north aisle, against the east wall, at the feet of St. Thomas de Cantilupe's monument, is seen the remains of his image painted in fresquo, with another image on ye other side the window after the same manner—supposed to be designed for Bishop Ethelston, only that this holdeth a crozier, the other an episcopal crook, and that whereas the episcopal habit of *this* is embroidered with many other ornaments, the letter T often repeated, *that* hath leopards' heads reversed swallowing *fleurs de lys.* Another curious of antiquity taketh this with ye T to be St. Thomas à Becket, and the other for our St. Thomas à Contelo. I incline most to believe ye latter opinion. Yet neither hath a glory about ye head.'[10] Dr. Stukeley also in his *Itinerary* speaks of the picture on the wall, and the hooks where the banners, lamps, or the like presents were hung up in his honour.

18. The history of the relics of St. Thomas is briefly this. When the shrine in the Lady Chapel was destroyed, the relics, or the greater part of them, must have been preserved, how or in what way is unknown, for in Queen Mary's reign they were in the custody of a Mr. William Ely, the Vice-President of St. John's in Oxford. All that is known of him is that he was born in Herefordshire, that though Catholic at heart he conformed out-

[10] *History in Marble.* Camden Society, p. clxxxix.

wardly to the new gospel; in 1563 he refused to acknowledge the spiritual supremacy of Queen Elizabeth, was deprived of his office, went abroad, and was ordained priest. He returned to his native county, and laboured in support of the old Catholic faith. A state paper of James I.'s time describes him as, 'an aged priest, and a great aider and abettor of the Jesuits, having such liberty as that he rideth up and down the country as he likes.'[11] He was thrown into prison, and died in the old Hereford Gaol in 1609. The following is a copy of an old MS. kept at Stonyhurst: 'Mr. Elie, a priest in Queen Marie's reigne, lived at Hereford, and had in his custody certain reliques formerly kept in ye greete church there, which were of St. Thomas, Bishop of that place ; this sayd Mr. Elie, dying many years after, delivered the said reliques to one Mr. Clarke, a lay gentleman, who afterwards delivered ye same to one Mr. Stephens, a priest, who lived many years after in ye same city of Hereford. The said Mr. Stephens having received those reliques, for a farther testimony and certainty of the authenticalnesse thereof, caused divers ancient Catholiques to meet him at Hereford, whom he examined about ye reliques, and they tooke their oath, in ye presence of ye said Mr. Stephens and others, that these were ye reliques

[11] *Records of the English Province S. J.*, vol. iv. p. 453.

wh. Mr. Elie used to show to them, and that they
had for many yeares seene and visited them as ye
reliques of St. Thomas, Bishop of ye place. And
this they knew by certaine signs and tokens. After
that, one Mr. Cuffauld, a priest, also living in Hereford, had those relics in his keeping and custody,
and gave one thereof (being, as wee conceive, an
arme bone of nine inches and somewhat more or
thereabout in length) to Mr. Evans, living in North
Wales, in ye year of our Lord 1664, to bee kept by
him.' In 1610, the year of the plague in Hereford,
the reliques were carried through the town in a secret
and night procession, and as our author states, 'it
gave a total succour to the same.' Two witnesses,
quoted in the Bollandist life, speaks to the pious
veneration with which the relics were then held, and
of their being exposed to the public veneration of
the faithful, 'as far as was possible amongst heretics.'
When the Parliamentary army under the Earl of
Stamford occupied Hereford in 1642, the Catholics
would have lost their treasure but for a Mrs. Ravens-
hill, a Catholic lady, who recovered it out of the
hands of the enemy. In the terror of the times which
followed it would seem that the relics were no longer
kept together, but committed to the care of individual
Catholics. The head fell to the charge of the Street
family—an old Catholic family of Herefordshire.

About the year 1670 one of the family took it with him to the monastery of Lambspring, in Germany, as is set forth in the following copy of a document in the keeping of the late Dr. Heptonstall, O.S.B. :

19. 'I, Brother Benet Gibon, Benedictine Monk of the English Congregation and professed of the Abbey of Lambspring, in the Diocese of Hildesheim, do declare that Brother Peter Street, Convers of ye same monastery, affirmed to me the manner with many particulars how he toke the head of St. Thomas of Hereford from his sister's house in Herefordshire, where it had been reposed long in ye family by ye Catholic clergé of England ; he out of a particular zeal for ye honour of ye Saint, not thinking it kept and exposed with due publick veneration, brought ye same to Lambspring as above, in order to a greater veneration of ye Saint, where with leave of the Bishop of ye place it has been permitted to be exposed to the devotion of ye publick, and his feast kept as a double annually upon the 2nd of Octobre. Now I, abovesaid Benet Gibon, do affirm that the said clergé reclaiming restouration of the same sacred head by a letter. writ to the Abbot Gascoigne, which letter he gave me to answer, and I none approving ye manner of this translation, did answer if they pleased to send any person approved to receive it back, it should be restoured, only desiring that some

particle of ye same head might remain at Lambspring, but no answer being given it there remains.
For satisfaction of my conscience before I dye, I
give this instrument about fifty years after this translation, Oct. 6th, 1720.'

20. Lambspring Abbey was suppressed by the Prus-
sians in 1803, and all trace of this relic has been
lost. The right arm bone, wrapped in green ribbon,
was taken by Father Poyntz in 1651, and first committed to the care of his sister in Paris, and afterwards given to the Jesuit College at St. Omer. After
the suppression of the Society this relic was lost.
The heart of St. Thomas, given to his friend the
Earl of Cornwall, was preserved in the Convent of
the Bonnes Hommes at Asheridge (Bucks), "in a
repository made with exquisite art in the north side
of the choir of the conventual church, but was afterwards removed by the Pope's authority, with the
Earl's heart, the portion of Christ's Blood, and other
sacred relics, and committed to an apartment finely
guilt by the Earl in his lifetime prepared for that
use."[11] This of course was destroyed at the Refor-
mation, as also Mortimer's bequest to the Abbey of
Wigmore of the finger of St. Thomas[12]—a second
' Mortimer's treasure' given to that favoured abbey.

[11] Kennet's *Parochial Antiquities*, p. 340.
[12] Robinson's *Castles of Herefordshire*.

So that the only authentic relic that remains of the Saint is the arm-bone given to Mr. Evans in 1664, which was carefully preserved at Holywell, and is now enshrined in a handsome reliquary at Stonyhurst College.

21. The Cantilupe Register, the oldest in the Episcopal Registry at Hereford, is still preserved, and contains at least one entry undoubtedly in the Saint's own writing.[13] The Hereford Missal, in the British Museum Library, contains special sequences in his honour.[14] The White Cross in Hereford and the Malvern Hill trench are monuments to his memory: the one is the record of his piety, the other of his fearless justice. The following extract from Blount's MS. shows the true history and meaning of the White Cross. 'His (St. Thomas's) usual residence was at his Palace at Hereford, and for his retirement he went sometimes to his house at Sugwas, and that usually on foot. In the way betwixt Hereford and this place he built a cross, where he rested himself and said his prayers; which cross was demolished by (Colonel Birch of) Garnons in the late civil wars, and in the place where it stood are since planted an oak, an elm, and an ash.' The present cross is of course a restoration on the old foundation. In all

---

[13] Swinfield's *Roll*, Webb's note, p. xcvii.
[14] See Appendix.

probability the north transept, with straight-ruled arches and unbending lines—one of the grandest features of the Cathedral—is the abiding work and record of that Bishop, who would not bend before oppression nor swerve from the straight line of right.

22. As to the miracles of this great English Thaumaturgus, some few remarks are necessary. There is a record, and this not a ·complete one, occupying nearly one hundred folio pages of the Bollandist life, of a series of marvellous facts—restorations to life, preservations from death, wondrous cures—and extending over some twenty years. These facts are sworn to by witnesses of every class and position, and from all parts of the kingdom, who sincerely believed that they had received favours from God at the prayer of St. Thomas, and under no compulsion but that of gratitude, and for no motive but the glory of God in His saints. Some of the things deposed to may admit of explanation by natural causes, but the greater part cannot· be explained except as miraculous.[15] Objection has been taken to the character of some of the miracles, such as the raising to life executed criminals, or the healing of sick animals—horses, falcons, and even pigs. It must be remembered that in those days men were

[15] See article on 'Catholic Miracles' in the *Dublin Review*, January, 1876, wherein many of the Hereford miracles are discussed.

hung for very small offences. Mediæval justice was
hasty as well as blind, and often hung the wrong
man. Cristina Cray, of Wellington, was hung because a strange pig joined her herd, and she sold it
as her own. And it is quite possible that even
criminals justly condemned, when restored to life
become wiser and better men. And if dumb animals
are worth man's caring for and praying for, there is
no reason to suppose that their Creator has put them
outside the possibilities of the prayer of faith. In
the history of the Cantilupe Miracles two curious
customs find frequent mention, measuring and coin-
bending. But these are not special forms of devotion to St. Thomas, but methods common in that
age for seeking the help of God or His saints.
Curiously enough, in Rietanger's record of miracles
at the tomb of Simon de Montfort, it is related that
Master Thomas de Cantilupe had his sick falcon
'measured' to Simon, and that it got well.

APPENDIX.

*Sequences transcribed from the Hereford Missal,
in the Library of the British Museum.*[1]

I.—FOR THE FEAST OF ST. THOMAS.

VI. Nonas Octobris.

Magnæ lucem caritatis
Meræ ducem veritatis
　　Hominem Angelicum.
Collaudantes veneremur
Operantes imitemur
　　Thomam Apostolicum.
Ob amorem paupertatis apostolum sequitur ;
Ob fervorem charitatis, martyri conjungitur,
In fide confessionis, primum Thomam sequitur,
Et in zelo passionis, secundum amplectitur.
　　Æmulator sanctæ vitæ
　　In Christo fecundâ vite
　　　　Insertus fructificat.
　　Exquirens in corde toto
　　Cum ferventiore voto
　　　　Subditos purificat.

---

[1] The Hereford Breviary, one of the literary treasures of the
Cathedral library, is anterior or more probably of the same date as
the Saint. His feast does not occur in the Calendar. It is full of
Gregorian notation. A witness says that St. Thomas used to *sing*
his Canonical Hours.

Virgulâ justitiæ, cecidit iniquos,
Mundos aquâ gratiæ fovit et pudicos.
Jugo temperantiæ pressus est amore,
Ut in throno gloriæ rutilet splendore.
O miranda sanctitas ! per quam Xti pietas
    Sic mundo patefecit.
Nam mutus et cæcitas, gutta claudus, surditas
    Et gibbus defecit.
    Per Thomam morbus curatur
    Et a carne mors fugatur
    Datur vitæ spiritus.
    Ergo, Pater, te precamur
    Ut laxentur quo gravamur
    Donis datis cœlitus.   Amen.

II.—FOR THE OCTAVE AND COMMEMO-RATION THROUGHOUT THE YEAR.

Summi Regis in honore præsulis memoria
Sancti Thomæ cum majori fiat reverentia.
Doctor plebem illustravit verbi vitæ radio
Pastor gregem confortavit frequenti subsidio.
Qui dum carnem domitavit pungenti cilicio
Sese Christo dedicavit hostiam servitio.
Thoma præsul gloriose, circumda præsidiis
Servos tuos gratiose servans in angustiis.   Amen.

III. FOR THE FEAST OF THE TRANSLATION OF HIS RELICS.

VIII. Kalendæ Novembris.

Novi plausus incrementum
Affert lux ad monumentum
Præsens corporis talentum
Qua Thomæ sustollitur.
Cœlum gratulatur ei
Crevit decus domus Dei

Dies adest nostræ spei
  Laus digna persolvitur.
Hunc honoris sub figurâ
Ferre docet nos Scriptura
Beatorum pondens jura
  Pro futuro debita.
Stola bina designata
Quam ejus carne suscitata
Tunc natura reformata
  Vestiet per merita.
Primum animæ sortitæ
Post decursum hujus vitæ
Congaudemus ejus rite
  Colentes memoriam.
Secundo cum hoc mortale
Post judicium finale
Redigetur, ad æquale
  Prevenimus gloriam.
Veneremur in præsenti
Vita per quod instrumenti
Sancti legem testamenti
  Domini perficere.
Curarunt resociatum
Subjectum appropriatum
Appetitum per innatum
  Optantes reficere.
Homo quam statuit Creator
Ademit prævaricator
Restauravit reparator
  Ex summâ clementiâ.
Sed intercedente morte
Qua sunt fractæ mortis portæ
Restituti pari sorte
  Sumus in potentiâ.
In hoc fide subarrhali
Sancti per spem confortati

Non timebant dira pati
　Pro dimissâ patriâ.
Disponentes mente sanâ
Pro salute se humana
'Terra ferri de profana
　In sanctorum atria.
Merces prima quam mens pura
Consequitur in futurâ
Constat ex terrura
　Triplicis materiæ.
Claræ Dei visionis
Fervidæ delectionis
Et securæ tentionis
　Sub prætexta serie.
Corpora tunc redimentur
Et a malis cruentur
Cum quaternis induentur
　Dotibus pro munere.
Hujus instar unionis
Christus his ditatus donis
Post effectum passionis
　Surrexit de funere.
Clara mens sit ad cernendum
Velle velox ad parendum
Fortis vis ad resistendum
　Subtilis ad solida.
Sic moraliter ornatos
Transfer Deus ad beatos
Carcer reddat liberatos
Nos ad regna florida.　Amen.

A

Select Catalogue of Books

LATELY PUBLISHED BY

BURNS AND OATES,

17, 18 PORTMAN STREET

AND

68 PATERNOSTER ROW.

LONDON:
ROBSON AND SONS, PRINTERS, PANCRAS ROAD, N.W.

𝕭𝖔𝖔𝖐𝖘 𝖑𝖆𝖙𝖊𝖑𝖞 𝖕𝖚𝖇𝖑𝖎𝖘𝖍𝖊𝖉

BY

BURNS AND OATES,

17, 18 PORTMAN STREET, W., & 63 PATERNOSTER ROW, E.C.

———◦———

Sin and its Consequences.   By His Eminence the CARDINAL ARCHBISHOP OF WESTMINSTER.   Second edition.   6s.

> CONTENTS : I. The Nature of Sin. II. Mortal Sin. III. Venial Sin. IV. Sins of Omission. V. The Grace and Works of Penance. VI. Temptation. VII. The Dereliction on the Cross. VIII. The Joys of the Resurrection.

' We know few better books than this for spiritual reading. These lectures are prepared with great care, and are worthy to rank with the old volumes of sermons which are now standard works of the English tongue.'—*Weekly Register.*

' We have had many volumes from his Grace's pen of this kind, but perhaps none more practical or more searching than the volume before us. These discourses are the clearest and simplest exposition of the theology of the subjects they treat of that could be desired. The intellect is addressed as well as the conscience. Both are strengthened and satisfied.'—*Tablet.*

' Of the deepest value, and of great theological and literary excellence. More clear and lucid expositions of dogmatic and moral theology could not be found. No one can read these very forcible, searching, and practical sermons without being deeply stirred and greatly edified.' -*Church Herald.*

' His Grace has added to Catholic literature such a brilliant disquisition as can hardly be equalled.'—*Catholic Times.*

' As powerful, searching, and deep as any that we have ever read. In construction, as well as in theology and in rhetoric, they are more than remarkable, and are amongst the best from his Grace's pen.'—*Union Review.*

The Prophet of Carmel: a Series of Practical Considerations upon the History of Elias in the Old Testament; with a Supplementary Dissertation. By the Rev. CHARLES B. GARSIDE, M.A. Dedicated to the Very Rev. JOHN HENRY NEWMAN, D.D. 5s.

'There is not a page in these sermons but commands our respect. They are Corban in the best sense; they belong to the sanctuary, and are marked as divine property by a special cachet. They are simple without being trite, and poetical without being pretentious.'—*Westminster Gazette*.

'Full of spiritual wisdom uttered in pure and engaging language.'—The *Universe*.

'We see in these pages the learning of the divine, the elegance of the scholar, and the piety of the priest. Every point in the sacred narrative bearing upon the subject of his book is seized upon by the author with the greatest keenness of perception, and set forth with singular force and clearness.'—*Weekly Register*.

'Under his master-hand the marvellous career of the Prophet of Carmel displays its majestic proportions. His strong, nervous, incisive style has a beauty and a grace, a delicacy and a sensitiveness, that seizes hold of the heart and captivates the imagination. He has attained to the highest art of writing, which consists in selecting the words which express one's meaning with the greatest clearness in the least possible space.'—*Tablet*.

'The intellectual penetration, the rich imagination, the nervous eloquence which we meet with throughout the whole work, all combine to give it at once a very high place among the highest productions of our English Catholic literature.'—*Dublin Review*.

'Is at once powerful and engaging, and calculated to furnish ideas innumerable to the Christian preacher.'—*Church Review*.

'The thoughts are expressed in plain and vigorous English. The sermons are good specimens of the way in which Old Testament subjects should be treated for the instruction of a Christian congregation.'—*Church Times*.

Mary magnifying God: May Sermons. By the Rev. Fr. HUMPHREY, O.S.C. Cloth, 2s. 6d.

'Each sermon is a complete thesis, eminent for the strength of its logic, the soundness of its theology, and the lucidness of its expression. With equal force and beauty of language the author has provided matter for the most sublime meditations.'—*Tablet*.

'Dogmatic teaching of the utmost importance is placed before us so clearly, simply, and unaffectedly, that we find ourselves acquiring invaluable lessons of theology in every page.'—*Weekly Register*.

By the same,

The Divine Teacher. Second edition. 2s. 6d.

'The most excellent treatise we have ever read. It could not be clearer, and, while really deep, it is perfectly intelligible to any person of the most ordinary education.'—*Tablet*.

'We cannot speak in terms too high of the matter contained in this excellent and able pamphlet.'—*Westminster Gazette*.

Sermons by Fathers of the Society of Jesus.

Third edition. 7s.

CONTENTS : The Latter Days : Four Sermons by the Rev. H. J. Coleridge. The Temptations of our Lord : Four Sermons by the Rev. Father Hathaway. The Angelus Bell : Five Lectures on the Remedies against Desolation by the Very Rev. Father Gallwey, Provincial of the Society. The Mysteries of the Holy Infancy : Seven Sermons by Fathers Parkinson, Coleridge, and Harper.

Also, printed separately from above,

The Angelus Bell: Five Lectures on the

Remedies against Desolation. By the Very Rev. Father GALLWEY, Provincial of the Society of Jesus. 1s. 6d.

Also Vol. II, in same series,

Discourses by the Rev. Fr. Harper, S.J. 6s.

Also, just published, Vol. III. 6s.

CONTENTS : Sermons by the Rev. George R. Kingdon : I. What the Passion of Christ teaches us ; II. Our Lord's Agony in the Garden ; III. The Choice between Jesus and Barabbas ; IV. Easter Sunday (I.) ; V. Easter Sunday (II.) ; VI. Corpus Christi. Sermons by the Rev. Edward I. Purbrick : VII. Grandeur and Beauty of the Holy Eucharist ; VIII. Our Lady of Victories ; IX. The Feast of All Saints (I.) ; X. The Feast of All Saints (II.) ; XI. The Feast of the Immaculate Conception ; XII. The Feast of St. Joseph. Sermons by the Rev. Henry J. Coleridge : XIII. Fruits of Holy Communion (I.) ; XIV. Fruits of Holy Communion (II.) ; XV. Fruits of Holy Communion (III.) ; XVI. Fruits of Holy Communion (IV.). Sermons by the Rev. Alfred Weld : XVII. On the Charity of Christ ; XVIII. On the Blessed Sacrament. Sermons by the Rev. William H. Anderdon : XIX. The Corner-Stone a Rock of Offence ; XX. The Word of God heard or rejected by Men.

WORKS WRITTEN AND EDITED BY LADY GEORGIANA FULLERTON.

The Straw-cutter's Daughter, and the Portrait in my Uncle's Dining-room. Two Stories. Translated from the French. 2s. 6d.

Life of Luisa de Carvajal. 6s.

Seven Stories. 3s. 6d.

CONTENTS: I. Rosemary: a Tale of the Fire of London. II. Reparation: a Story of the Reign of Louis XIV. III. The Blacksmith of Antwerp. IV. The Beggar of the Steps of St. Roch: a True Story. V. Trouvaille, or the Soldier's Adopted Child: a True Story. VI. Earth without Heaven: a Reminiscence. VII. Ad Majorem Dei Gloriam.

'Will well repay perusal.'—*Weekly Register.*
'Each story in this series has its own charm.'—*Tablet.*
'In this collection may be found stories sound in doctrine and intensely interesting as any which have come from the same pen.'—*Catholic Opinion.*
'As admirable for their art as they are estimable for their sound teaching.'—*Cork Examiner.*

A Sketch of the Life of the late Father Henry

Young, of Dublin. 2s. 6d.

Life of Mère Marie de la Providence,

Foundress of the Order of the 'Helpers of the Holy Souls.'

The materials of this Biography have been drawn from the 'Notice sur la Révérende Mère Marie de la Providence,' published in Paris in 1872; the work of the Rev. Père Blôt, 'Les Auxiliatrices des Ames du Purgatoire;' and some additional documents furnished to the authoress by the Religious of the Rue de la Barouillière. 2s.

Laurentia: a Tale of Japan. Second edition. 3s. 6d.

'Has very considerable literary merit, and possesses an interest entirely its own. The dialogue is easy and natural, and the incidents are admirably grouped.'—*Weekly Register.*
'Full of romantic records of the heroism of the early Christians of Japan in the sixteenth century. Looking at its literary merits alone, it must be pronounced a really beautiful story.'—*Catholic Times.*

Life of St. Frances of Rome. 2s. 6d.; cheap edition, 1s. 8d.

Rose Leblanc: a Tale of great interest. 3s.

Grantley Manor: the well-known and favourite Novel. Cloth, 3s. 6d.; cheap edition, 2s. 6d.

Germaine Cousin: a Drama. 6d.

Fire of London: a Drama. 6d.

OUR LADY'S BOOKS.
Uniformly printed in foolscap 8vo, limp cloth.

No. 1.

Memoir of the Hon. Henry E. Dormer. 2s.

No. 2.

Life of Mary Fitzgerald, a Child of the Sacred Heart. 2s.; cheap edition, 1s.

Meditations for every Day in the Year, and
for the Principal Feasts. By the Ven. Fr. NICHOLAS LANCICIUS, of the Society of Jesus. With Preface by the Rev. GEORGE PORTER, S.J. 6s. 6d.

'Most valuable, not only to religious, for whom they were originally intended, but to all those who desire to consecrate their daily life by regularly express and systematic meditation ; while Father Porter's excellent little Preface contains many valuable hints on the method of meditation.'—*Dublin Review.*
'Full of Scripture, short and suggestive. The editor gives a very clear explanation of the Ignatian method of meditation. The book is a very useful one.'—*Tablet.*
'Short and simple, and dwell almost entirely on the life of our Blessed Lord, as related in the Gospels. Well suited to the wants of Catholics living in the world.'—*Weekly Register.*
'A book of singular spirituality and great depth of piety. Nothing could be more beautiful or edifying than the thoughts set forth for reflection, clothed as they are in excellent and vigorous English.'—*Union Review.*

Meditations for the Use of the Clergy, for
every Day in the Year, on the Gospels for the Sundays. From the Italian of Mgr. SCOTTI, Archbishop of Thessalonica. Revised and edited by the Oblates of St. Charles. With a Preface by his Grace the ARCHBISHOP OF WESTMINSTER.

Vol. I. From the First Sunday in Advent to the Sixth Saturday after the Epiphany. 4s.
Vol. II. From Septuagesima Sunday to the Fourth Sunday after Easter. 4s.
Vol. III. From the Fifth Sunday after Easter to the Eleventh Sunday after Pentecost. 4s.
Vol. IV., completing the work. 4s.

'This admirable little book will be much valued by all, but especially by the clergy, for whose use it is more immediately intended. The Archbishop states in his Preface that it is held in high esteem in Rome, and that he has himself found, by the experience of many years, its singular excellence, its practical piety, its abundance of Scripture, of the Fathers, and of ecclesiastical writers.'—*Tablet.*

'It is a sufficient recommendation to this book of meditations that our Archbishop has given them his own warm approval. . . . They are full of the language of the Scriptures, and are rich with unction of their Divine sense.'—*Weekly Register.*

'A manual of meditations for priests, to which we have seen nothing comparable.'—*Catholic World.*

'There is great beauty in the thoughts, the illustrations are striking, the learning shown in patristic quotation considerable, and the special applications to priests are very powerful. It is entirely a priest's book.'—*Church Review.*

The Question of Anglican Ordinations discussed. By the Very Rev. Canon ESTCOURT, M.A., F.A.S. With an Appendix of Original Documents and Photographic Facsimiles. One vol. 8vo, 14*s*.

'A valuable contribution to the theology of the Sacrament of Order. He treats a leading question, from a practical point of view, with great erudition, and with abundance of illustrations from the rites of various ages and countries.'—*Month.*

'Will henceforth be an indispensable portion of every priest's library, inasmuch as it contains all the information that has been collected in previous works, sifted and corrected, together with a well-digested mass of important matter which has never before been given to the public.'—*Tablet.*

'Marks a very important epoch in the history of that question, and virtually disposes of it.'—*Messenger.*

'Canon Estcourt has added valuable documents that have never appeared before, or never at full length. The result is a work of very great value.'—*Catholic Opinion.*

'Indicates conscientious and painstaking research, and will be indispensable to any student who would examine the question on which it treats.'—*Bookseller.*

'Superior, both in literary method, tone, and mode of reasoning, to the usual controversial books on this subject.'—*Church Herald.*

May Papers; or Thoughts on the Litanies of Loreto. By EDWARD IGNATIUS PURBRICK, Priest of the Society of Jesus. 3*s*. 6*d*.

'There is a brightness and vivacity in them which will make them interesting to all, old and young alike, and adds to their intrinsic value.'—*Dublin Review.*

'We very gladly welcome this volume as a valuable addition to the now happily numerous manuals of devout exercises for the month.'—*Month.*

'Written in the pure, simple, unaffected language which becomes the subject.'—*Tablet.*

'We cannot easily conceive a book more calculated to aid the cause of true religion amongst young persons of every class.'—*Weekly Register.*

'They are admirable, and expressed in chaste and beautiful language. Although compiled in the first place for boys at school, they are adapted for the spiritual reading of Catholics of every age and condition of life.'—*Catholic Opinion.*

WORKS OF THE REV. FATHER RAWES, O.S.C.

Homeward: a Tale of Redemption.   Second
edition.   3s. 6d.

'A series of beautiful word pictures.'—*Catholic Opinion.*
'A casket well worth the opening; full to the brim of gems of thought as beautiful as they are valuable.'—*Catholic Times.*
'Full of holy thoughts and exquisite poetry, and just such a book as can be taken up with advantage and relief in hours of sadness and depression.'—*Dublin Review.*
'Is really beautiful, and will be read with profit.'—*Church Times.*

God in His Works: a Course of Five Ser-
mons.   2s. 6d.

SUBJECTS: I. God in Creation.   II. God in the Incarnation.   III. God in the Holy See.   IV. God in the Heart.   V. God in the Resurrection.

'Full of striking imagery, and the beauty of the language cannot fail to make the book valuable for spiritual reading.'—*Catholic Times.*
'He has so applied science as to bring before the reader an unbroken course of thought and argument.'—*Tablet.*

The Beloved Disciple; or St. John the Evan-
gelist.   3s. 6d.

'Full of research, and of tender and loving devotion.'—*Tablet.*
'This is altogether a charming book for spiritual reading.'—*Catholic Times.*
'Through this book runs a vein of true, humble, fervent piety, which gives a singular charm.'—*Weekly Register.*
'St. John, in his varied character, is beautifully and attractively presented to our pious contemplation.'—*Catholic Opinion.*

Septem: Seven Ways of hearing Mass.   Fifth
edition.   1s. and 2s.; red edges, 2s. 6d.; calf, 4s.; French Translation, 1s. 6d.

'A great assistance to hearing Mass with devotion. Besides its devotional advantages it possesses a Preface, in clear and beautiful language, well worth reading.'—*Tablet.*

Great Truths in Little Words.   Third edi-
tion.   Neat cloth, 3s. 6d.

'A most valuable little work. All may learn very much about the Faith from it.'—*Tablet.*
'At once practical in its tendency, and elegant; oftentimes poetical in its diction.'—*Weekly Register.*
'Cannot fail to be most valuable to every Catholic; and we feel certain, when known and appreciated, it will be a standard work in Catholic households.'—*Catholic Times.*

Hymns, Original, &c.   Neat cloth, 1s.;
cheap edition, 6d.

* *The Eucharistic Month.* From the Latin of
Father LERCARI, S.J.   6d.; cloth, 1s.

* *Twelve Visits to our Lady and the Heavenly
City of God.*   Second edition.   8d.

* *Nine Visits to the Blessed Sacrament.* Chiefly
from the Canticle of Canticles.   Second edition.   6d.

* *Devotions for the Souls in Purgatory.* Second edition.   8d.

* Or in one vol.,

Visits and Devotions.   Neat cloth, 3s.

.WORKS BY FATHER ANDERDON, S.J.

Christian Æsop.   3s. 6d. and 4s.

In the Snow : Tales of Mount St. Bernard.
Sixth edition.   Cloth, 1s. 6d.

Afternoons with the Saints.   Eighth edition,
enlarged.   5s.

Catholic Crusoe. Seventh edition.   Cloth gilt,
3s. 6d.

Confession to a Priest.   1d.

What is the Bible ? Is yours the right Book ?
New edition.   1d.

Also, edited by Father Anderdon,

What do Catholics really believe ?   2d.

Cherubini : Memorials illustrative of his Life.
With Portrait and Catalogue of his Works. By EDWARD
BELLASIS, Barrister-at-Law.   One vol., 429 pp.   10s. 6d.

Louise Lateau of Bois d'Haine: her Life,
her Ecstasies, and her Stigmata: a Medical Study. By Dr. F. LEFEBVRE, Professor of General Pathology and Therapeutics in the Catholic University of Louvain, &c. Translated from the French. Edited by Rev. J. SPENCER NORTHCOTE, D.D. Full and complete edition. 3*s.* 6*d.*

'The name of Dr. Lefebvre is sufficient guarantee of the importance of any work coming from his pen. The reader will find much valuable information.'—*Tablet.*

'The whole case thoroughly entered into and fully considered. The Appendix contains many medical notes of interest.'—*Weekly Register.*

'A full and complete answer.'—*Catholic Times.*

Twelve New Tales. By Mrs. PARSONS.

1. Bertha's Three Fingers. 2. Take Care of Yourself. 3. Don't Go In. 4. The Story of an Arm-chair. 5. Yes and No. 6. The Red Apples under the Tree. 7. Constance and the Water Lilies. 8. The Pair of Gold Spectacles. 9. Clara's New Shawl. 10. The Little Lodgers. 11. The Pride and the Fall. 12. This Once.

3*d.* each ; in a Packet complete, 3*s.*; or in cloth neat, 3*s.* 6*d.*

'Sound Catholic theology and a truly religious spirit breathes from every page, and it may be safely commended to schools and convents.'—*Tablet.*

'Full of sound instruction given in a pointed and amusing manner.'—*Weekly Register.*

'Very pretty, pleasantly told, attractive to little folks, and of such a nature that from each some moral good is inculcated. The tales are cheerful, sound, and sweet, and should have a large sale.'—*Catholic Times.*

'A very good collection of simple tales. The teaching is Catholic throughout.'—*Catholic Opinion.*

Marie and Paul: a Fragment. By 'Our
Little Woman.' 3*s.* 6*d.*; gilt edges, 4*s.*

'We heartily recommend this touching little tale, especially as a present for children and for schools, feeling sure that none can rise from its perusal without being touched, both at the beauty of the tale itself and by the tone of earnest piety which runs through the whole, leaving none but holy thoughts and pleasant impressions on the minds of both old and young.'—*Tablet.*

'Well adapted to the innocent minds it is intended for. The little book would be a suitable present for a little friend.'—*Catholic Opinion.*

'A charming tale for young and old.'—*Cork Examiner.*

'To all who read it the book will suggest thoughts for which they will be the better, while its graceful and affecting, because simple, pictures of home and family life will excite emotions of which none need be ashamed.'—*Month.*

'Told effectively and touchingly, with all that tenderness and pathos in which gifted women so much excel.'—*Weekly Register.*

'A very pretty and pathetic tale.'—*Catholic World.*

'A very charming story, and may be read by both young and old.'—*Brownson's Review.*

'Presents us with some deeply-touching incidents of family love and devotion.'—*Catholic Times.*

Dame Dolores, or the Wise Nun of Easton-
mere; and other Stories. By the Author of 'Tyborne,' &c. 4*s.*

CONTENTS: I. The Wise Nun of Eastonmere. II. Known Too Late. III. True to the End. IV. Olive's Rescue.

'We have read the volume with considerable pleasure, and we trust no small profit. The tales are decidedly clever, well worked out, and written with a flowing and cheerful pen.'—*Catholic Times.*

'The author of *Tyborne* is too well known to need any fresh recommendation to the readers of Catholic fiction. We need only say that her present will be as welcome to her many friends as any of her former works.'—*Month.*

'An attractive volume; and we know of few tales that we can more safely or more thoroughly recommend to our young readers.'—*Weekly Register.*

Maggie's Rosary, and other Tales. By the
Author of 'Marian Howard.' Cloth extra, 3*s.*; cheap edition, 2*s.*

'We strongly recommend these stories. They are especially suited to little girls.'—*Tablet.*

'The very thing for a gift-book for a child; but at the same time so interesting and full of incident that it will not be contemned by children of a larger growth.'—*Weekly Register.*

'We have seldom seen tales better adapted for children's reading.'—*Catholic Times.*

'The writer possesses in an eminent degree the art of making stories for children.'—*Catholic Opinion,*

'A charming little book, which we can heartily recommend.'—*Rosarian.*

Scenes and Incidents at Sea. A new Selec-
tion. 1*s.* 4*d.*

CONTENTS: I. Adventure on a Rock. II. A Heroic Act of Rescue. III. Inaccessible Islands. IV. The Shipwreck of the Czar Alexander. V. Captain James's Adventures in the North Seas. VI. Destruction of Admiral Graves's Fleet. VII. The Wreck of the Forfarshire, and Grace Darling. VIII. The Loss of the Royal George. IX. The Irish Sailor Boy. X. Gallant Conduct of a French Privateer. XI. The Harpooner. XII. The Cruise of the Agamemnon. XIII. A Nova Scotia Fog. XIV. The Mate's Story. XV. The Shipwreck of the Æneas Transport. XVI. A Scene in the Shrouds. XVII. A Skirmish off Bermuda. XVIII. Charles Wager. XIX. A Man Overboard. XX. A Loss and a Rescue. XXI. A Melancholy Adventure on the American Seas. XXII. Dolphins and Flying Fish.

History of England, for Family Use and the Upper Classes of Schools. By the Author of 'Christian Schools and Scholars.' Second edition. With Preface by the Very Rev. Dr. NORTHCOTE. 6s.

Tales from the Diary of a Sister of Mercy. By C. M. BRAME. New edition. Cloth extra, 4s.

CONTENTS : The Double Marriage. The Cross and the Crown. The Novice. The Fatal Accident. The Priest's Death. The Gambler's Wife. The Apostate. The Besetting Sin.

'Written in a chaste, simple, and touching style.'—*Tablet.*
'This book is a casket, and those who open it will find the gem within.'—*Register.*
'They are well and cleverly told, and the volume is neatly got up.'—*Month.*
'Very well told : all full of religious allusions and expressions.'—*Star.*
'Very well written, and life-like ; many very pathetic.'—*Catholic Opinion*

By the same,

Angels' Visits : a Series of Tales. With Frontispiece and Vignette. 3s. 6d.

'The tone of the book is excellent, and it will certainly make itself a great favourite with the young.'—*Month.*
'Beautiful collection of Angel Stories.'—*Weekly Register.*
'One of the prettiest books for children we have seen.'—*Tablet.*
'A book which excites more than ordinary praise.'—*Northern Press.*
'Touchingly written, and evidently the emanation of a refined and pious mind.'—*Church Times.*
'A charming little book, full of beautiful stories of the family of angels.'—*Church Opinion.*

ST. JOSEPH'S THEOLOGICAL LIBRARY.
Edited by Fathers of the Society of Jesus.
Vol. I.

On some Popular Errors concerning Politics and Religion. By the Right Honourable Lord ROBERT MONTAGU, M.P. 6s.

CONTENTS : Introduction. I. The Basis of Political Science. II. Religion. III. The Church. IV. Religious Orders. V. Christian Law. VI. The Mass. VII. The Principles of 1789. VIII. Liberty. IX. Fraternity. X. Equality. XI. Nationality, Non-intervention, and the Accomplished Fact. XII. Capital Punishment. XIII. Liberal Catholics.

xiv. Civil Marriage.   xv. Secularisation of Education.
xvi. Conclusion.   Additional Notes.

This book has been taken from the 'Risposte popolari alle obiezioni piu diffuse contro la Religione; opera del P. Secondo Franco.   Torino, 1868.'   It is not a translation of that excellent Italian work, for much has been omitted, and even the forms of expression have not been retained ; nor yet is it an abstract, for other matter has been added throughout.   The aim of the editor has been merely to follow out the intention of P. Franco, and adapt his thoughts to the circumstances and mind of England.

Considerations for a Three Days' Preparation for Communion.   Taken chiefly from the French of SAINT JURE, S.J.   By CECILIE MARY CADDELL.   8d.

' In every respect a most excellent manual.'—*Catholic Times.*
'A simple and easy method for a devout preparation for that solemn duty.'—*Weekly Register.*
'A beautiful compilation carefully prepared.'—*Universe.*

The Spiritual Conflict and Conquest.   By Dom J. CASTANIZA, O.S.B.   Edited, with Preface and Notes, by Canon VAUGHAN, English Monk of the Order of St. Benedict.   Second edition.   Reprinted from the old English Translation of 1652.   With fine Original Frontispiece reproduced in Autotype.   8s. 6d.

The Letter-Books of Sir Amias Poulet, *Keeper of Mary Queen of Scots.*   Edited by JOHN MORRIS, Priest of the Society of Jesus.   Demy 8vo, 10s. 6d.

Sir Amias Poulet had charge of the Queen of Scots from April 1585 to the time of her death, February 8, 1587. His correspondence with Lord-Treasurer Burghley and Sir Francis Walsingham enters into the details of her life in captivity at Tutbury, Chartley, and Fotheringay.   Many of the letters now published are entirely unknown, being printed from a recently-discovered manuscript.   The others have been taken from the originals at the Public Record Office and the British Museum.   The letters are strung together by a running commentary, in the course of which several of Mr. Froude's statements are examined, and the question of Mary's complicity in the plot against Elizabeth's life is discussed.

Sœur Eugenie: the Life and Letters of a

Sister of Charity. By the Author of 'A Sketch of the Life of St. Paula.' Second edition, enlarged. On toned paper, cloth gilt, 4s. 6d.; plain paper, cloth plain, 3s.

'It is impossible to read it without bearing away in one's heart some of the "odour of sweetness" which breathes forth from almost every page.'—*Tablet.*

'The most charming piece of religious biography that has appeared since the *Récits d'une Sœur.'—Catholic Opinion.*

'We have seldom read a more touching tale of youthful holiness.'—*Weekly Register.*

'The picture of a life of hidden piety and grace, and of active charity, which it presents is extremely beautiful.'—*Nation.*

'We strongly recommend this devout and interesting life to the careful perusal of all our readers.'—*Westminster Gazette.*

Count de Montalembert's Letters to a School-

fellow, 1827-1830. Qualis ab incepto. Translated from the French by C. F. AUDLEY. With Portrait. 5s.

'Simple, easy, and unaffected in a degree, these letters form a really charming volume. The observations are simply wonderful, considering that when he wrote them he was only seventeen or eighteen years of age.'—*Weekly Register.*

'A new treasure is now presented for the first time in an English casket—the letters he wrote when a schoolboy. The loftiness of the aspirations they breathe is supported by the intellectual power of which they give evidence.'—*Cork Examiner.*

'Reveal in the future ecclesiastical champion and historian a depth of feeling and insight into forthcoming events hardly to be expected from a mere schoolboy.'—*Building News.*

'Display vigour of thought and real intellectual power.'—*Church Herald.*

Ecclesiastical Antiquities of London and its

Suburbs. By ALEXANDER WOOD, M.A. Oxon., of the Somerset Archæological Society. 5s.

'O, who the ruine sees, whom wonder doth not fill
With our great fathers' pompe, devotion, and their skill?'

'Will prove a most useful manual to many of our readers. Stores of Catholic memories still hang about the streets of this great metropolis. For the ancient and religious associations of such places the Catholic reader can want no better cicerone than Mr. Wood.'—*Weekly Register.*

'We have indeed to thank Mr. Wood for this excellent little book.'—*Catholic Opinion.*

'Very seldom have we read a book devoted entirely to the metropolis with such pleasure.'—*Liverpool Catholic Times.*

'A very pleasing and readable book.'—*Builder.*

'Gives a plain, sensible, but learned and interesting account of the chief church antiquities of London and its suburbs. It is written by a very able and competent author—one who thoroughly appreciates his subject, and who treats it with the discrimination of a critic and the sound common sense of a practised writer.'—*Church Herald.*

LIBRARY OF RELIGIOUS BIOGRAPHY.
Edited by EDWARD HEALY THOMPSON.

Vol. I.
The Life of St. Aloysius Gonzaga, S.J.
Second edition.   5*s*.

'Contains numberless traces of a thoughtful and tender devotion to the Saint. It shows a loving penetration into his spirit, and an appreciation of the secret motives of his action, which can only be the result of a deeply affectionate study of his life and character.'—*Month*.

Vol. II.
The Life of Marie Eustelle Harpain; or
the Angel of the Eucharist.   Second edition.   5*s*.

' Possesses a special value and interest apart from its extraordinay natural and supernatural beauty, from the fact that to her example and to the effect of her writings is attributed in great measure the wonderful revival of devotion to the Blessed Sacrament in France, and consequently throughout Western Christendom.'—*Dublin Review*.

'A more complete instance of that life of purity and close union with God in the world of which we have just been speaking is to be found in the history of Marie Eustelle Harpain, the sempstress of Saint-Pallais. The writer of the present volume has had the advantage of very copious materials in the French works on which his own work is founded ; and Mr. Thompson has discharged his office as editor with his usual diligence and accuracy.'—*Month*.

Vol. III.
The Life of St. Stanislas Kostka.   5*s*.

' We strongly recommend this biography to our readers.'—*Tablet*.

'There has been no adequate biography of St. Stanislas. In rectifying this want Mr. Thompson has earned a title to the gratitude of English-speaking Catholics. The engaging Saint of Poland will now be better known among us, and we need not fear that, better known, he will not be better loved.'—*Weekly Register*.

Vol. IV.
The Life of the Baron de Renty; or Per-
fection in the World exemplified.   6*s*.

' An excellent book. The style is throughout perfectly fresh and buoyant.'—*Dublin Review*.

'This beautiful work is a compilation, not of biographical incidents, but of holy thoughts and spiritual aspirations, which we may feed on and make our own.'—*Tablet*.

'Gives full particulars of his marvellous virtue in an agreeable form.'—*Catholic Times*.

'A good book for our Catholic young men, teaching how they can sanctify the secular state.'—*Catholic Opinion*.

'Edifying and instructive, a beacon and guide to those whose walks are in the ways of the world, who toil and strive to win Christian perfection.'—*Ulster Examiner*.

Vol V.

The Life of the Venerable Anna Maria

Taigi, the Roman Matron (1769-1837). Third edition.
With Portrait. 6s.

This Biography has been written after a careful collation
of previous Lives of the Servant of God with each other,
and with the *Analecta Juris Pontificii,* which contain large
extracts from the Processes. Various prophecies attributed
to her and other holy persons have been collected in an
Appendix.

'Of all the series of deeply-interesting biographies which the untiring zeal
and piety of Mr. Healy Thompson has given of late years to English Catholics, none, we think, is to be compared in interest with the one before us,
both from the absorbing nature of the life itself and the spiritual lessons it
conveys.'—*Tablet.*

'A complete biography of the Venerable Matron in the composition of
which the greatest care has been taken and the best authorities consulted.
We can safely recommend the volume for the discrimination with which it
has been written, and for the careful labour and completeness by which it
has been distinguished.'—*Catholic Opinion.*

'We recommend this excellent and carefully-compiled biography to all
our readers. The evident care exercised by the editor in collating the
various lives of Anna Maria gives great value to the volume, and we hope it
will meet with the support it so justly merits.'—*Westminster Gazette.*

'We thank Mr. Healy Thompson for this volume. The direct purpose of
his biographies is always spiritual edification.'—*Dublin Review.*

'Contains much that is capable of nourishing pious sentiments.'—*Nation.*

'Has evidently been a labour of love.'—*Month.*

The Hidden Life of Jesus: a Lesson and

Model to Christians. Translated from the French of Bou-
DON, by EDWARD HEALY THOMPSON, M.A. Cloth, 3s.

'This profound and valuable work has been very carefully and ably translated by Mr. Thompson.'—*Register.*

'The more we have of such works as the *Hidden Life of Jesus* the better.'
—*Westminster Gazette.*

'A book of searching power.'—*Church Review.*

'We have often regretted that this writer's works are not better known.'
—*Universe.*

'We earnestly recommend its study and practice to all readers.'—*Tablet.*

'We have to thank Mr. Thompson for this translation of a valuable work
which has long been popular in France.'—*Dublin Review.*

'A good translation.'—*Month.*

Also, by the same Author and Translator,

Devotion to the Nine Choirs of Holy Angels,
and especially to the Angel Guardians. 3*s.*

'We congratulate Mr. Thompson on the way in which he has accomplished his task, and we earnestly hope that an increased devotion to the Holy Angels may be the reward of his labour of love.'—*Tablet.*

'A beautiful translation.'—*Month.*

'The translation is extremely well done.'—*Weekly Register.*

New Meditations for each Day in the Year,
on the Life of our Lord Jesus Christ. By a Father of the Society of Jesus. With the imprimatur of the Cardinal Archbishop of Westminster. New and improved edition. Two vols. Cloth, 9*s.*; also in calf, 16*s.*; morocco, 17*s.*

'We can heartily recommend this book for its style and substance ; it bears with it several strong recommendations. . . . It is solid and practical.' —*Westminster Gazette.*

'A work of great practical utility, and we give it our earnest recommendation.'—*Weekly Register.*

The Day Sanctified ; being Meditations and
Spiritual Readings for Daily Use. Selected from the Works of Saints and approved Writers of the Catholic Church. Fcp. cloth, 3*s.* 6*d.* ; red edges, 4*s.*

'Of the many volumes of meditations on sacred subjects which have appeared in the last few years, none has seemed to us so well adapted to its object as the one before us.'—*Tablet.*

'Deserves to be specially mentioned.'—*Month.*

'Admirable in every sense.'—*Church Times.*

'Many of the meditations are of great beauty. . . . They form, in fact, excellent little sermons, and we have no doubt will be largely used as such.' —*Literary Churchman.*

Reflections and Prayers for Holy Communion.
munion. Translated from the French. With Preface by the CARDINAL ARCHBISHOP OF WESTMINSTER. Fcp. 8vo, cloth, 4*s.* 6*d.*; bound, red edges, 5*s.*; calf, 9*s.*; morocco, 10*s.*

'The Archbishop has marked his approval of the work by writing a preface for it, and describes it as "a valuable addition to our books of devotion."'—*Register.*

'A book rich with the choicest and most profound Catholic devotions.'— *Church Review.*

Lallemant's Doctrine of the Spiritual Life.
Edited by the late Father FABER. New edition. Cloth, 4s. 6d.

'This excellent work has a twofold value, being both a biography and a volume of meditations. It contains an elaborate analysis of the wants, dangers, trials, and aspirations of the inner man, and supplies to the thoughtful and devout reader the most valuable instructions for the attainment of heavenly wisdom, grace, and strength.'—*Catholic Times.*

'A treatise of the very highest value.'—*Month.*

'The treatise is preceded by a short account of the writer's life, and has had the wonderful advantage of being edited by the late Father Faber.'—*Weekly Register.*

The Rivers of Damascus and Jordan: a
Causerie. By a Tertiary of the Order of St. Dominic. 4s.

'Good solid reading.'—*Month.*

'Well done and in a truly charitable spirit.'—*Catholic Opinion.*

'It treats the subject in so novel and forcible a light that we are fascinated in spite of ourselves, and irresistibly led on to follow its arguments and rejoice at its conclusions.'—*Tablet.*

Legends of our Lady and the Saints; or
our Children's Book of Stories in Verse. Written for the Recitations of the Pupils of the Schools of the Holy Child Jesus, St. Leonard's-on-Sea. 2s. 6d.

'It is a beautiful religious idea that is realised in the *Legends of our Lady and the Saints.* The book forms a charming present for pious children.'—*Tablet.*

'The "Legends" are so beautiful that they ought to be read by all lovers of poetry.'—*Bookseller.*

'Graceful poems.'—*Month.*

The New Testament Narrative, in the Words
of the Sacred Writers. With Notes, Chronological Tables, and Maps. Cloth, 2s.

'The compilers deserve great praise for the manner in which they have performed their task. We commend this little volume as well and carefully printed, and as furnishing its readers, moreover, with a great amount of useful information in the tables inserted at the end.'—*Month.*

'It is at once clear, complete, and beautiful.'—*Catholic Opinion.*

QUARTERLY SERIES.

Conducted by the Managers of the 'Month.'

———o———

VOLUMES PUBLISHED.

The Life and Letters of St. Francis Xavier.
By the Rev. H. J. COLERIDGE. Sec. edit. Two vols. 18*s.*

'We cordially thank Father Coleridge for a most valuable biography. . . . He has spared no pains to insure our having in good classical English a translation of all the letters which are extant. . . . A complete priest's manual might be compiled from them, entering as they do into all the details of a missioner's public and private life. . . . We trust we have stimulated our readers to examine them for themselves, and we are satisfied that they will return again and again to them as to a never-exhausted source of interest and edification.'—*Tablet.*

'A noble addition to our literature. . . . We offer our warmest thanks to Father Coleridge for this most valuable work. The letters, we need hardly say, will be found of great spiritual use, especially for missionaries and priests.'—*Dublin Review.*

'One of the most fascinating books we have met with for a long time.'—*Catholic Opinion.*

'Would that we had many more lives of saints like this! Father Cole-ridge has done great service to this branch of Catholic literature, not simply by writing a charming book, but especially by setting others an example of how a saint's life should be written.'—*Westminster Gazette.*

'This valuable book is destined, we feel assured, to take a high place among what we may term our English Catholic classics. . . . The great charm lies in the letters, for in them we have, in a far more forcible manner than any biographer could give them, the feelings, experiences, and aspirations of St. Francis Xavier as pictured by his own pen.'—*Catholic Times.*

'Father Coleridge does his own part admirably, and we shall not be sur-prised to find his book soon take its place as the standard Life of the saintly and illustrious Francis.'—*Nation.*

'Not only an interesting but a scholarly sketch of a life remarkable alike in itself and in its attendant circumstances. We hope the author will con-tinue to labour in a department of literature for which he has here shown his aptitude. To find a saint's life which is at once moderate, historical, and appreciative is not a common thing.'—*Saturday Review.*

'Should be studied by all missionaries, and is worthy of a place in every Christian library.'—*Church Herald.*

The Life of St. Jane Frances Fremyot de

Chantal. By EMILY BOWLES. With Preface by the Rev. H. J. COLERIDGE. Second edition. 5s. 6d.

'We venture to promise great pleasure and profit to the reader of this charming biography. It gives a complete and faithful portrait of one of the most attractive saints of the generation which followed the completion of the Council of Trent.'—*Month.*

'Sketched in a life-like manner, worthy of her well-earned reputation as a Catholic writer.'—*Weekly Register.*

'We have read it on and on with the fascination of a novel, and yet it is the life of a saint, described with a rare delicacy of touch and feeling such as is seldom met with.'—*Tablet.*

'A very readable and interesting compilation. . . . The author has done her work faithfully and conscientiously.'—*Athenæum.*

'Full of incident, and told in a style so graceful and felicitous that it wins upon the reader with every page.'—*Nation.*

'Miss Bowles has done her work in a manner which we cannot better commend than by expressing a desire that she may find many imitators. She has endued her materials with life, and clothed them with a language and a style of which we do not know what to admire most—the purity, the grace, the refinement, or the elegance. If our readers wish to know the value and the beauty of this book, they can do no better than get it and read it.'—*Westminster Gazette.*

'One of the most charming and delightfu volumes which has issued from the press for many years. Miss Bowles has accomplished her task faithfully and happily, with simple grace and unpretentious language, and a winning manner which, independently of her subject, irresistibly carries us along.'— *Ulster Examiner.*

The History of the Sacred Passion. From

the Spanish of Father LUIS DE LA PALMA, of the Society of Jesus. The Translation revised and edited by the Rev. H. J. COLERIDGE. Third edition. 7s. 6d.

'A work long held in great and just repute in Spain. It opens a mine of wealth to one's soul. Though there are many works on the Passion in English, probably none will be found so generally useful both for spiritual reading and meditation. We desire to see it widely circulated.'—*Tablet.*

'A sterling work of the utmost value, proceeding from the pen of a great theologian, whose piety was as simple and tender as his learning and culture were profound and exquisite. It is a rich storehouse for contemplation on the great mystery of our Redemption, and one of those books which every Catholic ought to read for himself.'—*Weekly Register.*

'The most wonderful work upon the Passion that we have ever read. To us the charm lies in this, that it is entirely theological. It is made use of largely by those who give the Exercises of St. Ignatius ; it is, as it were, the flesh upon the skeleton of the Exercises. Never has the Passion been meditated upon so before. . . . If any one wishes to understand the Passion of our Lord in its fulness, let him procure this book.'—*Dublin Review.*

'We have not read a more thoughtful work on our Blessed Lord's Passion.

It is a complete storehouse of matter for meditation, and for sermons on that divine mystery.'—*Catholic Opinion.*

'The book is—speaking comparatively of human offerings—a magnificent offering to the Crucified, and to those who wish to make a real study of the Cross will be a most precious guide.'—*Church Review.*

Ierne of Armorica : a Tale of the Time of Chlovis. By J. C. BATEMAN. 6s. 6d.

'We know of few tales of the kind that can be ranked higher than the beautiful story before us. The author has hit on the golden mean between an over-display of antiquarianism and an indolent transfer of modern modes of action and thought to a distant time. The descriptions are masterly, the characters distinct, the interest unflagging. We may add that the period is one of those which may be said to be comparatively unworked.'—*Month.*

'A volume of very great interest and very great utility. As a story it is sure to give much delight, while, as a story founded on historical fact, it will benefit all by its very able reproduction of very momentous scenes. . . . The book is excellent. If we are to have a literature of fiction at all, we hope it will include many like volumes.'—*Dublin Review.*

'Although a work of fiction, it is historically correct, and the author portrays with great skill the manners and customs of the times of which he professes to give a description. In reading this charming tale we seem to be taken by the hand by the writer, and made to assist at the scenes which he describes.'—*Tablet.*

'The author of this most interesting tale has hit the happy medium between a display of antiquarian knowledge and a mere reproduction in distant ages of commonplace modern habits of thought. The descriptions are excellent, the characters well drawn, and the subject itself is very attractive, besides having the advantage of not having been written threadbare.'—*Westminster Gazette.*

'The tale is excessively interesting, the language appropriate to the time and rank of the characters, the style flowing and easy, and the narrative leads one on and on until it becomes a very difficult matter to lay the book down until it is finished. . . . It is a valuable addition to Catholic fictional literature.'—*Catholic Times.*

'A very pretty historico-ecclesiastical novel of the times of Chlovis. It is full of incident, and is very pleasant reading.'—*Literary Churchman.*

The Life of Dona Luisa de Carvajal. By Lady GEORGIANA FULLERTON. 6s. (See p. 6.)

The Life of the Blessed John Berchmans. By the Rev. FRANCIS GOLDIE, S.J. 6s.

'A complete and life-like picture, and we are glad to be able to congratulate Father Goldie on his success.'—*Tablet.*

'Drawn up with a vigour and freedom which show great power of biographical writing.'—*Dublin Review.*

'One of the most interesting of all.'—*Weekly Register.*

'Unhesitatingly we say that it is the very best Life of Blessed John

Berchmans, and as such it will take rank with religious biographies of the highest merit.'—*Catholic Times.*

'Is of great literary merit, the style being marked by elegance and a complete absence of redundancy.'—*Cork Examiner.*

'This delightful and edifying volume is of the deepest interest. The perusal will afford both pleasure and profit.'—*Church Herald.*

The Life of the Blessed Peter Favre, of the

Society of Jesus, First Companion of St. Ignatius Loyola. From the Italian of Father GIUSEPPE BOERO, of the same Society. With Preface by the Rev. H. J. COLERIDGE. 6*s.* 6*d.*

This Life has been written on the occasion of the beatification of the Ven. Peter Favre, and contains the *Memoriale* or record of his private thoughts and meditations, written by himself.

'At once a book of spiritual reading, and also an interesting historical narrative. The *Memoriale, or Spiritual Diary,* is here translated at full length, and is the most precious portion of one of the most valuable biographies we know.'—*Tablet.*

'A perfect picture drawn from the life, admirably and succinctly told. The *Memoriale* will be found one of the most admirable epitomes of sound devotional reading.'—*Weekly Register.*

'The *Memoriale* is hardly excelled in interest by anything of the kind now extant.'—*Catholic Times.*

'Full of interest, instruction, and example.'—*Cork Examiner.*

'One of the most interesting to the general reader of the entire series up to this time.'—*Nation.*

'This wonderful diary, the *Memoriale,* has never been published before, and we are much mistaken if it does not become a cherished possession to thoughtful Catholics.'—*Month.*

The Dialogues of St. Gregory the Great.

An old English version. Edited, with Preface, by the Rev. H. J. COLERIDGE. 6*s.*

'The Catholic world must feel grateful to Father Coleridge for this excellent and compendious edition. The subjects treated of possess at this moment a special interest. . . . The Preface by Father Coleridge is interesting and well written, and we cordially recommend the book to the perusal of all.'—*Tablet.*

'This is a most interesting book. . . . Father Coleridge gives a very useful preface summarising the contents.'—*Weekly Register.*

'We have seldom taken up a book in which we have become at once so deeply interested. It will suit any one ; it will teach all ; it will confirm any who require that process ; and it will last and be read when other works are quite forgotten.'—*Catholic Times.*

'Edited and published with the utmost care and the most perfect literary taste, this volume adds one more gem to the treasury of English Catholic literature.'—*New York Catholic World.*

The Life of Sister Anne Catherine Emme-
rich. Edited, with Preface, by the Rev. H. J. COLERIDGE.
5*s.*

St. Winefride; or Holywell and its Pil-
grims. By the Author of 'Tyborne.' Second edition. 1*s.*

Summer Talks about Lourdes. By Miss.
CADDELL. Cloth, 1*s.* 6*d.*

Blessed Margaret Mary Alacoque: a brief
and popular Account of her Life; to which are added
Selections from some of her Sayings, and the Decree of her
Beatification. By the Rev. CHARLES B. GARSIDE, M.A.
1*s.*

A Comparison between the History of the
Church and the Prophecies of the Apocalypse. Translated
from the German by EDWIN DE LISLE. 2*s.*

CATHOLIC-TRUTH TRACTS.

NEW ISSUES.

Manchester Dialogues. First Series. By the
Rev. Fr. HARPER, S.J.

> No. I. The Pilgrimage.
> II. Are Miracles going on still?
> III. Popish Miracles tested by the Bible.
> IV. Popish Miracles.
> V. Liquefaction of the Blood of St. Januarius.
> VI. 'Bleeding Nuns' and 'Winking Madonnas.'
> VII. Are Miracles physically possible?
> VIII. Are Miracles morally possible?

Price of each 3*s.* per 100, 25 for 1*s.*; also 25 of the above
assorted for 1*s.* Also the whole Series complete in neat Wrap-
per, 6*d.*

Specimen Packet of General Series, containing 100 assorted,
1*s.* 6*d.*

www.ingramcontent.com/pod-product-compliance
Lightning Source LLC
Chambersburg PA
CBHW030627030726
47497CB00006B/1665